BONDED AGENT

David B. Riley

WolfSinger Publications Security, Colorado

FOREWORD
David Lee Summers

I first "met" David B. Riley's interplanetary claims adjuster Sarah Meadows in a story he submitted for the anthology *Space Pirates*, which I edited back in 2008. That story appears in this book as the second chapter. Back when I first encountered Sarah, I was captivated by her no-nonsense approach to her job and I wanted to know more about her background. After all, how many insurance agents could match wits with a band of pirates?

David continued to write about Sarah and this book is the result. The first chapter gives us a glimpse of Sarah's background and he tells more of her backstory as the novel unfolds. After Sarah's encounter with space pirates, she has to deal with a mysterious phantom space station and then she's sent into a war zone where she teams up with the dinosaur-like Tau.

David Riley had a degree in history, which served him well as he imagined human society in the distant future. In a 1941, WorldCon talk, Robert A. Heinlein suggested the power of science fiction came from the way it allowed readers to engage in time-binding. According to Heinlein, time-binding was the human capacity to reconstruct the past and imagine the future through reading and writing. In *Bonded Agent*, David Riley used his knowledge of human settlement, cultural clashes, and warfare to build a plausible future.

Not only is Riley's future a plausible one, it's colorful. In addition to space pirates who traverse the solar system, Sarah encounters a haunted derelict abandoned in the depths of space, and a dragon who manages an interstellar corporation. David Riley once told me he didn't write space cowboy stories, but I immediately saw his love of the old west when Sarah Meadows steps into the Martian settlement of Dry Gulch.

As it turns out, David Riley shared a few traits with his protagonist, Sarah Meadows. He rarely minced words and he could be fearless when he set his mind to something. He enjoyed a good beer and a good dessert. He could be a loyal friend in times of trouble. Unfortunately, David Riley left us much too soon, but we're fortunate he left us this peek into a possible future where Mars has declared independence from Earth, pirates roam the solar system, and dinosaur-like aliens fight for freedom. Turn the page and let David sweep you into the world of Sarah Meadows, bonded agent for Gompers Insurance.

1
SALES

Sarah found herself wishing for a window—dearly, dearly wanting one. Her cubbyhole of an office had no window, just a door. It was at the end of a long hallway. The other agents were mostly in the bullpen, a consortium of desks and tables in a large airy chamber that overlooked the Mars City Mall. And it had plenty of windows. But, she didn't like to complain–and she was the newbie. So, she looked around at her gray walls and wondered where to put her framed diploma from The Martian School of Economics and her newly issued all lines insurance license from the Ministry of Banking and Insurance.

Then, there was a knock at the door, even though the door was open. She looked over at a nondescript little man of about 40, with thinning blond hair and a pathetic excuse for a moustache. "Can I help you?" she asked.

"That bald lady in the lobby said to see you?" It seemed like more of a question.

"Come in." She pointed at the vacant chair across from her desk. "I'm Sarah. What can I do for you?"

"I need to buy some life insurance," he said.

"Well, you've come to the right place." She turned on her notebook. "Can I get your name?"

"Phillip."

"Last name?" she asked.

"Phillips."

"So, that's Phillip Phillips?" she confirmed, wondering if this was a joke being played on her by the other agents out in the bullpen.

"That's right," he confirmed. "Phillip P. Phillips. Wanna know what the P. Stands for?"

She didn't. She really didn't. "Address?"

"Two zero one Tulip Esplanade," he said.

"Tulip Esplanade?" That was the infamous Mars City sewage

treatment plant. This had to be a joke. "You live at the sewage plant?"

"That's right. I have a little apartment above the office, me and Curtis. In case something bad happens, they can come get us," he said.

"Something bad?" she asked.

"You don't want to know," he said. "What are you?"

"Excuse me?" she asked.

"What are you? You kind of look like a redhead, but not?"

"I'm a strawberry blonde," she said.

"Oh. You have pretty eyes," Phillip said.

"Uh, thank you, Let's finish this up. How much coverage did you want?" she asked.

"Enough to cremate me and take care of me mother," he said. "That's why I'm here. I worry about me mother. And, I may not have long to live."

"Are you ill?" she asked. She pulled a health questionnaire out of the drawer.

"Na, I ain't sick or nothing. But, the government's out to get me," he stated, rather matter-of-fact. "I think they want me dead."

This had to be some kind of joke. "Out to get you?" she asked.

Philip nodded. "That's why I need insurance. They could push me in some vat. One minute I'm there, the next minute me mother is all alone. She doesn't live with me. She has her own place. Nobody but me and Curtis lives at the plant. I get free rent."

"I guess that's a good deal," Sarah agreed.

"They're already monitoring my communications. I figure it's just a matter of time before they take me out. They keep making me get fired," he said. "Though, they haven't messed with me since I got the sewage job."

"Who, precisely, are *they*?" Sarah asked. This had to be some kind of joke.

"The government," Philip said. "You know."

"Why are they so interested in you?" she asked. This had to be a joke.

"It's a conspiracy," he explained. "They want to keep me from running for office. They wouldn't let me run for mayor."

"Why is that, Philip?" she asked, then immediately regretted it.

"They said I didn't provide the required signatures with the form. How was I supposed to know all the people who signed the form are already dead?" he explained. "It could happen to anyone."

"Were they dead when they signed them?" Sarah asked.

Phillip sort of shrugged. "Beats me. Some guy got the signatures for me."

"I see." She turned her notebook around so Phillip could look at it. "Well, a lot of people buy a million doubloon policy, but there are plenty of other options. This is the amount of coverage and the right figure in blue is the monthly premium. And you can save ten percent by paying it every six months instead of monthly."

"I guess I'll go with the million. Me mother will like that," he decided.

"Excellent," she said.

It took another half hour to get everything filled out and signed. She walked him out to the front door. Then, she headed out to the break area. No one was snickering or even paying any attention to her. She looked over at the bald lady who worked in reception. "I'm Sarah," she said.

"I know that," was the reply.

After a few awkward moments, Sarah asked, "What's your name?"

"I can't give that out to just anyone," was the answer.

Sarah took a bag of some orange stuff from Martian Hydroponics out of the vending machine and retreated back to her gloomy little cubbyhole office. Suddenly, she sensed a presence at her doorway. An Almerian dragon completely filled the entrance. "May I help you?" She'd never seen one so close. They sure were large. They were usually about five meters long with big, pointed heads and small wings on their backs. The wings were from an era when their ancestors actually flew. This one was at least that big, though it extended out into the hall, making its exact dimensions merely a guess.

It looked at her with its big golden eyes. "Are you Sarah Meadows?" it asked.

Its presence was baffling to her. "Yes. Did you want to buy insurance?"

It made an odd cackling sound. "That is rich." It cackled some more. "I'm Dragon. I own the Gompers Insurance Company. Humans can't pronounce my Almerian name. Everyone just calls me Dragon."

"Own it? Isn't Gompers a publicly traded company?" she asked.

"Oh, that's just for the regulators." Dragon stared at her again, then finally said, "Here at Gompers, everyone starts out as an insurance agent or underwriter. Then, most agents stay as agents. Being an agent is an important job, obviously. But, for some of our employees, their careers may take a different track."

"Un, I'm not sure I understand? I just started two days ago," Sarah pointed out.

"I know that. Time is irrelevant, Miss Meadows. The important thing for all of our employees is that they achieve their full potential."

"And what is my potential, exactly?" Sarah asked.

"We have an opening in our Special Operations Division. Interested?" Dragon asked.

"What does special operations do?" she replied. She didn't recall any mention of special operations at orientation.

"I like to think of them as glorified claims adjustors," Dragon said.

"And what do they actually do, precisely?" Sarah asked. She wasn't really sure about the term glorified claims adjustor.

"Whatever it takes," Dragon replied.

She looked at her gray walls for a second. "I guess I could give it a try."

"Splendid. We'll start your training tomorrow. One of my assistants will call you later this evening to give you directions to the training facility," Dragon said.

"Okay, I guess," Sarah said.

"Most of our employees enjoy our training," Dragon said, "those that live through it, anyway."

She wasn't sure what to say to that. "Uh?"

"That's a joke. A little dragon humor," Dragon said. "We'll start you out on weapons training, then go on to other things."

Sarah looked over at the door. Dragon was gone. "Weapons training?"

2
CLAIMS

One year later

Sarah released the buckle from the shoulder harness and glided over to the porthole. "I think I know what they are," she said.

"The computer counts twenty-seven of them," Tanager said. "Unknown objects."

"They're Pinkertons," Sarah said.

"Pinkertons?" Lt. Commander Nick Tanager asked. "Enlighten those of us who are less worldly."

"They're like private marshals," she explained, "from Earth." As if to underscore her point, one of the objects bounced off the front window of the Armored Personnel Carrier. There was a human face.

"They're bodies?" Ensign Wayne asked.

"How do you know they're these Pinkertons?" Tanager asked.

"The gray and white uniforms," Sarah answered. "Of course, they may not have been dead until after they hit space."

"I'm going to be sick," Ensign Wayne declared as she fled toward the head.

"What do we do with them?" Tanager asked.

"Nothing, they're already dead," Sarah said.

"You can't just leave them there?" Ensign Wayne returned.

"We're not equipped to recover twenty-seven dead bodies in an APC. Besides, we've got company." She gestured toward the LYDAR.

"Something big is coming in fast." Tanager said. "Really big." The computer screen changed as it identified the approaching vessel's transponder. "Earthforce ship *Enterprise,* listed as a heavy cruiser."

"Martian vessel," someone with a booming male voice was now saying over the com system, "state your business in Earth territory."

"We were answering a distress call," Tanager explained. "We found this transport adrift, bodies are floating everywhere."

"Withdraw," the unidentified earthman ordered.

"Gladly," Tanager replied. "Ensign, reverse course, space normal speed. Com off. Oh, thank you for your help. Think nothing of it. Jerkwad."

"Aye, sir," Ensign Wayne acknowledged. "What's a jerkwad?"

~ * ~

Sarah banged her head on the low ceiling of the bathroom. She rubbed the sore spot as she wandered back to the chair next to the bed of the deluxe room. Sarah was only of average height. She couldn't believe how often she kept banging her head. She looked over the report she'd written, then pressed the transmit on her clipboard. It was time for bed. She wondered what the economy rooms looked like if this cramped room was a deluxe. How she hated Fremont Station. But she'd missed the last shuttle down to Mars City.

She rested all of five minutes when her clipboard started chirping, but there wasn't a caller listed. She thought it was a message failure until she unfolded the clipboard. There was a new message coming in from Mars. It was that bald woman from the Mars City office. "Yes?"

"We've got a new claim. I'm transmitting it now," the bald woman said.

"Wonderful. Where is it this time?" Sarah asked.

"Right next door to you."

"Oh." Sarah turned off the link without saying goodbye and loaded up a schematic of the floor. The unit next door was a private apartment with its own garage. She ventured out and pressed the door buzzer.

A man in black pajamas soon appeared at the door. "Can I help you?"

"Greg Steele? Sarah Meadows, Gompers Insurance."

"I just filed the claim five minutes ago?" he said.

Sarah slid by him and entered the apartment, although she hadn't really been invited in. "We pride ourselves in prompt service. Where's the runabout?"

He moved away from the door. "This way. I've got my own garage."

A private residence at Fremont Station was darn near impossible to get. There were only three of them. Based on his credit history, that she'd just checked, she really wondered how he had one. The vehicle was scorched pretty bad. Sarah recorded the images onto her clipboard. "It says Johnson LeClark tried to board you?"

Steele sort of shrugged. "That's what he said his name was. Came out of nowhere. We were lucky to get away."

Sarah turned off her clipboard. "Well, Mr. Steele, it seems like everyone these days is getting robbed by that guy."

"They've got to do something," he said.

She started moving toward the door. "Well, I'm sure *they* will. In the meantime, your claim is denied."

"What?"

"Funny thing about blaster burns like these, when they're done in atmosphere, they look like this, all scorched. In the vacuum of space, it's completely different. You did this here, in the garage, though I have no idea how you disabled the fire suppression system."

His tone changed. "Why would I do that, you stupid redheaded cunt?" He picked up a full wine bottle and swung it at her.

A moment later, he found himself face down on the floor with his arm pinned behind his back. "Martian Hydroponics composite wine? Composite? Yuk. By the way, I'm a strawberry blonde, not a redhead. Now, back to our conversation and stop squirming or I'll break your arm. Perhaps you faked it because you're three months behind on your payments for this thing and they're about to evict you from this apartment, for starters," Sarah said. "Goodnight, Mr. Steele." She left him on the floor screaming at her and returned to her deluxe room.

It was time for bed. How she missed her Mars City apartment.

What it lacked in accommodations, Fremont Station also punished its visitors in food service. Sarah had no idea what the cafeteria had given her on the tray, except that she got something yellow and warm and something blue that was cold. Any resemblance to actual food was strictly in the realm in the imagination.

Ensign Wayne was staring at her, from about ten meters away. She was in her khaki MDF uniform and holding a tray. Sarah smiled and the ensign approached and seated herself across the table from Sarah. "You've got some of that sliced green stuff. You're a braver soul than I," Sarah said.

"I guess it's an acquired taste." She took a bite. "I've been wondering something? How do you get rides on Martian Armored Personnel Carriers? You're not military?"

"Gompers insures those APCs," Sarah explained. "We have a longstanding business relationship with the Martian Defense Force."

She looked surprised. "You can insure warships?"

"You can insure just about anything," Sarah said.

"Did that ship we were looking for have insurance?" Wayne asked.

"Probably, but not from Gompers. We set out looking for the Martian cargo ship, *Luger,* as you'll recall. Then, we got a distress call from the *Botany Bay.* The *Botany Bay* is an Earth transport ship. Gompers doesn't do business on Earth." Sarah explained. "Lloyds of London insures most Earth vessels, to answer your question."

"Why did the Earth ship have all those Pinkertons on it? I've done some checking. No Earth ship has ever been raided by Johnson LeClark's band," the ensign said.

Sarah shrugged. "The Pinkertons, they were probably coming to Mars. Sure wish I knew who hired them." Sarah tossed the rest of her food in the recycling bin and stacked her tray. "I've got a shuttle to Mars City. Nice seeing you."

There was no shuttle waiting at the docking bay. There was nothing there at all except a sign that read DELAYED. Sarah sat on an uncomfortable orange plastic bench and turned on her clipboard. There was a message from that bald woman in Mars City.

~ * ~

Ensign Wayne stepped into an Armored Personnel Carrier. She was startled to find Sarah there.

"I could sure use a ride to Mars," Sarah said.

"Funny, I just got assigned to take this APC to the shipyard," Ensign Wayne said.

Sarah strapped herself in and wondered why Ensign Wayne hadn't done the same. The ensign just sat down and stared out the front window. Sarah looked at her expectantly.

"It's just, I was assigned to take this thing to the shipyard. If it's just me, that's fine. But, if we're carrying passengers, regulations require two crew members," the ensign explained.

"I see. How long have you been with the MDF?"

"I graduated from the academy six months ago," the ensign said.

"Rookies." Sarah unclamped the docking clamps, then fired the thrusters to pull away from the station. "You might radio for permission to disembark," Sarah suggested. "The controllers like that sort of thing."

Fremont Station sat in orbit opposite of Deimos. It was normally a short and uneventful run to Mars City. But, that was not their destination. They were going to the MDF maintenance yard, which was on the far side of the planet. They were going to have to make a full trip around Mars in an oddball orbit to line up for atmospheric entry.

"Did you bring anything to eat?" Sarah asked.

"There are all sorts of rations in back," Ensign Wayne said.

"Did you bring anything to eat?" Sarah repeated. Martian Hydroponics latest offerings seemed less and less disgusting the longer she was away from the surface. At least Martian Hydroponics food didn't have a twelve-year shelf life. MDF rations were made for storage. The package of sliced green stuff had three years to go, according to the package. Sarah tossed the packet to Ensign Wayne. It glided easily across the zero G cabin.

Sarah took a bottle of water and floated back to the cockpit area. She popped her water cap and noticed her companion hadn't started on the sliced green stuff. "Not hungry?"

"We're making a course correction in five minutes. I'll eat after that." Ensign Wayne looked at the navigation computer, then did a double take. "Two ships off of Deimos are about to collide."

"Warn them off," Sarah said.

"Only one of them has a transponder." Ensign Wayne

touched the transponder image on the screen. "What do I tell them?"

"Tell them they're going to collide. And say it with authority," Sarah suggested.

"Cargo tree-niner-four, this is MDF AP…MDF four-fife-one you are about to collide with an unregistered vessel. Alter your heading."

"We know that! They're shooting at us," the cargo ship replied.

The ensign asked, "Cargo tree-niner-four, have you radioed Mars Central?"

"They're jamming the Martian Relay Network. We didn't know there was a ship close enough to hear us."

"You didn't want them to know we're just an Armored Personnel Carrier. Good idea," Sarah said.

Ensign Wayne looked at the navigation console. "They're moving straight at us. So is the attacker."

"Well, you're in command, Ensign, as I'm just a civilian, but I'd increase speed," Sarah suggested.

"I haven't got any crew. We've only got laser canons. They're designed for suppression fire when you're landing troops."

"Make do with what you've got," Sarah said.

Her voice seemed to be getting higher. "Make do? I'm reading energized hull plating. And, whoever they are, will be in range in three minutes."

"I'll man the laser canon," Sarah said.

"This is suicide," Ensign Wayne protested.

"Ensign, you are in command of an MDF vessel. A Martian vessel needs your help. So, go and help them." Sarah activated the laser canon. "Try a heading of thirty-two mark twelve."

"That's a collision course!" the ensign yelled.

Sarah glared at her. When the APC turned toward the other ship, Sarah opened fire.

"That laser cannon isn't powerful enough to do much damage," Ensign Wayne cautioned.

"I'm trying to blind their targeting sensors so they don't blow us out of the sky," Sarah explained.

"Oh." The phantom ship veered off at heavy thrust, then went into hyperspace and was gone. "What just happened?"

Ensign Wayne asked.

Sarah turned off the laser canon. "We won."

~ * ~

Sarah rolled over on her back. She couldn't tell what time it was. "I must have the crappiest security system on Mars." She couldn't tell the time because there was someone between her and the clock on the wall of her apartment.

"Pretty much," a voice said from the darkness.

There was no conversation for about a minute.

"No protests? No screams that I've invaded your home?" the voice asked.

"If you were going to kill me, you would've already done so," Sarah said. "Why are we speaking?"

"I was surprised to learn I'd been defeated in battle by an insurance agent. Where'd you learn a maneuver like that?"

"The Martian School of Economics," she said.

The intruder said, "That seems unlikely. It was such a brazen move; it caught me by surprise. Trying to ram me. They used to call it a game of chicken when I was younger."

"Again, why are we speaking?" Sarah asked.

"You would've made a good pirate."

She could see the clock once again.

~ * ~

"Ya know, this pirate nonsense is getting really bad for business," Sarah said.

"How so?" Nick Tanager asked.

"The cost of insuring cargo on a Terran ship from Earth to Titan is half that of the same cargo on a Martian ship." Sarah showed him a chart on her clipboard.

"Why is that?" Ensign Wayne asked.

"Because this Johnson LeClark character only attacks Martian or alien ships, never ones registered on Earth," Sarah said.

"What about the *Botany Bay?*" Ensign Wayne pointed out.

"Well, that one's actually owned by Martian freight even though it has an Earth registry," Sarah said. "Besides, it was full of Pinkertons who were going to hunt down this pirate. It's kind of an aberration."

"I suppose." Ensign Wayne gobbled up the rest of her sliced green stuff.

"Well, the rest of the Pinkertons will be better prepared," Sarah said.

"There are more?" Ensign Wayne asked.

"Yep, lots of them. They're coming up tomorrow on the *Discovery,*" Sarah said.

Tanager's eyebrows shot up. "The *Discovery?* MDF is getting involved? Finally?"

"Looks that way," Sarah said. The *Discovery* was a Martian Defense Force military cargo ship.

"Why these Pinkertons?" Ensign Wayne asked.

"There are times when the government prefers to hire people who don't ask a lot of questions and who don't worry much about regulations," Sarah said.

~ * ~

Avery Heathcliff III was waiting at the airlock when Sarah and Nick Tanager boarded. "Miss Meadows, Commander Tanager, welcome aboard."

"Thank you, Captain," Tanager said.

The Captain gestured to his left. He took them to the ship's command center. Ten officers and crew were busily navigating and communicating and doing what they do to run a ship.

"Mighty impressive," Tanager said. "A far cry from my APC."

"Which fits inside the hold of this ship," Avery pointed out.

The next hour was routine, with the crew going about their business. "I don't like flying without running lights, it seems cowardly," Avery said.

"It's necessary," Sarah pointed out.

"I suppose. I just hope we haven't come all this way for nothing," Avery said. "We were called off another mission for this little errand of yours."

"Incoming ships, coming in fast," the tactical officer announced. "Three of them. They'll be in weapons range in two minutes."

"Battle stations," Avery ordered. He strapped himself in the captain's chair.

"Receiving a message," the tactical officer announced. A Jolly Roger Flag appeared on one of the screens. "It says, 'prepare to be boarded.' If we resist, the crew will be slaughtered. They are now in weapons range."

"Lieutenant, change our transponder signal from the cargo ship *Discovery* to our correct designation," Avery told the tactical officer. "And reply this is the Martian Cruiser *Defiant*. Stand down or you will be destroyed."

"The lead ship has opened fire, laser cannons," the tactical officer said.

"That's all they've got? Return fire, all blaster batteries, all lasers. Blow them to hell," Avery said.

"Two ships hit, one is destroyed and the other is disabled. The third one is retreating into the asteroid belt – Earth side," the tactical officer said. "Sir, do you want to give chase?"

"No. Prepare a boarding party for the disabled ship," Avery ordered. "Let's see who's been causing all this ruckus."

Nick Tanager and Sarah went as far as the security team would let them. They could hear a lot of small arms fire on the boarded ship, which was now joined by one of the *Defiant's* airlocks. Finally, the all clear was given and they boarded the raider.

"Not very impressive," Nick remarked.

"Sir," a sergeant reported, "they all fought to the death. There are no prisoners."

Sarah ventured to one of the weapon stations. "This ship has virtually no armor. Laser cannons and maybe a few other systems, but they're not state-of-the-art weapons."

"That's for sure. I use them on my APC, but that's just for landing troops," Nick agreed. "Of course, you don't want to destroy the cargo you're trying to steal."

"Good point." Sarah looked over the helm area, then scanned the instrument panel with her clipboard. "This is interesting."

~ * ~

Johnson LeClark rolled over on his soft, comfortable bed. It was the best bed he'd ever owned. Unfortunately, the asteroid didn't provide enough gravity for him to fully enjoy it. He noticed he couldn't see the clock on the wall. He sat up in his bed.

"I would assume," Sarah said, "your real name isn't Johnson LeClark."

"It's sort of a franchise," he answered. "Someone else will replace me."

"You don't seem too surprised that I'm here," Sarah said.

"Well, we got sloppy. You don't attack a heavy cruiser with raiders, unless you've got a hundred of them. It never occurred to me you'd substitute a warship for a cargo vessel. It's too sneaky for MDF."

"I'm not MDF," Sarah reminded him.

"Outsmarted by an insurance agent," LeClark said.

"Backtracking the helm settings on the raider led us straight to this base," Sarah said.

"I suppose this place is crawling with Martian troops? Is there a prison cell with my name on it?" the pirate asked. "Bread and water or that dreadful Martian Hydroponics crap?"

"No, actually there isn't. There won't be any prison in your future, I'm afraid. The shipping consortium really did hire the Pinkertons. They're here right now and they're not too happy about what you did to their chums," Sarah said. "Good day, Mr. LeClark."

"You would've made a good pirate," LeClark said.

~ * ~

Sarah watched Ensign Wayne eat the last of her sliced green stuff. Sarah put down her Martian Hydroponics tea and leaned back in her chair. "Well, it's good to have this piracy stuff taken care of. It was really bad for business."

"I guess," Ensign Wayne said. "I'm sure there will be more someday."

"No doubt. Especially, since they can get corrupt military officers to help them out," Sarah said.

"How so?" Ensign Wayne asked.

"Well, when Johnson LeClark paid me a visit, he knew who I was and that I'd been on board the APC when we mixed it up with him. Thing is, I sure didn't tell anyone. So, how'd he know?"

"It was in my report. We did fire on an unknown vessel," the ensign argued.

"But your report hadn't been filed then. Commander Tanager

hadn't approved it. It was still in queue. I checked the time stamps. The only way he knew I was on that APC was because you told him," Sarah said. "That's why we didn't take you to the *Defiant* or tell you it was masquerading as a cargo ship to draw the pirates out."

"No," Ensign Wayne protested.

"Tell it to your court martial," Tanager said. "Those two provost marshals standing behind you have plans for you, Ensign. Take her away."

~ * ~

Sarah noticed she couldn't see her clock. "And you're the new franchisee?"

"Yes, indeed," a voice said. "And we've got a score to settle, you and I."

"I suppose we do." With a quick move, Sarah pulled the particle gun out from beneath her pillow and fired. Small metallic particles blasted across the room and sliced into the new Johnson LeClark. "The insurance industry is a lot tougher business than most people think."

"Madam, so is piracy," the dying heap on her floor replied.

3
WHERE D THAT THING COME FROM?

Sarah's eyes couldn't focus on the clock. The numbers were so blurry. That was the problem with Martian Red Ale, at least when you drink a huge amount of it. That chirping sound was getting annoying, too. Finally, she realized it was the terminal. It was Gompers, Mars City. No, it was Gompers, but not Mars City. She sat up. Gompers HQ? They never called her direct. She tried to remember how to answer. "Whuluh?"

"Sarah Meadows?" some guy was asking.

Sarah wondered if she had any clothes on. She wondered who this guy was. "What do you want?"

He seemed to be saying something about Fremont Station. "Why do I have to go there? I'm tired. I want to sleep."

"Dragon says to get up to Fremont Station on the next available shuttle," the guy was saying. "Now!"

"Who's Dragon?" she asked, though the name seemed familiar.

"He owns the company," the man said. This man seemed a little testy.

"Oh, him. Dragon always wants stuff," Sarah said. "I'm going back to bed." She turned off the terminal and let her head fall back to the pillow. She noticed she didn't have any clothes on and she'd flashed some guy she didn't even know. "I'll bet he'll remember me."

She climbed out of bed and struggled to find the shower in the tiny apartment. It was proving difficult to find. She finally found it next to the bathroom. The hot water hit her face. She wondered what some guy she didn't know was thinking about some girl sitting in front of the terminal stark naked. She wondered where it was she was supposed to go. "Fremont Station," the voice inside her head told her.

Sarah had no idea how she got to the Mars City Space

Terminal. But she was there. She accepted the boarding pass and staggered over to one of the orange plastic chairs in the waiting area. Sarah wondered what the guy from Gompers HQ was worried about. She'd made it with five minutes to spare. Lord, she wanted to pass out. *Can pass out on the shuttle. Can throw up on the shuttle. No, we can't.* Some man was talking to his lady friend. Sarah grabbed his carry on and upchucked into it, then put it back unnoticed. *Enjoy your lunch, sir. Can't believe I just did that.*

They were boarding now. She staggered through the airlock and grabbed hold of the first seat she saw. The shuttle was swirling around. They didn't used to do that. The attendant was waking her. They were there. That was fast. She wandered out into Fremont Station.

Some short little bald guy was standing by the window holding a sign that read Sarah Meadows. "Are you Sarah Meadows?" she asked.

He said, "No. I'm Smedley, from finance."

"Well, Smedley from finance, I'm Sarah Meadows, too."

"There's an MDF transport waiting at Level D," Smedley said.

"Lead on, my good fellow," Sarah said, though she knew the way and could probably walk it blindfolded. She was feeling much better. Sleeping on the shuttle and the simple passage of time was eliminating the effects of lack of sleep and too much Martian Red Ale. "Uh, where are we going again?"

"Pittsburgh," Smedley replied.

That didn't seem right somehow. "I don't go to Earth. I hate Earth."

"The other one," Smedley explained.

That didn't make any sense at all. "The space city?"

"That's the one," Smedley insisted.

"But, it disappeared twenty years ago?" Sarah asked. She sort of remembered the guy from HQ might have mentioned some of this.

Smedley nodded. "And yesterday, it suddenly reappeared."

"The biggest underwriting loss in the history of Gompers Insurance Company is suddenly back?" Sarah pointed toward the stairs that went down to Level D. "No wonder HQ called me. Why are you here?"

"They said to come. Beats me. I work in a cubicle," Smedley replied.

The airlock was open. Two crewmen clad in the khaki uniforms of the Martian Defense Force looked them over.

"Sarah Meadows and Smedley from Gompers," Sarah said. She wondered if Smedley was a first name or a last. She decided she didn't really care.

"Welcome aboard," one of them greeted. They were both quickly strapped into the space couch things by the crewmen.

An officer climbed down from the cockpit. "I'm Lt. Commander Skip Ferguson. Folks just call me Skip."

"Sarah Meadows. This is Smedley."

"Pleased to meet you. My orders are to head out to the Pittsburgh Station and try and figure out what the heck is going on," Skip explained. "I got called out of bed by the Minster of Defense himself for this one."

"Sounds like a plan," Sarah agreed.

"There's a small group of five MDF engineers already on board Pittsburgh Station," Skip added. "They got there a few minutes ago."

Fremont Station, from where they were disembarking, was obsolete the day it opened—too small, too limited in its features and services, lacking the space for cargo transfers and not enough hotel rooms for people to sleep during layovers. And, perhaps most important, nearly everyone who went there thought it was ugly.

Pittsburgh Station was to have ended all that. Massive in size and scope, grand and sparkling in appearance, and simply too far from Mars, many said. It was so big it had to be placed in a parallel orbit around the sun, rather than in orbit around Mars. It was feared that, over time, it would alter the orbits of Deimos and Phobos and perhaps cause them to crash into Mars itself. So, it was going to be more of an independent city in space than simply a space station. Two days before its planned opening, the entire facility vanished without a trace. The cost of building it had been astronomical, with much of the materials coming all the way from Earth. And the Gompers Insurance Company had made the unfortunate decision to insure it.

"I've never been on a mission before," Smedley said.

"Why are you here, exactly?" Sarah asked.

Smedley explained, "If it really is back and operational, Gompers owns it unless the Martian Government wants to repay the millions they got from the claim and have long ago spent. They may decide to lease it. That's what I do, negotiate leases on property Gompers owns."

"Makes sense," Sarah agreed.

They could see Pittsburgh Station long before they arrived. It was a glistening little star in space. As they got closer, it was not all that little. It's docking area was bigger than the entire station they'd just left.

"Prepare for docking," Skip said over the intercom. There was a gentle thud a few moments later. "Welcome to Pittsburgh."

The docking area opened out into a huge atrium with large skylights and pleasing indirect lighting. "Wow," Sarah said.

"The operation center is four flights up, if the elevators work," Skip said. "Let's check in with the engineers."

"Lead on," Sarah replied.

One of the engineers looked up from a heating duct. The others kept on working. "Hey Skip."

"Anything interesting?" Skip asked back.

"Heck yeah. There were twenty-three construction workers on the station when it disappeared. There's no sign of any of them. And," he paused for just a moment, "some of the escape pods are gone. No idea where they went."

"Place looks brand new," Skip said.

"That's why we were checking the ventilation. It's hardly been used. Thing is, everything was running when we got here."

"It's been running on empty for twenty years?" Skip asked.

"I'm not so sure what's going on," the engineer explained. "I want to check out a few more things." He started back for the ventilation system. "Hey, one more thing. The bar's fully stocked."

"Well, then maybe this won't be a wasted trip after all," Skip said.

"Wasted?" Sarah asked.

"It's not a military station. I don't know what I'm doing here. This is the future of space commerce," Skip explained. "It's not a MDF facility."

"Well, for Gompers, this is a big deal. But we've got to figure out what happened or people will be afraid to come here." She gazed out one of the many enormous windows for a moment.

"Where have you been all this time?" she asked the station. There had been plenty of theories from falling through a wormhole to being stolen by aliens. Truth was, no one knew for sure. It had simply reappeared at the exact precise location it had vanished from 20 years earlier. The Gompers HQ guy had told her that. She was starting to remember things, including the billions Gompers lost.

"Hey, Smedley, let's go check out one of the penthouses. I used to dream of living in them when I was a little girl. They told us about this place in school. It was going to be this wonderful city. Then, it was gone."

Smedley cautiously approached an elevator. The doors sensed him and opened. "Penthouse please." The doors closed and they were quickly taken up to the penthouse level.

"Ooh." Sarah looked around in amazement. The entire ceiling was an open skylight view of space. She touched a button and the windows instantly clouded up. "Ooh." Then she saw the bathtub, in many ways it looked more like a little pond. It even had its own cascading waterfall. "Ooh." She turned it on and the warm water began to cascade into the tub. "If a man wanted to sleep with me, all he'd need do is bring me here. That'd work." For a space station, this was beyond fancy.

Smedley seemed uncomfortable with that revelation. "Hey, it's got its own bar." Smedley poured himself a glass of Martian Red Ale and took a sip. "Not bad for twenty year old brew. Want one?"

The thought made Sarah's head start hurting again. "Uh, not right now."

"Not bad at all." Smedley collapsed into one of the big comfy lounge chairs that filled a conversation pit next to the bar. The little terminal at the edge of the bar started chirping. "May I help you?" Smedley asked.

A rather sexy computer voice asked, "Shall I put through a call for a Smedley?"

"Nobody ever calls me? Uh, okay, put it through," Smedley decided.

"Smedley?" A face appeared on the tiny screen. Smedley pressed a button and the face also appeared on half of the wall. He pressed it again and the image went back to just being on the small screen. "Smedley, are you there?"

"I'm here sir," Smedley assured him.

"Is the station salvageable?" There was something odd in his speech, like it was taking too long between words. "I've," there was a quick skip, "got a meeting," another skip, "with the Chancellor."

Sarah recognized the man, though she had never actually met him in person. He was Malcolm Collier, Director of Finance for Gompers Insurance. "Sir, Sarah Meadows with Special Ops, we're hopeful. Everything seems in good shape, but it's a big station. A lot to check out." She looked back at the bathtub. "Water system is in great shape."

"Who's in shape?" he asked. "You're not coming in too good. Maybe it's sun spots."

"We'll keep you informed, boss," Smedley said. He terminated the call from a new bunch of controls he found underneath the armrest of his comfy chair.

"Damn, I so wanted to take a bath in that tub," Sarah said.

"Oh?" Smedley asked.

"Sunspots my ass. We've got to get back over to operations," Sarah said.

"What for? I haven't finished my beer."

"I didn't like that call clarity," Sarah said. "I want to check something." Sarah headed for the elevator. The doors opened. "Central Operations." The doors closed. She noticed Smedley was still with her.

The engineer looked up from his work doing whatever it was with the vents. "These vents are amazing."

"Do you have a name?" Sarah asked.

"Chuck."

"Well, Chuck, I need help with something," Sarah said.

"Oh?" Chuck looked anxiously.

"Can you set up a hyperspace link with the MDF Research Lab in Mars City?" Sarah asked.

"We're not that far away. A regular link is all we use," Chuck explained as he looked longingly at his vents.

"Can you set up a hyperspace link with the MDF Research Lab in Mars City?" Sarah asked for the second time. "The Martian Defense Force Research Lab? In Mars City?"

"Yes, it's no different than calling some other planet. System here was state of the art in its day." He went over to a station next to a window that overlooked the main promenade where shops and recreation were going to be. He touched a panel. "But, why a hyperspace link? It's really not necessary."

"Just connect it," Sarah said.

Marshall Fenton, civilian director of the lab, appeared on the screen. He looked curiously at them.

"It's your party?" Chuck said.

"Dr. Fenton, Sarah Meadows with Gompers," Sarah explained.

"How (there was kind of a skip) help you?" he asked.

"Behind you is the atomic clock. Can you show, not tell, us the time? I know it's an odd request," Sarah explained.

He spun his terminal around to a digital display on the wall. The time was 6:22.

Sarah pointed to the clock in the operations area. It was 6:43. "Doesn't this clock align itself with that very clock we are looking at on Mars?"

"I don't understand?" Dr. Fenton asked.

"I went to the Martian School of Economics. Time theory is not my strongest area, but I think this station is existing in different time than Mars. Doctor, is there any possibility that some sort of rift in time is going on? This station does not appear twenty years old. It is brand spanking new."

"Possibly. Frankly...know," Dr. Fenton said.

"I think we missed some of that, say again?" Sarah asked.

"I don't know. It may be possible...may be fluid. Not much...research." He looked kind of blank.

Sarah pointed at the clock. It now read 6:58. The one on Mars was reading 6:44. "Either we've got a defective clock or we are in big trouble," Sarah said.

"What should we do?" Smedley asked.

"Abandon ship!"

"This is not a ship," Chuck pointed out.

"Evacuate! Get the heck out of here." Sarah pressed a red

button that was labeled ALL STATION ADDRESS SYSTEM. "All hands, this is Sarah Meadows. Evacuate! Evacuate now!"

"Madam, I think you're over reacting," Chuck protested. "I'm going back to my vents. This station looks rock solid to me."

"Suit yourself, Chuck." She started running for the elevator. "Coming Smedley?" She noticed he was right on her heels. The bidirectional elevator whisked them directly to the docking ring.

The MDF crew were already on board. "What's wrong?" Skip asked.

"We need to get away from this station, pronto," Sarah said.

Skip looked down the hallway toward the docking airlock of the transport the engineers had used. There was no activity. "Aren't the engineers coming?"

"I don't know what they're doing," Sarah said. "If I'm right, this station is going to do another vanishing act."

Skip pressed the talk button on the communicator clipped to his shoulder. "Get us out of here now. Straight away course, maximum speed."

"Aye, aye," came the reply. The airlock door slid shut. "All hands prepare for departure. I'll get us in hyperdrive as soon as we clear the station."

"No!" Sarah yelled.

"What?" a confused Skip asked.

"I think it's worse in hyperspace than regular space," Sarah said.

"Stay in regular space drive," skip ordered, "maximum thrust."

The shuttle jerked as it pulled away from the station. "I'm heading topside. Get strapped in." Skip bolted up the ladder to the cockpit on the top level.

Smedley managed to get himself buckled in. "I don't know much about hyperspace. I've never been off Mars before."

"Neither do I, frankly. It's just a gut feeling. I've got this rudimentary vision in my head of holes in time that I can't begin to explain right now. It's like my brain is solving this, but can't quite explain it to me yet." The shuttle craft jolted hard as the pilot blasted into full speed. It was a violation of the Uniform Space Act to use anything other than thrusters within two kilometers of a docking space station.

"I may puke," Smedley said.

Sarah was so glad the Martian Red had worn off. "Think happy thoughts. These shuttles are pretty tough."

Time went by. Sarah wasn't sure how much, or which time. Where they in Martian time again or something else?

"Sarah Meadows, topside," Skip announced over the intercom.

Sarah floated over to the ladder and held on. Small transports didn't have artificial gravity. Gravity ceased the instant they uncoupled from the space station. She grabbed the ladder rung and pulled up. She easily floated up into the cockpit, which was very dark, illuminated only with the greenish glow from some of the instrument panels. She looked expectantly at Skip.

He pointed out the window. Pittsburgh, the space city of the future shined in the sky, directly ahead of them.

"I don't understand," Sarah said.

"This ship also has an aft view." He pointed behind them. There was a small porthole style window. Sarah floated over and looked out. Pittsburgh, the space city of the future shined brightly in the sky, directly behind them. "Care to explain that?"

"I, uh." She looked back at the front, then again at the same image behind them. "Uh."

"Yeah." Skip looked at some of the reading. "I don't know where to turn."

"Think three dimensionally, commander. They're both on the same plane. Head up or down."

"Might as well," Skip agreed. He nodded to the helmsman. Take us down ninety degrees. "There's really no up or down in space, they say at the academy. Down compared to Mars, anyway."

Then, in an instant, the station behind them was gone.

"This is getting weird," Smedley said.

Sarah wondered how long Smedley had been there. "That's for sure."

"Golly," Skip said.

Sarah looked back to the front of the ship. Because of the change in angle, the station was now high up on the front window. Then, it was gone. "Golly."

"What just happened?" Skip asked.

"I think the one in front was yet another view from a different time, of the same station," Sarah said. "Though I could be wrong."

~ * ~

Sarah noticed Dr. Fenton and the two men who were never actually introduced to her were no longer looking at her drawings that tried to depict how her brain had tried to tell her what was happening with time and space and the enormously expensive Pittsburgh Station. "Maybe, in time, I'll figure out what my brain was trying to tell me. It's hard to explain."

"There is no known link between hyperspace and time," Dr. Fenton said. "Why did you think the hyperlink would be no different than the regular com transmission for such a relatively short distance?"

"I didn't. I knew it would be immune to interference from the sun. That's all. I could rule out solar interference with a hyperlink call. The rest started coming together when we called you," Sarah explained.

"I sure wish the engineers would have believed you that they were in danger," he said.

"So do I," Sarah said.

"That will be all, Miss Meadows," Dr. Fenton said.

Sarah went down the Mag Lev station. She had a strong suspicion Dr. Fenton knew more about this than he was admitting to.

4
FULL COVERAGE

Sarah had no idea what time it was, but the console near her bed was chirping. She reached over and touched one of the buttons. It never actually seemed to make any difference which button she pressed. The bald lady from the office appeared on the screen. "Oh good, you're up."

Sarah looked and seemed fairly certain she was still tucked in underneath the covers of her nice warm bed. "Leave me alone," she protested.

"I've got a priority assignment for you," the bald lady said.

A file came in on the system. Sarah dragged herself out of bed. "Lovely." The screen went blank. "Goodbye to you, too." She looked over the file. "They've got to be kidding," she said aloud to an empty room. "They have got to be kidding."

She took a quick bath, then opened up her closet and stared at the blue jumpsuit. The jumpsuit wasn't that bad. The white helmet was another matter. And the boots were also white. "What moron designed this getup?" She started to get dressed, wondering why she couldn't have stayed in sales. "I went to the Martian School of Economics," she said. She seemed to talk to her apartment a lot, lately. "I was born to sell insurance. Not this crap."

Sarah decided to carry the helmet. Only a dork would wear it around the city. Twenty minutes after being woken up, she stepped on the tram heading out of Mars City. Next stop, the Martian Defense Force maintenance yard.

Lt. Commander Nick Tanager kept looking at his notebook. The orders were plain enough. He just couldn't believe them. "Tartarus?"

"Tartarus," Sarah repeated. "That's where I need to go."

"Miss Meadows, I don't know what dirt the Gompers Insurance Company has over the Martian High Command, but it must be something incredible. You people are always using us as your personal taxi service, but to get them to risk a ship in a war zone. That is no small favor."

"When do we leave?" was all Sarah had to say.

"The ship is ready now," Tanager said.

Sarah strapped into one of the seats in the back of the cramped cockpit of the armored personnel carrier. She nodded that she was ready.

Tanager swiveled around toward her as the copilot taxied the ship out of the hangar. "This is Ensign Yee," he said, then pointed at the seat next to her, "and Chief Watson."

Sarah nodded.

"And," Tanager continued, "just so we understand each other, this is drop you off and skedaddle. My orders do not include rescue missions."

Sarah nodded again.

"I hope they pay you a lot," Chief Watson said.

The APC shot off into the Martian sky.

"Not nearly enough, chief." Sarah dozed for a while after the ship went into hyperspace. There was nothing for her do or even to look at as the APC sped toward its destination.

Then, somebody was tapping on her shoulder. It was Chief Watson. "Time to get ready." He pointed to the aft area where troops usually rode.

Sarah followed.

"Didn't think Gompers did business with Earth," the chief said.

She put on her backpack, then the chute. "We don't."

His eyes seemed to get bigger. "You're working with the lizards!"

"So, it would seem," Sarah replied.

The chief helped her get strapped into the parachute. "You ever done a high altitude jump?"

"Once."

"Well, this time we'll dump you out at five thousand meters. Your chute will deploy automatically. That's in case you black out on the way down. And you want to get down on the ground as fast as possible. The chute won't pop until you're down to a thousand meters above the surface, so don't panic. That ground comes up fast. You're an easy target floating in the breeze," the chief explained.

Sarah nodded.

A light near the door flashed yellow. "We're out of hyperspace," the chief said.

Almost immediately, the APC began jerking violently. "Turbulence?" Sarah asked.

"Nah, someone's shooting at us," the chief said.

"Which side?"

He shrugged. "Does it matter?"

The cold night air slammed into her like getting kicked in the gut. The APC was too high and moving too fast. The force from being tossed out into the atmosphere tried to rip the mouthpiece from the breathing apparatus right out of her mouth. And that was from the "thin" air up high. She bit down all the harder. Still, she blacked out.

When Sarah came to, the chute was deployed. The ground was coming up really fast. And, then, she was on the surface. Her ears hurt. Her neck hurt. Her back hurt. Her head hurt. She had to force her body to get out of the parachute harness and get to something that would provide some cover.

She took refuge next to a large boulder and pulled the handheld unit out of a pocket in her jumpsuit. It quickly told her she was only a kilometer off target. Not bad. She unfolded a laser rifle from her pack. The barrel extended and the butt clicked into place. She hid the parachute under some rocks. It was dark. Tartarus was a moon slightly larger than Mars that orbited a gas giant. She adjusted the straps on her backpack and headed out.

Tartarus seemed an odd place to be fighting over. It was usually described as a hell hole. Way too hot. The air contained a sulfur quality and stunk most of the year. The water was barely drinkable. And, the vegetation was mostly bushes and scrub grass etching out a humble existence in the rocky surface. Then, there were the earthquakes caused by the gas giant's gravity.

Right, precisely at the assigned coordinates sat a hover tank. Earthforce called them prairie schooners. It was a misnomer. They were not slow and even could change color to mimic their background. She rapped on the hull with the butt of her laser rifle.

A hatch slowly opened. "Hello. I'm Miss Meadows of the Gompers Insurance Company."

"At least you're on time." A green reptilian head stuck up out of the conveyance. "What weapons you carry?"

"Barkisko folding laser rifle."

"What else?" the reptile asked.

"A folding knife."

"Anything else?"

"Maybe."

"Get inside."

She climbed down inside the tank. It was staffed by a crew of three.

"Do not like having to deal with human," the reptile said. "We fight them. Kill them."

"I appreciate that," Sarah said. "But I remind you, I am from the Martian Republic and I have nothing to do with Earth. And, if you want to deal with my company, I'm the only rep trained in battlefield assessment available. It wasn't my idea to buy a war policy. It was *your* emperor's."

"I Marshal Zuto."

"Let's get on with it," Sarah suggested.

Zuto pointed at a reptile with much less elaborate insignia on its uniform. "Tink."

The tank lifted slightly on its air cushion and they began to move. They went along for a few minutes, then the reptiles became agitated. Some of the instruments were flashing and beeping. "They think you brought them here," Zuto said.

"I didn't bring them. If we die, I die with you." The truth was, she probably had brought them. The Earthforce planes were more than likely looking for whomever jumped out of an unidentified space ship and parachuted to the surface.

Two Earthforce Jumper Jets dumped a load of Z Palm that barely missed the tank. Most of the area around them seemed to explode from the flaming gel. The planes dropped below a nearby ridge.

Sarah said, "A suggestion, Jumpers only carry one load of the stuff. If they come around, it'll just be with their guns. They can't carry missiles and Z Palm at the same time."

As the planes returned, the tank started firing its very fast revolving guns. When the planes emerged over the ridge, they took a lot of the dart shaped projectiles. The planes' engines were smoking and they soon retreated out of sight.

They rode for some time, then stopped at what remained of a burned out set of Quonset huts. The hatch opened and Zuto climbed out. He moved so fast Sarah struggled to keep up with him. The other two reptiles took positions at the rear, with their hand-held mini cannons. "This where it all began," the Grand Marshal of the Tau Army explained.

"The Sandner Colony." Sarah looked around. Everything was burnt. It was hard to imagine the thriving community that once stood there.

Zuto started back for the tank. Sarah had to run to keep up with them. The Tau reminded her of small dinosaurs. These guys were about a meter and a half tall. They had considerable teeth. And, as she huffed to keep up, were amazingly fast. She was grateful for the Gompers translator she carried on her belt. They weren't real talkative, but at least she was able to communicate. She climbed into the tank and the hatch closed.

Their next stop was a bunker a few kilometers away. They passed through a narrow canyon and eventually went underground. The place was full of several hundred Tau warriors. They all seemed incredibly busy, and they all managed a suspicious glance or two at Sarah.

Zuto led the way deeper into the cavern. An entourage quickly formed behind them. They were soon in an office of sorts. At least, there was something that looked like a conference table. Zuto took a seat at the end. "What do you require?"

"A tank crew. Two days should do it." She held up the clipboard she'd extracted from her backpack moments earlier. She scanned the troop positions on a map on the wall. "Client information is always confidential."

"She could give that to our enemy," another of the reptiles warned.

"Gompers is the most reliable insurance company anywhere in the galaxy. And, frankly, those of us who live on Mars have little more use for Earth than you do," Sarah said.

There was some discussion, then Zuto pounded on the table. Nothing else was said.

Then another reptile brought her a tray. It had a cup of water and two Earthforce nutrition bars. "Thanks, I guess." She tried one of the bars. It was supposed to be cherry flavored. "Earthforce?" They were quite a bit chewier than she remembered.

"We have plenty of them. We do not like them," Zuto said. He made some sort of grunting noise the translator could not handle. The room cleared except for the reptile previously introduced as Tink. "Tank Commander Tink is assigned for you. They will leave whenever you are ready." Zuto stood and walked out of the room.

"Let's go, then," Sarah said. She wanted out of the cavern. There were simply too many of the reptiles giving her the evil eye. She slammed down the water.

Tink led her back to the tank. Two other Tau stood next to it. "Kosh and Pepo."

Sarah nodded, then climbed into the tank. "Commander, the computer in my clipboard has randomly selected battlefield grid areas. All we have to is go there and I'll record some information. From that, the computer at the home office will rate the risks and your emperor will get his insurance policy."

"I wouldn't insure a war," Tink said.

"All risks can be broken down, if you have the stomach for it," she said. "But, quite frankly, I wouldn't either, if it was up to me."

There was some chatter amongst them. There seemed to be a second reptile dialect the translator didn't pick up.

The survey of the first sector was unremarkable. The clipboard computer wanted data and Sarah entered it. She carried a small visualizer in her pack which gave excellent information on distances and temperatures and such.

They'd just started section two when she noticed something interesting in her visualizer. "Guys I've got a human male dead ahead, at the base of those jutting rocks."

They stopped well away from the man. "We do not detect any others. What is he doing?" Tink asked.

"Why don't we go ask him?" Sarah suggested.

"More likely a trick," Tink warned. "If you want to know, you go ask."

"Okay," Sarah agreed, "I will." The hatch opened.

"Kosh sharpshooter," Tink said. "Put both hands together

above your head if you are in trouble."

She climbed out and made her way around the scrub brush to an open area near the rocks. "Hello."

The man held a clipboard computer similar to her own. He seemed completely absorbed in his work and actually startled at her presence. "Huh. Who are you?"

"Sarah Meadows. I'm from Gompers Insurance."

"Should've known they'd send in a Martian slitch."

"We just met and you've already resorted to name calling."

"Just go back to Mars. I didn't ask you to come out here," he said. No question, he was from Earth with the accent and rudeness to match.

Suddenly, there was a gun in his hand. "I'm military intelligence. We got a report there was a Gompers man doing a survey. We couldn't believe they'd be stupid enough to do a policy for a war. But, it lets me locate their supply dumps unmolested. Two patrols have already left me alone. "Then, you show up."

The tank's camouflage was so good it was hard to see. She hoped Kosh was out there. "Well, now what?" She slowly raised her hands above her head. "Looks like you got me."

"I'll cover your body under some rocks and get on with things," he said.

"Well, there is one thing. I'm not alone," Sarah warned.

The Earth man's head sort of exploded.

"Military intelligence. There's an oxymoron." Sarah turned back toward the tank and ran as fast as she could. She dove into the tank.

"The man is dead now. There was no need to run," Tink said.

Sarah didn't say anything until she caught her breath. "He was pretending to be me, from Gompers. Wandering around, spying." She looked at Kosh. "Nice shooting."

"Do not understand humans. You are here with us, not out there." Tink nodded and Pepo started up the tank. "And you are female human. They must think we are double stupid."

Sarah handed Tink the dead man's clipboard. "Have your people find out what he was after."

Tink looked at it for a moment, then nodded.

It soon turned dark. They parked next to a ridge. The reptiles covered the tank with large rocks, which they tossed around with ease.

Sarah took the opportunity to eat another Earthforce nutrition bar and doze for a little while. Her slumber was interrupted by a tap on the shoulder.

It was Tink. He pointed at the tank's infrared screen. An Earthforce tank was moving toward them. It looked like an infantry patrol of eight men were walking along behind the tank.

The tank stopped where the body of the man Kosh shot was still lying. The soldiers put it in a body bag and strapped it on the back of the tank.

The tank turned around and the soldiers piled up on top of it. "Must be search party. Tau not so careless. Dead man dies twice." He touched a panel. It turned red. He touched it again and a missile shot out of the tank. It raced to its target and ripped the back half of the Earthforce tank right off its treads. Bodies of soldiers flew everywhere.

Pepo immediately had their tank in motion. It glided across the rough terrain on its air cushion as the rocks on top of it tumbled off. And they were going in the opposite direction. "Human base will detect lost signal from their tank. They will send more. We will be gone."

They took a different route to get to the final survey zone. It was much the same—rocks and weeds and little else. Sarah finally closed her notebook. "That's about it, guys."

"Finished?" Tink asked.

"Yes."

"We celebrate." They'd all been standing on a hill. Tink walked down to a dried up stream bed and pulled a plant out of the ground. He returned with it, pulled the leaves off, then washed it off from a canteen. He then smashed the bulb part that had been growing underground against a rock, then pulled it into four pieces. "Humans think we just eat bugs."

"Even put fake bugs out with bombs in them," Kosh added.

Tink gave everyone a piece of the plant. "These don't grow on our home world, only here."

Sarah looked it over. It seemed harmless enough. She took a bite. The fruit was amazingly sweet. "This is good." Her companions were too busy eating to say anything.

"Aren't you curious at what might be on that Earth guy's

clipboard?" Sarah asked.

"No," Tink said. After a minute or so, he added, "already know." He scraped around in the ground and brought up some tiny metallic flakes. "He was looking for this. Doesn't pick up from satellite."

Sarah looked at the material. "Carenthium? Used to power space ships?"

"Humans built settlement. Our governor of planet sent emissary to see why they were here. Humans killed emissary and ate him. Roasted him over open fire," Tink said. "But, war not really fought over that, is it? Does this change your report?"

"Not that much. Gompers doesn't really care why a war is fought. Surprisingly, it doesn't affect the outcome that much," Sarah said. "Boy, that's different from the Earth version of things."

"They call it massacre," Tink added.

"That they do," Sarah agreed.

Then, everything turned to hell. A mortar round exploded right next to them. Sarah was behind Pepo. His body absorbed the blast, leaving her relatively unscathed. Pepo's head was missing. Tink and Kosh were down, but still alive.

Sarah ran down the hill and got into the tank. She'd seen enough that she thought she could drive it. She powered it up and brought it to the top of the hill. There were five Earthforce grunts out in the open, approaching the hill. They must've thought they were taking on sentries. The tank's rapid fire guns tore them to pieces in seconds.

She wasn't strong enough to drag the reptiles into the tank. With a little coaxing, she was able to get Kosh and Tink inside. Then, she drove in the opposite direction as fast as the tank would go. When she found a secluded spot, she parked it.

"Why you stop?" Tink asked.

"I don't know where your base is. I can't read the writing on the computer screen. I could just as easily be driving right into Earth's main lines."

"Proceed forward," Tink said.

She did just that. The trail got narrower, then descended underground. There were five other tanks parked in the cave. One of the Tau was welding on one of them. She popped open the hatch, then helped Tink out.

He said something in the dialect the translator didn't understand, then reptiles came running. They took him and Kosh off somewhere. Sarah sat herself on the floor. She had nowhere to go. She certainly wasn't going to wander around the base by herself. She looked too much like the enemy for that.

Finally, a reptile approached her. He just stared at her.

"Can I help you?" she asked.

"Never see human before," it answered.

"Well, today's your lucky day, then," she replied.

"You are to come with me. Commander Tink say so," the reptile stated. He took her farther inside the cave, then pointed at a console. "You transmit report to insurance company from here."

"Okay." She did just that.

There was some commotion at the front entrance. She followed a group of reptiles to the entrance. Two more tanks were entering. The hatches opened up and a number of Tau climbed out, including Marshal Zuto. Everyone sort of bowed toward him.

He walked up to Sarah. "Are you finished?"

"Yes."

"Good." He headed for the interior of the cave.

Once again, she sat herself down next to the tank. She waited there a long time. Then, Zuto returned.

"Commander Tink say you drove tank without permission," Zuto said.

"Uh, I guess that's one way of looking at it," she agreed.

He sort of swatted her on the shoulder. The other reptiles all started making some sort of chatter in the second dialect. Then, Zuto said, "That was joke."

"Oh."

"Tink say you saved tank crew. Even killed Earth soldiers. Is this true?" Zuto asked.

"Yes."

He said something in the second dialect to a subordinate, who quickly scurried off. The subordinate soon returned with a small wooden case. Zuto handed it to her.

She stared at it a moment, then gave Zuto a puzzled look. "I don't understand."

"Open case," he said.

She opened it. There was a medal on a gold braided rope. There was writing on it, but she could not read it. The medal looked like it was made from platinum.

"Put medal around neck," Zuto said.

"Oh." She did as instructed. "Thank you."

Zuto picked her up and tossed her into the air. He caught her on the way down. The other reptiles let out some sort of yelp. "Now, go outside."

"Outside?" she asked.

"Outside," he repeated. He pointed at the entrance to the cave.

She started that way and noticed a lot of the Tau were following her. Once outside, she noticed a small ship was landing. It looked like a Tau version of an armored personnel carrier.

Two Tau in blue uniforms came out through the hatch. When they saw her medal, they snapped to attention.

"Ship take you back to Mars, if it not get shot down by Earthforce," Zuto said.

"Thanks. No worries. It's insured."

5
CHEAP TRANSPORTATION

Sarah counted four Tau crew members, though she hadn't been to the bottom deck of the transport. None of them had introduced themselves to her. She'd just sat down and buckled herself in. The chair took some adjusting to fit her. Anything that flies was becoming her motto. At least she was off Tartarus. One ship buzzing through hyperspace was pretty much the same as another. Though, she was starting to wonder if Dragon ever actually paid for transportation. She usually got where she needed to go by bumming a ride from someone.

The Tau seemed to mostly talk in that odd second dialect her translator could not seem to pick up. She wrote a quick note to transmit to Special Ops Division, warning them of the problem.

Then, abruptly, the reptile with the most garishly decorated uniform turned toward her. "I'm Commander Goth. We've never been to Mars."

"Well, today is your lucky day, then," Sarah said.

"We can't find it," he reported.

"What? It's a big red planet. Fourth one from star 341," Sarah said.

The reptiles all made some sort of odd noise. "That was joke," Commander Goth said.

Sarah grinned. She had no idea what to say to them.

"We come out of hyperspace soon. Not enough fuel to land on Mars. We go to Fremont Station."

"That will be fine. I can catch a shuttle back to Mars City. They run twice a day." How she hated that space station.

"What is it like?" Goth asked.

"Fremont Station? Well, it's a space station," she said. "You guys might like the refectory." Her most evil grin took over her face. "Hey, I'll buy lunch for your crew. You'll love it. A beautiful view of Mars and Earth and all you can eat dining."

"We have crew of five," Goth said.

"The more the merrier. I've got an expense account," Sarah

said.

The Tau reverted back to that second dialect, but the crew seemed suddenly energized.

That tone changed when they left hyperspace. In fact, Goth suddenly seemed quite agitated.

Sarah unstrapped from her seat and went over to the control area. "Something wrong?"

"All he say is gibberish. Can't understand him."

"Maybe their translator isn't as good as mine. May I try?" She put on and adjusted a headset without waiting for an answer from Goth. "Fremont Station, this is Tau Transport requesting approach clearance."

There was a long, awkward silence, then a voice replied, "Repeat please?"

"This is Tau transport requesting approach clearance," Sarah repeated.

"Tau?"

"Tau," she assured him.

There was another awkward silence. "What planet are you arriving from?"

"Tartarus."

And another silence. "We are having trouble locking onto your ship."

"Tau systems are not compatible with your Lydar based docking system. It will have to be a manual docking," Sarah explained.

"Tau shuttle, you are clear for approach to docking ring two. We are turning on docking lights now."

Sarah took off the headset. "Just follow the flashing blue lights and glide right in. Then, remember to stop."

Goth gave her a funny look, like he was offended at the notion he would forget to use his thrusters and stop. Sarah retreated back to her seat. It was a perfect docking.

Two Martian customs officers dressed in white uniforms looked at Sarah, then at her companions as they exited the airlock. "Welcome to Fremont Station," one of them said.

"Thanks." Sarah handed them her Martian identity card, which was quickly scanned and handed back.

Then, the customs officers looked at the reptiles. "What is

your business on Fremont Station?"

"We were invited to come and eat," Goth said.

"And you are?" the customs guy asked.

"Commander Goth of the Army of the Tau Empire. This is my crew."

The two customs officers whispered to each other, then looked at Sarah. "We don't have any policy on the Tau. They've never come here before."

"Well, do you have any policy prohibiting them?" Sarah asked.

"Well, no, not really," he admitted.

"They'll only be here a little while," Sarah assured them.

"Enjoy your stay," the customs guy said.

"This way, guys," Sarah said.

The cafeteria was fairly crowded. Sara found them a table near one of the sky view windows. "Grab a plate and load up, guys."

"What do we need plates for?" Goth asked.

"Uh, that's the way they do it here," she said.

"That was joke," Goth said as they headed for the buffet line.

Sarah grabbed some salad and beat the reptiles back to the table. She managed one bite.

"You!" It was Greg Steele. "I got foreclosed on account of you!" he screamed.

"You were in financial trouble long before I met you," Sarah pointed out. "Go away now."

"It would've worked out. I was counting on that insurance payment," he screamed.

Sarah glared at him for a moment. "Two words. Insurance fraud."

"I'm going to kick your worthless..." He looked at the reptiles who were now standing next to him.

"These are my friends," Sarah said.

He looked over the Tau soldiers for a second time, then quietly walked away. He wouldn't have been a match for even one of them.

Sarah was amazed they'd taken mounds of Martian Hydroponics green stuff. They'd also loaded up on other things that looked like meat. It wasn't long before their plates were spotless. "You can have more," Sarah pointed out. She didn't have to tell them twice.

They were finishing their second run through the desert aisle. She hadn't figured these guys as cream pie connoisseurs, but they couldn't get enough of it. Then the mood changed, and not for the better.

"Sure stinks in here!" someone was yelling.

Each Tau soldier said at the exact same moment, "Earthforce."

"I had no idea they would be here. Earthforce hardly ever comes here," Sarah said.

A potato bounded off Goth's nose. "What is the custom in this situation?" Goth asked.

"Well, you can be civilized and ignore them," Sarah said as another potato bounced off her head, "or you can kick their damn ass."

The Earthforce guys, all eight of them, had probably never seen a Tau in person before. They certainly didn't seem prepared for how fast they moved. Sarah remembered a lot of people and chairs went flying, some Earthforce guy picked up a carving knife from behind the buffet line, then he was knocked out cold when she smashed a chair over his head. Then, there was the stun gun from the Martian Marshals. Then, she was waking up on the floor of a holding cell.

The five reptiles were all sitting quietly on a bench. There wasn't any room for her. She decided to stay on the floor. It was closer to the ground, anyway. Then, there was a large presence at the bars.

It was Dragon. "Miss Meadows, I see you have regained consciousness. I must say, your conduct reflects rather poorly on the Gompers Insurance Company."

"Uh, yeah, I guess so," she admitted. She struggled to sit up. Her throbbing head liked it better on the floor.

"Well, they've agreed to drop the charges as long as restitution is paid to repair the damages to the refectory," Dragon explained. "And that will come out of your pay." He looked over at the Tau. "And I'll let your commanding officer deal with you. The Martian government wants you to go back home as soon as possible." The door slid open.

"One other thing," Dragon asked, "Did you win?"

"Of course," Sarah said.

Dragon was gone.

"I wonder how he does that." Sarah walked the reptiles back to their ship.

The other four went on board. Goth remained a moment. "Sarah Meadows, this is the best time we ever had."

"You really need to get out more," Sarah said.

Goth went on board his ship. The airlock closed behind him.

Sarah went home briefly and changed clothes. For some reason, she smelled like vomit. It must've been the cell Next, she wandered down to the Mars City Brewery. How badly she'd wanted an ice cold glass of beer on Tartarus. Then, she noticed a familiar face. She moved down the bar. "Hi sailor, I almost didn't recognize you with your clothes on."

"Huh?"

"I've never seen you out of uniform."

"Oh." Nick Tanager looked at himself. "I was supposed to be off today. Then, I had to go and escort a Tau ship out of Martian space. High Command was afraid that, without an escort, Earthforce might go after them. Just got back a little while ago."

"Don't be mad. I was just doing my job," Sarah said.

"Well, your job lately seems to keep bumping into my job," he said.

"And how lucky you are," she said.

He got up and started to leave.

"That was a joke," she insisted.

He kind of rolled his eyes and headed for the escalator to the lower levels.

"Lighten up." She finished her glass of beer, then headed back to her apartment. Instead of a tank, she got to sleep in a nice warm bed that night.

6
THE BAKER

Karl unwrapped the tray and placed it on the table in the break room. He noticed most of the office staff were standing around, expectantly. He cut into the brown, perfectly formed crusty round loaf and handed the first slice to the bald lady.

She smelled it, then took a bite. "What is it?"

"Fungus bread."

There was kind of a gasp from some of the people.

"We need a better name," Karl admitted.

The bald lady took another bite. "It's actually pretty good." She took another mouthful. "Darn good, actually."

Once she'd pronounced it edible, the bread was quickly devoured. The ritual was always the same. Once the bald lady pronounced his creation edible, then everyone else would try it. They were always edible. They were always way more than that.

He sat at his bullpen desk in the corner. Then, he noticed he wasn't alone. Someone was staring at him. "May I help you?" he asked.

"I'm Phillip Phillips," the man said. "That bald lady said to see you."

"How can I help you?" Karl said.

"I have an insurance policy with your company," Phillip said.

"Okay? Life insurance?"

"Yes," he answered.

"And what can I do for you?" he asked.

"You may have to pay a claim on it. Some guys are trying to kill me," Phillip said.

"What makes you think that?" Karl asked.

"How come you're purple?" Phillip asked.

"He's an alien, you moron!" the rest of the bullpen chimed.

"Where from?" Phillip asked.

"Chiron," Karl said.

"Where's that?" Phillip asked.

"Can we get back to the killing you part?" Karl asked.

"These men pushed me in the primary tank. I work at the sewage plant." Phillip took a bite of fungus bread. "Could've drowned. Bacteria break down the urine and stuff. I had to get a prescription to keep my ears from going deaf. This stuff is really good, the bread, I mean."

"I know it is. Did you know these men?" Karl asked.

"Government. The government's after me," Philip insisted.

"Show me where this happened," Karl said.

"Okay. We take the Mag Lev out to the end of L Line. We get off at Tulip Station. Can I have some more bread?"

"It's all gone, Phillip," Karl said. "Let's go."

It took quite a while to get to the sewage processing plant. Phillip showed Karl where he went in and how he managed to climb out.

"What did they look like?" Karl asked.

"Like them guys there," Phillip said.

Karl, at that moment, dearly wished he'd brought a gun with him. The two guys Phillip pointed out each had stun guns. He remembered going down on the pavement, then being rolled over the side and splashing into the liquid sewage. Stun guns make no noise. They leave no marks on a body. They're non-lethal in name only, Karl was thinking as his lungs filled with the vilest liquid he'd ever smelled or touched.

Then, it seemed like somebody was pulling on him. And someone was slapping his face.

"Your majesty, are you okay?" Sarah was asking him.

"Earthforce," he muttered, after a series of coughs. "Earthforce." There was so much sewage in his mouth and lungs that talking was nearly impossible. Then, he passed out.

Hours went by. Perhaps days? Perhaps only minutes? "What's your name?" Some lady was asking him.

He struggled to open his eyes. The lights were far too bright.

"Do you know your name?" the lady asked again.

"King Karl Phillip Geste the third," he said.

"He may have brain damage," the lady said.

"I am King Karl Phillip Geste the third," he repeated.

"Where do you work?" she asked.

"Gompers Insurance."

"You sell insurance?" she asked.

"No, I am a claims adjustor," he said.

"Well, King Karl Phillip Geste the third, welcome to Mars City General Hospital. I'm Dr. Gates."

The soup they gave him wasn't very good. The antibiotics made him feel sick. They were just guessing on dosage. They knew nothing about his alien physiology. He figured if the bacteria he swallowed didn't kill him, the hospital surely would. A nurse came in and looked at the monitor next to his bedside. "Can't you monitor me from your desk?" he asked.

"Of course," she said. "But, I can't talk to you from there. How are you feeling?"

"Like death," he said.

"Well, King Karl Phillip Geste the third, can I get you anything?" she asked.

"No. Just let me die in peace," he pleaded.

"Very well. Press the button if you need me."

"How did I get here?" Karl asked.

She shrugged. "No idea."

"Did Phillip Phillips come here, too?"

"He's down the hall. He's sleeping," she said.

"Good deal," he said. "Somebody tried to kill me."

"You don't say. It says you fell in a sewage vat."

"It was more of a tank, a really big tank." King Karl Phillip Geste III, ruler in exile of the planet Chiron, drifted off to sleep.

~ * ~

There was someone staring at him. He could always tell when someone was staring at him. He opened his eyes. Phillip Phillips was standing next to his bed. "May I help you?"

"I was wondering if you were alive," Phillip replied. "You didn't seem to be breathing."

"I assure you I am not dead, Mr. Phillips," Karl said.

"Okay, then," Phillip said. "I'll go back to my room. I told you the government was out to get me."

"Yes, but you didn't say which one, Mr. Phillips," Karl pointed out.

"There's more than one?" Phillip asked.

"Oh yes, hundreds of them."

That seemed to confuse him. Phillip Phillips scratched his

head and went back to his own room.

Karl closed his eyes. His head hurt. The bacteria he'd breathed in and swallowed were playing havoc with his immune system. The drugs they'd given him had made things even worse. "Get me out of here before they kill me," he pleaded.

"How did you know I was here?" Sarah asked.

"I know." He still didn't open his eyes.

"I was waiting for Mr. Phillips to leave. He's kind of annoying," she said.

"Really?"

"So, are they really after him? You kept saying 'Earthforce' before you passed out," she said.

"No doubt on that count. Earthers have a heck of a time blending in. They can't get the walk right in our low gravity."

"I know that," Sarah reminded him.

"But, why they would be interested in him, that's confusing the heck out of me."

"I've done a full background on him. I'm not getting anything. He's just some clod with a very unglamourous job. Doesn't seem to have any friends," Sarah said. "Except for Carl, a coworker."

"What does he do with his money?" Karl asked.

"He saves it up. Every couple of months, he takes it out of the bank and spends it," she said.

"On what?" Karl asked.

"He goes to one of the brothels over in Jackass Flats," she said.

"Oh." Karl opened his yellow eyes. "Did you get any fungus bread?"

"It was gone before I got to the office. I slept in a whole hour. My trip to Tartarus really left me exhausted," she said. "I tried to catch up to you. You were floating in a pool of sewage when I got there. If you want to take up swimming, there's a pool over at the recreation center with water in it."

"I can still smell it. I can still feel it on me. It's in my lungs. I keep coughing it up. At least I'm bald and it's not in my hair," Karl said.

"I'll see about getting you out of here, your majesty," she said.

"Bless you, my child," he said. "I'll name a city after you when I return to power."

"I can hardly wait," Sarah said. "I'd rather have a knighthood."

"We don't have knighthoods."

7
EFFLUENT

The Mag Lev train quietly came to a stop at the edge of the platform at Hospital Station. Sarah started to get on board, then turned away at the last moment. She went downstairs and picked up another train that also was leaving the station.

It took a half hour to reach Dry Gulch, the first settlement on Mars. Where Mars City was bright and airy, Dry Gulch was dingy and confined. It was a series of various modules and connectors that were tunneled together in an L shape. It was antiquated in every respect. Every time there was a major election, someone would advocate demolishing the town for scrap. It never seemed to happen. Dry Gulch, formerly called Jackass Flats, had found a niche.

There was gambling in the gulch–lots of it. There was a place where you could smoke mushrooms from a cave grown underneath the town that supposedly gave you lots of feelings. And, on a world where men still outnumbered women by nearly two to one, there were the brothels–places men could do what men do, all without disrupting the sensibilities of the decent folk in Mars City.

And Sarah got off the train and went out onto L Street, right in the middle of it. She didn't really care for the toothless man who was rubbing his crotch as he looked her over. She cared even less for the guy behind her who seemed to be following her. She knew where she was going. It wasn't any criminal backwater. It was the Ritz Hotel. A dive, by Earth standards. A last choice for someone in Mars City. In Dry Gulch, the nicest place to stay. She knocked the red dust off her boots and entered the establishment.

"Hi," she said to some guy without a name tag on, who was standing behind the front desk.

"May I help you?" he asked, not offering a name. This was Dry Gulch. People weren't big on names.

Sarah opened her notebook. "This guy? What room?"

"Uh, I don't know him," the desk agent replied.

"Martian doubloons. One hundred of them," Sarah offered.
"Let's see them?"

She held out her handheld notebook. "Deposited anywhere."

"No way. Cash only," he insisted. He looked up.

Sarah was already out the front door. The guy raced after her.

"Wait," he said. "Come back inside. Check in. I'll refund the money in cash and keep it."

"You got a deal," Sarah whispered.

"Let's go back inside, lady," the desk agent urged.

Sarah nodded and followed him back into the Ritz. "What will you put down for the reason for my refund?"

"That you're a whore and your client never showed. And you never used the room," he said.

Sarah asked, "You get a lot of freelancers with five brothels in this town?"

"Six, actually, but one of them's not for men. No. Never. But then, the owners from Mars City never actually come here," he said. "Deal?"

"Deal," she agreed.

"Guy you want is staying in room one thirteen, at the end of the hall. Cheapest room we got," he said.

"Transferring funds now," Sarah said.

One of the many refinements tech support had made to the hand held folding clipboard issued to all Gompers agents and claims adjustors was function 43, in that the special ops people had 43 functions an insurance agent's clipboard did not have. It was her favorite function.

The door popped open. No electronic key or combo code required. She always wondered how they did that, but it worked on just about any electronic door.

Curtis seemed, on first appearance, to be an even more pathetic individual than Phillip Phillips was. He was lying there, stroking himself in the dark, then squinting when the lights came on. "What is this?"

"How much did the people pay you?" Sarah asked.

"What? Who are you?"

"How much did they pay you?" She pulled the stool away from the work desk and sat on it, then opened her clipboard. "It's a rhetorical question, Curtis, I already know the answer."

"Who are you?" Curtis repeated.

"Convincing your friend the government was out to get him. That wasn't too tough." She looked at the screen for a moment. "It seems like a lot of bother, though. Taking a sewage job, manipulating Phillip that way, just to get someone completely different to come to the sewage plant. A lot of bother."

"Not really. It worked. That alien guy came. Phillip told everyone he had a big life insurance policy. Those people from Earth, they're real smart and figured it would be easy to get him down there. Famed ruler falls to his death in vat of sewage. Nobody would investigate that, nobody," Curtis said. "Now, if you'll leave my room?"

"Nobody but me." Sarah said

"Get out!" he screamed. He lunged off the bed. She had no idea where the knife in his hand came from. The stool to the side of his head stunned him and dislodged the knife from his hand. He learned how painful certain pressure points can be as his arm was forced around behind his back and he was driven to the floor.

"I'm not sure if it would be possible to convict you. I know a sewage vat trial is the last thing his majesty would want. So, there's not much I can do with you." She released him and headed out the door. "But, don't think this is the end of it."

He picked up the knife and raced after her. Two steps out in the hallway he noticed there were laser sights trained on him. He stopped moving.

"Yep, bring a knife to a gunfight. A real clever fellow, he is," Sarah said. "I said it wasn't the end of it, Curtis."

"Gunfight?" the bewildered Curtis asked.

"On the ground!" someone was yelling.

"The Federal Police have a unit that investigates diplomatic crimes. Did you know it's a crime to work on behalf of a foreign power without registering as an agent with the Foreign Ministry, Curtis?"

"On the ground!" one of the armored officers repeated.

"And it seems you've done other jobs for Earth, according to your bank records. These fellows are taking you somewhere for a nice long chat," Sarah said.

She was glad to leave the hotel. For just an instant, her mind wondered through the law on foreign registry. At the time, while a student at the Martian School of Economics, she'd thought it odd there was a special exemption pertaining to licensed insurance professionals. Suddenly, it didn't seem so odd anymore.

She headed for the train station. She hated Dry Gulch. She hated the dry, dusty air. She hated the dingy light. She hated the men, so many creepy men. The toothless bastard was still standing in the street, rubbing his crotch as he looked at her. Some other guy was vomiting in the gutter.

Right before she got to the train station, she turned off the street and knocked on a bright orange door. The door quickly opened and a short lady ushered her inside. She hated how the town seemed to drive everyone to their base instincts, their caveman genes, as she used to call them. "I've never been here before. I understand a woman can get a bath and a massage and then handsome young men will bang her into the mattress for as long as she wants," Sarah said.

"You got money?" the short lady asked.

"Oh yeah," Sarah said. "I've got money." She handed the short lady her Gompers Card, the most widely accepted travel card in the known galaxy. She'd given her the cranberry red one for official travel expenses, not the emerald green one for personal charges. "It's been a rough week. Pamper me."

~ * ~

Karl was busily reading something on the little terminals the hospital let patients have if they were feeling better. "Ah, Sarah," he said without looking at her. "Apparently, I am to live, after all."

"The folks at Earth won't be so happy," Sarah said.

"That's the amazing thing. You figured out Earth was behind this? I am impressed. Even I didn't realize Phillips wasn't the real target."

"Phillip Phillips told everyone in town he had a large policy out. So, if somebody was trying to kill him, it would get our attention," Sarah said.

"It could have been you?"

She shrugged. "But they knew I was on Tartarus. You would get the draw, in all probability. And, no one was going to investigate a dead deposed king who died falling in sewage tank, at least not very closely. So, they kill you and don't rile up the

Martian authorities."

"Remarkable. And this Curtis person?" Karl asked.

"They paid him a little to grease it along and feed Phillip's paranoia. I think he's done a few other odd jobs for them. He's being questioned by the folks at the Federal Police about it," Sarah said. "Glad you're feeling better."

"They contacted a Chironese doctor. He got them to undo what they did to me. I can go home tomorrow," Karl said. "I was just getting caught up on some of the paperwork."

"Where'd they find you a physician?" she asked. There weren't an abundance of his countrymen on Mars.

"On Earth, actually. Contacting one on Chiron was out of the question," he said.

"How ironic."

"Yes," Karl agreed.

Sarah started for the door. "Good night, your majesty."

"Uh, there is one little matter," he said.

"Yes?"

"Well, an odd charge just came in on your expense card. From Dry Gulch," he said.

"Uh, yes?" she asked. "What about it?"

"Oh, never mind," Karl said. "Good night."

"Good night, your majesty."

8
CIVILIZED FOLKS

Sarah stretched out on her bed. It was the deluxe model from Martian Mattress. It cost a little more, but it was worth it. She'd used it so little, always gone some place or another. She drifted off to sleep on her cloudlike bed. And, sleep she did, for a few hours anyway. Then, the blasted terminal started chirping. "Sleep is overrated," Sarah told her apartment.

Fortunately, no public conveyances were required. This assignment did not require a space ship or even a ride on Mag Lev. She merely had to take the escalator down five levels. There were few people out and about so early in the morning. She found two uniformed members of the Mars City Marshal's Office chatting with a man in green coveralls with museum insignia on the shoulder.

One of the marshals looked at her. "May I help you, Miss?"

"Gompers Insurance," Sarah said. "What did they get?"

"Some paintings," the marshal answered.

"Could you be a little more specific?" Sarah asked.

"About ten million in paintings," somebody coming out of a side door said. He looked at Sarah. "I'm Inspector Potts. Like you, I got called out of bed on this. I take it Gompers insured the collection?"

"Yes, indeed," Sarah said. "Sarah Meadows, claims adjustor."

"Well, get in here and I'll show you what happened," he suggested.

Sarah raced after him.

"I'm Inspector Potts, Avery Potts," he said. He pointed at the floor where there was a yellow plastic pod with the number twelve on it. "Security guard was out cold. He's at the hospital. Maintenance guy who you just saw outside was letting the robot floor cleaners loose and he heard a loud bang as the cargo door blew open. He passed out on the way up the stairs. I'm thinking some sort of gas." He ushered her into a side room near the loading area. The sign on the door said security. There were two terminals and various screens. "Surveillance system crashed seconds before the door blew open. That's not easy to do."

That was true, though Sarah's own chipboard could crash it—function nine. "What'd they get?"

"Well, I won't know for sure until the curator gets here. The maintenance guy says they're definitely missing seven paintings by Paul, he's that hot Earth artist that died a while back. And there may be more. Curator's on the way in. He lives in that north dome complex. The first Mag Lev doesn't come into Mars City until," he checked his watch, "about now."

"You've certainly got a handle on things, Inspector," Sarah said.

"This is a serious theft," he replied.

"That's for sure," Sarah agreed. "I'll contact you later today for an update on the exact items taken. I've got to get things rolling with Gompers," she said.

Sarah had never used her pass code to get inside the Gompers Mars City office. There was always somebody there. And, it was usually the bald lady. Today, it was too early for anyone. She'd been called out by the computer center, which was always manned and fielded any calls from anywhere when the offices were closed. She connected to the computer center.

"Good morning. I need a secure line to tech support," Sarah said. "And, after that call, I'm going to need to track down Dragon."

"Dragon's assistant is on the way in, actually," the technician said.

"I don't want Dragon's assistant. Wherever Dragon is in this galaxy, find him," Sarah said.

"Do you need Karl. He's out of the hospital and on the way home?"

"No."

"He is your supervisor," the technician pointed out.

"No. That will not be necessary. Tech Support, then Dragon," Sarah repeated.

"The secure communications room is ready."

Sarah went across the lobby. A small light on the edge of an ordinary glass door was flashing green. She placed her hand on a flat panel next to the door. The panel turned green and the door opened. As she sat down, the window to the lobby frosted over. Some bearded guy appeared on the screen in front of her. "I'm Sarah Meadows, Special Ops, Mars City, authorization one, Omega, Epsilon."

"Authority confirmed. How may I help you this morning?" the technician asked.

"The Martian Museum of Art has just been robbed. I'm working off a partial list." She pointed her clipboard at the terminal. "We'll start with seven Paul paintings. I am determined to not let them get off of this planet. Can you activate the alien tracking devices?"

His jaw dropped. "We've never used them real time. The museum doesn't know they're even in the paintings. This could get rather sticky."

"That's why I'm calling Dragon," Sarah said.

"I'll start the process, but Dragon's going to have to okay this," he said.

"Fine."

The screen went blank. She waited for several minutes, then pressed the intercom button. "Any luck on Dragon?"

"No. He may be in transit somewhere. His assistant is outside," the bald lady advised. Apparently, she had now arrived for work.

"Send him in," Sarah said.

Don Don Walker was an unlikely assistant for Dragon, at least to Sarah. For starters, he was an Earth man. Most of the Gompers people despised Earth. The Harvard educated man with perfect teeth and perfect blond hair just rubbed Sarah the wrong way. And, he would never admit there was nothing he did not know. They said he'd been the top producing sales agent before Dragon promoted him. Add to that he'd tried to have Sarah fired because no woman just out of college was going to work in special ops if he had anything to say about it. And what kind of a name was Don Don?

Karl had appealed directly to Dragon over that decision. Obviously, Karl won that battle.

And, there he stood. "Good morning," Sarah said.

"Good morning, Miss Meadows." Don Don plopped himself down in the other vacant chair. "We're up early this morning.

Museum job?"

"Yep," Sarah said. "Just talked to tech support and asked them to activate the alien tracking devices. They're a bit reluctant."

Don Don stared off at the ceiling for a moment. "Sarah, this is a touchy subject. You know the museum doesn't actually know we placed the trackers in their paintings. The Martian Customs Department doesn't know we brought them onto the planet. There are a lot of issues here. I didn't realize you even knew about them, actually."

"What is the purpose of having them if we cannot use them?" she asked.

"They'll be used, eventually," he said. "Just not right now. In a few months, the marshals or maybe even the federal police will get a tip on where a painting is. That sort of thing."

"We could grab them all and the thieves this morning," Sarah said.

"That's just not doable, I'm afraid," Don Don said. He got out of the chair, then reached over and turned off the secure terminal. The window unfrosted and the door lock clicked open. "Do get claims processing a full list of the stolen paintings, Miss Meadows."

"Yes, sir," she said. There was little enthusiasm in her voice. Sarah returned to the museum and asked for the curator.

A surprisingly young and handsome man soon came up the stairs. "Ah, Miss Meadows, I'm Dr. Jenkins." He extended his hand. "But everyone calls me Mike."

"Pleased to meet you," she said. "I was hoping to get photos of the stolen paintings."

Mike gestured down the hallway. "Right this way."

Mike's office overlooked the main exhibit floor of the museum. He had a picture of one of the paintings up on one of the terminals. "This one is 'Workers' Rape of Society.'" He picked up a handheld unit. "The full catalog information is in here on all of them."

Sarah downloaded it to her clipboard. "Is there much of a market for this stuff?"

"No and yes. It's all about the collectors. Some people obsess about a particular artist or type of art. They'll do anything to have it. It's not the sort of thing one can just blast around the known galaxy that you have it for sale, though." He scratched his chin. "There is something else."

"Yes?" Sarah asked.

"Well, it's so unrelated to the paintings. Still, I'd swear it was in the exhibit hall yesterday." He pressed a button on his terminal. A picture of an insect appeared. The insect was made out of some sort of metal.

"That's a sculpture?" Sarah asked.

Mike explained, "A small sculpture, from a small exhibit we have called 'Art by non-human artists.'"

"Non-human?"

"It's a sculpture by a Tau artist known as Frock," Mike explained. "It's value is negligible. Even on its home world, art is not a highly traded commodity. It's of so little value. We had it just as a study piece. Still, it is suddenly missing."

"It seems to have little in common with the paintings." Sarah downloaded the information. "Still, if it is missing, it needs to become part of the insurance file. Thank you for your time, Mike."

"My pleasure," he said.

Sarah wandered toward one of the mini domes that connected Mars City with some self-contained homes or groups of homes. The one she wanted was at the end of a short tunnel. The tunnel even had an occasional window, or porthole, to look out through. At the end of the tunnel there was a T shape connection. The tunnel leading to the left was blocked off. The one to the right went about 20 meters to a set of large doors. On one door was a gold placard EMBASSY OF THE PLANET CHIRON.

The government of Earth had demanded the placard be removed. The Martian foreign office sent a hand delivered letter to Karl. Karl did something to the letter that could not be discussed in polite company, but saved the Gompers Insurance Company a very small amount of money on toilet paper.

Sarah rang the door buzzer.

A moment later, some tall guy answered–human. "May I help you?"

"Sarah Meadows from Gompers Insurance," she said.

"This way." He led her into an atrium. Small birds were

actually flying around.

Karl was playing some flute-like instrument. "Ah, Sarah."

"Sorry to bother you, your majesty," she said.

He handed the instrument to the tall guy. "It's no bother. What can I do for you?"

"There was a big robbery at the Museum of Art this morning," Sarah said.

"So I heard," he agreed.

"I wanted to try the alien tracking devices."

"Oh." He opened a side door and motioned for her to follow him. He went into a small office. The view of the red mountains was spectacular. "The tracking devices." He sat in a very ordinary chair and motioned for her to take the vacant one on the opposite side of the desk.

Sarah explained, "Don Don said no. I couldn't get a hold of Dragon."

"It always seems Dragon is never available when these matters come up. I sometimes wonder if that's on purpose," Karl said. "Ten million doubloons is the hit for us?"

"Well, if we accept their appraised value, we have a half million deductible," Sarah said.

"A big loss, even for Gompers," Karl said. "Still, the use of the tracking devices may have unintended consequences."

"What do you suggest?" she asked.

"The paintings are not far away." He handed her a plain envelope. She opened the envelope and there were coordinates on plain paper with no letterhead.

"You activated the trackers in violation of Don Don's orders?"

"He did not order me to do anything," Karl said. "I haven't spoken to him in at least a year."

"You knew I'd be coming here? I've never come to your home before," Sarah said.

"It was a pretty good hunch."

"I'll do what I can," Sarah said.

"Of that, I am certain," Karl said. "Would you like some tea?"

~ * ~

Though the paintings were not far away, they might as well have been on Deimos. Sarah looked over the two sentries in their crisp green uniforms, then approached them. They stood rigidly at attention outside the gold inlaid doors of the Embassy of the Planet Earth. When she was right in front of them, the one on her right opened the door. She went inside. Another Earthforce soldier sat behind a large wooden desk. He appeared to be some class of sergeant. Sarah wasn't that up on Earthforce ranks.

"May I help you?" the sergeant asked.

"I'm Sarah Meadows, from the Gompers Insurance Company," she said.

"So?"

"I need to see whomever is in charge," she said.

"Do you have an appointment?" he asked.

"No."

"I'm pretty sure the ambassador doesn't need any insurance," the sergeant smugly replied.

"I'm not selling any," Sarah said. "It's a special matter. I think your embassy can help my company locate some stolen art work."

"I'll see if somebody's available," the sergeant offered. The sergeant went into a back office, then returned with a small gray haired man. "This is Mr. Hicks. He's our cultural attaché."

"Sarah Meadows, Gompers Insurance."

"Let's go to my office." He led her past a few desks and into a small room. "How may I help you today?"

"I'm trying to locate some stolen artwork," Sarah said.

"And you think the items are on Earth?" he asked.

"No, a little closer. We have a tip they're right in this building," she said. "There is a reward for their safe return."

"I see." He sort of slunk back into his chair. "Well, why don't you bring in the marshals and confiscate them?"

"Because, as you know all too well, the Martian government considers this building foreign soil. And, I'm sure you have diplomatic immunity should you venture out its front door," Sarah said.

"Then, I guess we have nothing to discuss," he said. "Though, those tracking devices will keep the fellows at Earth Labs busy for months. They're nearly microscopic, yet I would bet they could be tracked all the way to Earth from here on Mars. We can't find any power source. I'd love to know where they came from."

"So, my visit was not a complete surprise," she said. "But, you'll still crate up the paintings and place a diplomatic seal on the box and ship them off to Earth?"

"I retire next month. Though it's been an honor to serve my planet, our pension system is not as rewarding as other streams of revenue," he said. "I want a comfortable retirement. A very comfortable retirement."

"How nice, at the expense of the Martian people"

He smugly asked, "Was there anything else?"

"A small sculpture by a Tau artist was also taken. It had minimal value?"

"I don't know anything about that. But, my kids always like for me to bring them a present from my travels with the diplomatic service. Good day, Miss Meadows."

"Good day, Mr. Hicks." As soon as she poked her head out of the office, soldiers escorted her to the front door.

All she could do was go home.

~ * ~

The Skylight Refectory was only a short walk from her apartment. They had trees and flowers growing everywhere and a panoramic view of the city. It was a nice place to relax. She was surprised to see a familiar face sitting at a table. He gave her a wave.

"You must be feeling pretty good to have ventured all the way over here," Sarah said.

"Bored, more likely." Karl pointed at a full mug of Martian Red Ale. "I can't drink that stuff with the meds I'm on. I've got water." He picked up his mug and took a sip.

"Am I that predictable?" Sarah asked.

"I felt you'd either go here or your apartment, which I can see from this table," Karl said.

Sarah took a sip of the ale. "Ah."

Karl unwrapped a piece of cake. "Blue root cake. Don't let its blue color scare you off. Fresh out of the oven."

"Excuse me, you can't have outside food here," Some guy in a white shirt was saying.

Karl handed him a piece of cake on a napkin. The waiter gobbled it up and actually seemed to be trying to suck the crumbs out of the napkin. He didn't bother them again.

Sarah devoured her cake before anyone tried to take it. "Damn, this is good," she said with her mouth full.

"I was afraid you might do something stupid to get those paintings back," Karl said.

"Define stupid?"

"The law firm of Ernst and Wilder, which we have on retainer, informed me you wanted to file suit against this Hicks fellow in an Earth court. That could take years, Sarah. Don Don would never approve," Karl pointed out.

"Okay. I guess there's always plan B," she said before gulping down some more ale.

"We'll settle the museum's claim tomorrow," Karl said.

"Okay by me," Sarah said. "Thanks for the ale. I'll meet you at the museum, then."

"Am I going to find out what plan B is?" Karl asked.

"Eventually."

"That's what I was afraid of," Karl said. He gulped down the rest of his water.

Right after they opened, Karl, Sarah and Don Don entered the Martian Museum of Art. The curator, Mike, and some other people they had not met before were waiting for them. Everyone went into the board room.

"There are some papers to sign," Karl said. "And, the highlight of these papers is the understanding that the Gompers Insurance Company takes ownership of the stolen art. If it is ever recovered, the museum can repurchase the items pursuant to clause fourteen. I mention this all the time we settle a large claim. We seem to have problems with that one. You don't get the settlement money and the paintings."

"Understood," Mike agreed.

The documents were signed. Then Karl handed Sarah a blue handheld unit that was smaller than the standard clipboard and had only one real purpose. Karl had signed off on the first line. Sarah signed off on the second line and entered her security code. She offered the device back to Karl.

He didn't take it. "You do the honors."

Sarah told the device to complete the funds transfer. In a few seconds, the little screen turned green and displayed a transaction code. "Done," Sarah announced.

Hands were shook. Minor small talk was completed. And Sarah was out of there. Don Don had barely said a word. Sarah liked it that way. He was probably still fuming about the tracking devices Karl activated. Don Don was at least two steps in rank above Karl, yet Karl openly defied him. Being a former king might have something to do with that, Sarah reasoned.

~ * ~

An ensign of the Martian Defense Force was looking over his team. Two technicians and a sergeant. The fate of their world was in their hands. They were the night shift at the MDF Operations Command Center, protecting Mars from enemy attack. The ensign wondered why the lady from Gompers was poking around. She had authorization, but it was unusual to have visitors in the middle of the night.

"We are on Defcon one," he announced. He sort of wanted to impress her that he was a capable officer. And, she was kind of cute. "That's our lowest threat level."

"And why they left an ensign in charge," the sergeant mumbled so low Sarah could barely hear him.

She suppressed a laugh. And pretended to be interested in the fire panel.

"Ensign Prost, we have traffic," one of the technicians said.

"Transponder USS *Calcutta*," the Sergeant confirmed. "I believe that is an Earth ship traveling from Mars City to Earth Chicago spaceport."

"What sort of traffic?" the ensign anxiously asked.

"They are under attack, sir," the sergeant said. The big screen on the wall lit up and showed the relative position of the vessel with a white dot and transponder code. A second dot, in orange, was right next to it. It had no transponder code.

"Who's attacking them?" the ensign asked. He opened the plastic cover and moved his hand toward the red button. If that button were pressed, they would definitely no longer be at Defcon one and the pilots at a number of sites would no longer be sleeping peacefully. He realized another hand was blocking his.

She had soft, warm hands. She'd managed to move his hand away from the general alarm button.

"Attacking is a relative concept, ensign. It's not my place to tell the MDF what to do, but perhaps you should get a little more information before pushing that button and getting everyone all upset," Sarah said.

"What kind of information?" he asked.

"Who's attacking them, perhaps?"

"*Calcutta*, say again, who is attacking you?" the sergeant asked.

"Can you put it on speaker?" Sarah asked.

"This is the USS *Calcutta*. We are being boarded."

"Boarded does not necessarily mean attacked," Sarah pointed out.

"Who is boarding you, *Calcutta*?" the sergeant asked.

"It's nothing of ours," the technician added.

"Lizards. We're being boarded by Tau lizards," the voice on the speaker said. "Help us."

"Oh my!" He wanted to go back to the comfort of his big red button, but Sarah was in his way. "We can't have this. They're in Martian space."

"Just barely," the sergeant grunted.

"Perhaps, well, the Tau ship, you could ask them why they're boarding the *Calcutta*," Sarah suggested.

"Open a channel," he said.

"Channel open," the technician replied.

"Tau vessel, this is the Martian Defense Force. Why are you boarding a ship in our territory?" he asked. There was no reply. He waited a few seconds. "Tau vessel, let's not create a military incident. Why are you boarding the *Calcutta*?"

"Perhaps," Sarah said, "they may be having problems with their translator. They're not all that used to our language." She held her clipboard up. "May I?" Without waiting for an answer, she went over to the technician's station and plugged the clipboard into the console.

"Stolen antiquities," came out of the speaker. "Tau are searching vessel for stolen antiquities."

"Oh dear. Can they do that?" he asked.

Sarah smiled at him with her most disarming look she could muster. "I'm not sure, ensign. But it doesn't sound like the passengers are in any grave danger."

"I'm not so sure," he said. "I think I should call somebody."

"By all means," Sarah said. "Just make sure whomever you call understands the *Calcutta* is an Earth ship and they've now officially drifted into neutral space." She pointed at the big screen on the wall.

"But it came from a Martian port," he protested.

"And it's underway," the sergeant reported. "The *Calcutta* is moving away, back to its original course for Earth."

"I guess I should write a report or something," the ensign said.

"Oh, absolutely," Sarah agreed. She unplugged her clipboard from the console. "I'll be going now. Nice meeting everyone."

~ * ~

Customs station one, on the main docking ring of Fremont Station, was a ghost town. There were no ships scheduled to arrive for hours, yet two Martian customs inspectors still were required to be there at all times. The card game was getting very boring.

The senior agent looked out the window. A warship was coming toward the station, fast. It didn't look like anything he'd ever seen before. He was going to call central ops, but they were on the line before he had the chance. "What?"

"Beats us," the ops lady said. "That is a Tau cruiser, you know, them lizard people. It wants to dock and drop off some antiquities."

"Antiquities?" He scratched his head. "Well, we wanted something to do."

"Be careful what you wish for, my grandma always said," the other customs inspector said.

Three Tau soldiers exited the airlock. Two of them carried a large crate. The other one, with the more garish uniform, seemed to be in charge.

"Welcome to Fremont Station. How can we help you today?"

The crate was placed on the floor. The customs agents were not comforted by the fact that what looked like the remnants of a diplomatic seal had been blasted off the edge of the container. "I am Commander Goth of the Tau Army. My ship recently boarded an Earth vessel. We were looking for stolen antiquities. In the ensuing search, we found these paintings, which we believe to be stolen property from the Martian Museum of Art. The Emperor of the Tau has directed me, Commander Goth, to return these paintings to the nearest Martian facility." He snapped to attention. So did the other soldiers. "We would like a receipt, please."

At that precise moment, the communications machine let out a ding. "Excuse me just a moment, commander," the inspector said. He looked over the text communication. "The text says some lawyers in Mars City have just filed a motion claiming ownership of the seven paintings by the artist Paul believed to be in the custody of the Martian Customs Department and directing me, I wonder how they got my name, to take custody of any such paintings and bring them before a magistrate. That is positively incredible." He looked at the Tau Commander. "Are these paintings by that Paul person?"

"I am not art expert, but that is the name on them," Goth said.

The customs inspector wrote up a receipt for the paintings and handed a copy to Goth. "Did you find any?"

"Any what?" Goth asked.

"Any Tau antiquities on the ship you boarded?"

"Yes. We found a sculpture that is one hundred years old by the artist Frock. I confiscated it in the name of the Tau Empire. We take it back to our world." Goth explained.

"Very good commander."

9
BUSINESS

"Miss Meadows, could you come by my office for a moment, please?" Don Don was asking over the intercom.

"Yes sir," she answered. She finished her slice of pie that Karl had just brought in. Karl's baked goods only lasted a few minutes in the office. You had to be quick to get some. She doubted Don Don even knew the pie was out there. She sauntered down the hallway as slowly as practical. "You wanted to see me?"

Don Don pointed at the empty chair across from his desk. "Sarah, I just received an invoice."

"We get invoices all the time," Sarah said. "Could you be a bit more specific?"

"Not like this we don't. It is an invoice from the Emperor of the Tau requesting payment of one million Martian doubloons?"

"Does it say why?" she asked.

"They are claiming the finder's fee for returning the Paul paintings," Don Don said.

Sarah pointed out, "Gompers does offer a ten percent reward for the return of stolen artwork, sir. It's been policy for quite some time."

"We haven't got it back," he grumbled.

"It's just a formality. The Tau confiscated it off an Earth ship and turned it over to the magistrate on Fremont Station. There's a hearing tomorrow. Our lawyers, you know the ones I can call at any hour because we have them on retainer, are handling it," Sarah said.

"The Tau just happened to pop up and seize this art out in space? Out of the blue" Don Don asked.

"We know so little about them," Sarah said.

"And, when were you going to tell me all this?" Don Don asked.

"I was working on my report when you called me in here," she said.

"I see. Well, get back to your report, then."

"Yes sir." Sarah went back to her desk. The pie was gone. She smiled, comforted by the fact Don Don would not get any of it.

"Take it Don Don was not all that pleased with Plan B?" Karl asked.

"One gets that impression, though I saved the company millions," Sarah said.

"Well, maybe I should set aside a piece of pie for him next time," Karl suggested. After a glare from Sarah he said, "Or not."

Sarah sent Don Don the report that had been compiled for hours in her clipboard. "There."

"I sometimes think I should spank you," Karl said.

"I might like that," she replied.

"Let's just say I would not have had the guts to have an Earth ship boarded by a foreign military and expect that military to hand over such expensive art. You have an exceptionally creative ability to solve problems," Karl said.

"Thank you, your majesty," Sarah said. "Do you want to see if the museum wants to repurchase the paintings or shall I?"

"Actually, let's let Don Don handle that. We've got another assignment that came in while you were in his office," Karl said.

"We do?"

"Fancy a trip to Margrave Station?" Karl asked.

"Uh, I didn't think you could go there," Sarah said.

"I can't. When I said we, I really meant you," Karl replied. "Earthforce would attack immediately if they got word I was there. And they have plenty of spies running around."

"How do you tell who the spies are?" she asked.

"Basically, anyone who's not purple," Karl said.

"That would kind of include me," she said.

"Well, humans aren't really popular there right now, but the company has a problem," Karl explained.

~ * ~

Martian Spaceways offered luxury accommodations at affordable prices according to their advertising. The opposite seemed more true. But, they were the only commercial service going from Mars City to Margrave Station. One couldn't always get the military to transport oneself. So, Sarah relaxed in her seat and turned on the music and drifted off to sleep as her transport zipped through hyperspace to her destination.

She had never been there before, but was impressed at how much nicer it seemed than the Martian-run Fremont Station. Where Fremont was cramped and gloomy, Margrave seemed spacious and well lit.

"Welcome to Margrave Station," some guy who looked a lot like Karl said. "Purpose of your visit?"

Sarah handed him her passport. "Business meeting."

He seemed to perk up when he realized she had a Martian passport. He scanned it, then stamped it, then handed it back to her. The stamp read "Margrave Station." It made no mention of Chiron at all. Nor did his uniform. The two security people eyeing her from a distance also had no insignia on them that mentioned the word Chiron.

She followed the signs to the Majestic Hotel. The front desk was staffed with a Chiron and a human. The purple guy showed no inclination on waiting on her. "May I help you?" the human offered.

"Sarah Meadows, I have a reservation," Sarah explained. She offered her Gompers Card.

"I'm afraid we don't take that," he said. "Do you have Earth Express or Master Card by chance?" Both were Earth products.

Having already checked payment options before coming, she held her clipboard up. "How about a direct transfer in Earth dollars from the Mars City Bank for the lodging, tax and a thousand-dollar deposit for any incidentals?"

The clerk pressed a few buttons. "Transmit when ready." He waited for acknowledgment, then handed her a room key.

The day Sarah Meadows would use an Earth credit card was the day she stopped traveling. She knew they wouldn't take the Gompers Card, but had offered it anyway.

The room, the deluxe plus, was gorgeous. Karl had advised her well. It had a view and comfortable furniture and an enormous bath tub. Karl told her to come a day early. She was already glad she had. The bath tub was calling to her.

The next day, after hours in the bath and a large supper ordered from room service, she ventured off in search of Promenade 366. It wasn't on any of the public maps or directories. After asking a few people, she finally arrived at the administrative offices.

"May I help you?" a tall Chironese lady asked.

"Sarah Meadows to see Administrator Chaconne," Sarah said.

"Follow me, please," the tall lady invited. They walked past a few doors and into a conference room.

Sarah was not surprised to see a human on the other side of the table. "Sarah Meadows, Gompers Insurance."

He smiled at her. "Glad you could come, Miss Meadows. Thank you, Agnus." The Chironese lady departed.

He was Martian. She could tell by his accent. That was a surprise.

"Can I get you something to drink?" Ainslee Chaconne offered.

"No thank you," Sarah said.

"Well, I do appreciate your coming all this way in person. So much business is over conference calls," Ainslee said.

"Yes, we do use them, but mostly for internal matters. We prefer to meet with clients and potential clients in person," Sarah explained.

"We find ourselves in need of insurance," Ainslee said.

"If we means this magnificent station, the answer would be no," Sarah said.

"No? You came all this way to turn us down, without even hearing my case," Ainslee protested.

"Yes. It's a sitting duck. Our underwriters say it's simply out of the question," Sarah said. "Perhaps an Earth based insurer like Lloyds could help you."

"We really need insurance. No one will invest."

"I didn't say you don't need it. I said we can't possibly write it," she said.

"You company insures Fremont Station?" he pointed out. "You insured that thing that disappeared."

"True, but that is owned by the Martian Government. This station is in some sort of perpetual limbo. Earth invaded the planet Chiron, but left this facility alone. You have a Board of Directors appointed by a government that doesn't exist any longer. Any disgruntled individual could blow it up. Then, there's the matter we do not consider it economically viable. There is little traffic to Chiron or its moons these days. In fact, Martian

Spaceways is dropping its service next month."

"You insure wars for gosh sake," Ainslee said. "We're not under attack."

"A fleet of ships or tanks, when engaged in battle, will usually only suffer a small percentage of loss in that one event. Believe it or not, the battlefield can be amortized. One giant big target, on the other hand, cannot." Sarah paused for just an instant, then decided to change the subject.

"Gompers would like to open an insurance office here. It would be to insure ships and cargo passing through the sector. In spite of the Earth occupation, there is still commerce going on and we'd like a share of the shipping business. As for insuring this station, we are not interested. Think over what I've said. I'll call on you tomorrow," Sarah said.

The station seemed so incredibly empty. It was built for ten times more commerce than it was getting. As she looked over the menu in the restaurant she'd found, she sensed she was not alone and lowered the card she'd been reading.

There was a Chironese man sitting across from her. "May I join you?" he asked.

"Since you already have, it is pointless to ask," Sarah said.

"You are Martian, then?"

"What of it?"

"The manager of this station is Martian," the fellow said.

"What of it?" Sarah asked again.

"You can't come here. More business for Earth means it harder to get them to leave," he said.

"It doesn't look like there is much business," Sarah said.

"My point, exactly. Gompers not wanted here. Go back to Mars." He left the table after that observation.

Being the only customer in the restaurant didn't really bother her, although not all the people of Chiron were excellent bakers. Her desert was particularly disappointing and she'd hoped it would be the highlight of her meal.

She returned to her room at the hotel. A message light was flashing on the console by the window. She pressed the button. A text message invited her to level four, room one hundred.

It took about a minute for the elevator to take her to that level. She was a little surprised at who owned the suite she'd been invited to. Sarah pressed the button below the gold placard for the Consulate of the Republic of Mars. The door quickly opened.

The surroundings were neat and tidy, but rather modest by what she'd seen of diplomatic establishments. Only one door was open. Sarah poked her head inside. The lights were set very low. "Hello?"

Someone was standing by the window. It was a woman, a tall woman with black hair and brown eyes. She turned around. "Sarah Meadows." She pointed at a vacant chair in front of the desk, then sat at the other one. "I'm Becky Hudson."

Sarah found the chair surprisingly uncomfortable. "The Martian foreign minister?"

"That's me."

"I'm just a little surprised to see you here," Sarah said.

"In this backwater location? Let's say it's just a stopover on my way somewhere else." Becky stared at Sarah for a moment then said, "Sarah Meadows, I've been following your career for some time. It's no wonder Dragon snatched you up. I wish we'd been faster."

"Uh, thank you," Sarah said.

"Getting the Tau to take back those stolen paintings, absolutely brilliant," Becks said.

"Uh, thank you," Sarah repeated. Talking about herself was one thing Sarah was never comfortable with.

"So, when I realized you were here, I just had to meet you," she said.

"Uh, thank you."

"Which leads me to the question, why does the Gompers Insurance Company send its top field agent all the way out here. Look around you, there is nothing going on. This station is a basket case. Nobody wants to come here, except for the Chironese, and that's just because they want off their planet so bad."

"We want to establish a field office to write more cargo insurance," Sarah said.

"Okay, then don't tell me," Becky said. "You're not insuring the station are you?"

"Heavens no," Sarah said. "They might as well put a sign on it that says subsidiary of Earth, Inc. We want nothing to do with the station, in terms of insurance."

"That's a relief. Since the Martian Republic was founded, Earth has bullied us constantly over everything from tariffs to the routes the MDF can fly. Now, with the most militant government in place in Earth history, we find our position unusually strong. Do you know why that is?"

Sarah pointed to the bright blue planet that looked like a small ball out the window. "Occupying that planet, and war with a reptilian race some distance from here have left Earth seriously overextended."

"For the first time in our history, Earth couldn't invade us if they wanted to. They can't even really tell us what to do," Becky said. "For my job, that makes things a heck of a lot easier."

"For now," Sarah said.

"For now? Earth can't extract themselves from the mess they've created on Chiron. They'll be bogged down there for years," she said. Then Becky smiled. "His majesty hasn't got you believing he'll be back in power, soon?"

"That seems unlikely. When Earth invaded Chiron, the planet fell so fast he couldn't even get any money out. That's why he works for Gompers," Sarah said. "All common knowledge."

"True," Becky agreed. "Still, that brings me back to my original question. Why is Gompers trying to set up shop and do business with the puppet regime," she turned and pointed out the window, "down there."

"I assure you, Minister, it's a limited venture as I described it. This beautiful station has few customers, but we'd like to sell to the ones there are," Sarah said.

"The real commodity on this station is information. Who's supporting whom. That's why we keep a consulate here. I'm sure that's why Dragon wants a foot in the door," Becky said.

"You would have to take that up with Dragon. The station master was trying to get an insurance policy out of us to come here. I've recommended against it. Still, I expect to be overturned on that. Was there anything else, Minister?" Sarah stood from the chair.

"Thanks for coming by, Sarah," Becky said. "And, if you get tired of the insurance business, come see me."

"Thank you, Minister," Sarah said.

Two minutes later, Sarah was back in her room. She was not surprised there was a new message waiting.

As she curled up in the warm comfy bed, she read the label on the comforter. It was filled with something called goose down feathers from the Siberia region of Earth. She wondered what a goose looked like and vowed to look one up when she got home. She was too warm and comfortable to bother with it then.

The next shift cycle found Sarah in the station master's office. Ainslee looked at her expectantly. "My company has made a decision."

"And that is?" he asked.

"The current business climate is unfavorable for us to further explore any operations at this station," she explained. "I'll be leaving on the ship to Mars City in a few minutes."

"I'm sorry to hear that," he said.

"Good day," Sarah said. She headed for the Martian Spaceways waiting area

She suddenly was not alone. "Heading home?" Becky asked.

"This trip was a total waste of time," Sarah said.

"For you, perhaps, but not for the station," Becky said.

"How do you figure?"

"Your mere presence here brought about a panic on Earth. The station being insured by a Martian company was a hot topic yesterday around Congress, I hear. Lloyds has offered the station insurance and is opening a cargo office as soon as they can get a rep out here from Earth," Becky explained.

"You are well informed," Sarah said.

"That's my job. Have a nice trip home, Sarah," Becky said.

"Thank you, Minister."

"And His Majesty's precious space station is suddenly insured, should someone blow it up," Becky added. "I keep underestimating that man. Maybe he will return to power."

Sarah was so relieved when they started boarding the ship.

10
TOURISM

There wasn't anything good to eat at the office, yet Karl's station was active. He'd been spoiling everyone, bringing in stuff so often. But Sarah didn't feel particularly spoiled. Eventually, Karl came out of Don Don's office. He found Sarah sitting in his chair with her feet up on his desk. "You're back," he said.

"That was a complete waste of time, Karl," she said.

"How so?" he asked.

"We didn't insure them. We didn't set up any agreements. We did nothing. I did nothing."

"The station has a new insurance policy. The people of Chiron could never afford to rebuild that thing if something happened to it," Karl pointed out.

"You mean *you* couldn't rebuild it," Sarah countered. "It's really *your* station."

"Nothing is mine, Sarah, it's only in my name, but held for the people," Karl pointed out. "And the people need that station. It's their future."

"It had nothing to do with insurance, at least not Gompers insurance," she said.

Karl picked her up and carried her over to her desk and placed her on it, then returned to his. "I don't recall you ever calling me 'Karl' before," he said. "You must be miffed."

Sarah got off the top of her desk and planted herself in her chair. She glared at him, but did not say anything. After a few minutes she got up and walked out of the office. She headed for her apartment. She hadn't asked. She'd only been at work for a few minutes. She dropped her clipboard off at her apartment and went to the nearby atrium and plopped herself down in the corner, with her back to the trees. They were just opening.

"What can I get you?" the cute new guy asked her.

"Martian Red Ale, in the tall glass." She'd never drank that early. Not ever. Still, since she was a salaried employee, Gompers owed her for thousands of unpaid hours spent in every ungodly hell hole in the galaxy. Sarah decided she deserved a day off.

Then, she realized she was not alone. "Hello, Minister."

"They said you'd gone home for the day," Becky said. "I was heading by your apartment and I saw you here."

"I decided I needed some me time today. I've been working a lot, lately," Sarah said. "What brings you up to A level?"

Becky handed Sarah a small envelope. It had her name printed on the front. On the back was an actual golden seal. "Is this an official diplomatic note?"

"It is," Becky said. "It came in this morning, right after I got back."

"How does an insurance agent on Mars rate a diplomatic note?" Sarah said.

She suggested, "Why don't you open it and find out?"

Sarah admired it in her hands for a moment. "Don't you have people to deliver things like this, Minister?"

"I do." Becky pointed at Sarah's glass and the new guy brought her a glass of Martian Red. "But the Foreign Ministry does not have a bar next door to it."

"What a shame. They'd probably do a heck of a business." Sarah opened the envelope. She pulled out a piece of very heavy paper with gold leaf lettering.

The Emperor of the Tau People Requests Your Presence at Okemodon Palace in Commemoration of the Twenty-fifth Anniversary of His Ascension

It went on with date and time and such. "Wow."

"No human has ever been invited to any Tau function. Not ever. We don't even officially have diplomatic relations with them," Becky said. "This came from their embassy at Artamus, Almeria and was delivered to our embassy there." She took a long sip of beer. "Ah, drinking in the morning. Reminds me of my days at the MSE."

"You're an MSE grad?"

Becky nodded. "Sure. So, when something like this turns up, well it does tend to get the attention of the Foreign Office."

Sarah stared at her invitation. "I wonder if I'll have to take Karl."

"He got one too," she said. "I dropped it off at Gompers when I was looking for you. That's how I knew what it said." Becky finished off her glass. "He is a king. It would rude to invite you and snub him. Thanks for the beer." She headed for the escalator. "And, Sarah, you're the first human most of them have ever seen. Try not to make an ass out of yourself."

When the check came, Sarah realized she was paying for both beers. "Thanks, Minister."

After paying the check, she looked over her two Gompers Credit Cards, each issued by Gompers Bank of Almeria. One was her personal account and was an emerald green color. The one for her official travel expenses was cranberry red. She wondered if this was going to be a personal expense or a business expense. She put the green one away and headed down the escalator for Talbott's Fashion Store. Sarah Meadows needed something to wear to the party and Don Don was not going to like the bill.

II
DIPLOMACY

"I'm going to a diplomatic function and I need something to wear," Sarah announced to the wiry little man behind the counter of Talbott's.

"You look familiar," he replied.

"I should. I sold you a life insurance policy, once," Sarah said.

"Ah."

"So, what have you got that says 'I'm hot'?" she looked around the store. There were so many dresses and such.

"Did you have a price range in mind?" he asked.

"Expensive. Definitely something expensive," she answered.

"The insurance business must be doing rather well," he said. "How do you look in gold?"

She liked the sound of that. "Let's find out."

He brought out a white dress that had actual gold woven through it. "We have one in platinum, too."

"Let me try this one on, first," she said.

An hour later, Sarah emerged from the store. The dress had been easy. The shoes had been the problem. They had plenty that matched, but she'd been wearing *something she could run in* since that fateful day she'd started her current position. These shoes were definitely not for running, but they sure looked good. She put her cranberry Gompers card in her pocket and started for her apartment with her bright blue Talbott's bag.

"It won't make any difference," Karl said.

"What won't?" Sarah asked.

"You could show up at the party in a plastic trash bag. Few Tau have ever met a human before. They won't know the difference."

"That may be so, but I'll know," she said.

"You found garments you feel are suitable?"

"Oh yeah."

"You're sending the bill to Don Don?"

Sarah showed him the receipt.

"His head will explode," Karl predicted.

"I sure hope so."

"My vacation to Dragon's home is delayed. I'll go there after the party. You're invited too," Karl said. "We're booked on a ship leaving tomorrow."

"I'll be there," Sarah said.

The little console started chirping way too early. She'd packed the night before. She grabbed her travel bag and headed down the escalator to the Mag Lev platform. In no time at all, she was on her way out to the spaceport.

Karl was sitting in the boarding lounge when she got there. "Is Gompers springing for steerage?" Sarah asked. There was no such thing. They called it economy class. It was simply her way of asking if they were in the cheap seats.

"Not this time. We're booked first class," Karl said.

"Does Don Don know?" Sarah asked.

"He will when he gets the bill." Karl held up one of the cranberry Gompers cards. "You're not the only one with one of these."

Sarah squealed. "Don Don's head will explode."

"I sure hope so," Karl said.

The first class cabin was just that, first class. The seats were roomy and comfy. They gave Sarah a warm comfy blanket. The instructions even said she could fold her seat down into a bed. But that would be after her lobster.

She wondered if they were getting Martian lobsters. These were creatures that were clones from Earth stock, but raised in tanks on Mars by Martian Hydroponics. The frightfully expensive Earth raised lobster, actually grown in an ocean on Earth, were quite a lot better. And they didn't have that weird gray color. When the tray arrived, Sarah was a happy girl. These lobsters were not gray.

There were no direct ships to the Tau world. There was barely any commerce between Mars and Tau. They had to go to Dragon's home world, Almeria, then take another ship to the Tau planet.

Sarah was glad they'd gone first class. The long ride had been spent sleeping and eating. Leaving the spaceport at their destination, Sarah discovered one thing about the world she was visiting. It was hot, really hot. She wasn't used to such a climate and hoped they didn't have to go far to their hotel.

As it turned out, a moving walkway took them right there. Karl was sure good with travel arrangements. Her room was enormous, far larger than her apartment on Mars. If only people weren't all staring at her.

She was the hated human race. These people were at war with Earth. She wasn't sure if they actually hated her or were just curious. Karl had advised her not to wander around by herself, especially at night. That was not going to be a problem. She didn't know where to go, anyway.

Sarah was debating whether to take a bath or a nap. The plush comfy bed was calling to her even though it was hardly bedtime. Somehow, the big ceiling fans had a hypnotically soothing effect on her. She'd never seen ceiling fans, as living in climate controlled domes made them unnecessary. This place had air and wind and heat. Damn it was hot. She opted for a bath to cool off. Before she could get started, the doorbell rang. Sarah was surprised to see two Tau soldiers standing at her door.

"Are you Sarah Meadows?" one of them asked.

"Who wants to know?" They didn't have any particularly garish colors on their uniforms, so she surmised they were of fairly low rank.

"We have orders to bring you to His Majesty's palace."

"Orders from who?" she asked.

They both looked at her like she was stupid. "His Majesty."

"The party isn't until tomorrow," she replied.

They both looked at her like she was stupid. "We know when the party is."

"Very well." She followed them downstairs and they got into a square sort of vehicle. She sat on an uncomfortable bench in the back while they drove to the palace.

The palace was a domed building decorated with gold and turquoise. The soldiers only went to the large wooden doors, where she was pawned off to two other Tau who wore different uniforms, of crimson and gold. These guys were the palace guard.

They walked her down a long, narrow corridor that seemed to go on forever. Every few minutes, they passed by a fountain or pool of water. Then, they opened a large door. She went inside.

The guards did not.

This room was very dark and uncomfortably warm, even compared to everywhere else she'd been. The reason became apparent. The only apparent light source was the glowing embers from a fire in a fireplace that took up about half of one wall. She wondered why anyone would want a fire when it was already so hot.

Sarah sat herself down in one of the many chairs in the room. The Tau didn't fit in chairs, as such. They preferred benches, couches, and used a sort of bench with a backrest in the ships she'd seen. She knew many of Karl's people lived on the planet. They were shaped much like humans and used chairs. She wondered if this was a room to meet foreigners.

Meeting them in the dark made little sense. Then, back to the fire. Why would they have a fire burning? She puzzled over it for a moment, then figured it out, though it made little sense. She went over near the corner and sat down on the floor, with her back against the wall. "I find the chair more comfortable."

A Tau individual moved from against the wall. He'd been pressed in the corner. "I'm surprised you could see me."

"I couldn't. I heard you breathing," Sarah said.

"In ancient times, monks tried to precisely match their body temperature to the surrounding air. It was an exercise in self-control. Unless someone is looking for you with an infra-red sensor, it has no real value." He moved over to a bench in the opposite corner. "Lights." The lights came on to reveal a Tau wearing a purple outfit. "Do you like Tau wine?"

"Never had any," Sarah replied.

He dipped two goblets in a bowl and handed her one. He sat on the bench and pointed at one of the chairs.

Sarah waited for him to take a sip, then she tried the wine.

"In our culture one always waits for the host to take the first drink. I am impressed," he said.

"It's the same on Mars," she said.

"I am Sing. I am the Emperor of the Tau people. It is a pleasure to meet you, Sarah Meadows."

"Likewise." Sarah took a sip of the wine. She placed the goblet on a small table next to her chair. "Uh."

"You don't care for the wine?" It wasn't really a question.

"The Earthforce units on what you call Tartarus actually used to think we ate bugs. They would put material that smelled oddly, but attracted insects over booby traps, thinking we would rush at the opportunity to dine on the local insects. They were quite surprised when we stole their wine."

"I can imagine," Sarah said.

"Earthforce wine came in a green box with red letters. They brought me back some. My first reaction was much the same as yours, just now. Do you like Earth wine, Sarah Meadows?" Sing asked.

"I suppose. The Martian version has a different flavor. I guess I've come to prefer it." Sarah said.

"We don't have grapes. Our wine is made out of a big red berry called the qusaghav. Like many delicacies, part of the experience is based on physiology, partly on what we learn, partly just on what our reaction to a sensation is. I've now become a fan of Earthforce wine in a box, though I have none to offer you right now. Don't tell them that. They'd poison the entire supply and leave it at my doorstep." He held out his hand.

Instantly, a servant stood next to him. Sing took a small disk from the servant. The servant, just as quickly, was gone. He got off the bench and went over to Sarah and handed her the disk. "A gift from the Tau people." He returned to the bench.

"Thank you." She examined the disk and wondered what information it contained. "I'm anxious to see what it contains."

"I think you will be most pleased. You are coming to the party tomorrow?" Sing said.

"Of course."

"Until then. My drivers will return you to your hotel," Sing said.

Sarah stood, bowed toward Sing, then went out into the hallway. Another servant escorted her back outside, where the same uncomfortable vehicle was waiting.

Karl was hovering around in the hall at the hotel. "Where have you been? I was afraid something happened to you."

"Oh that's sweet. Actually, something did happen to me." Sarah opened the door to her room after entering her door code. "The emperor sent for me."

"The emperor? Sing?" Karl seemed to be having trouble

grasping the situation. "Sing sent for you? Just now?"

"Yeah, they took me over to the palace." She took her shoes off. In the hot weather and twenty percent more gravity her feet seemed to be swelling up a little, something that never happened on Mars.

"For what? Why? What happened?" Karl asked.

She handed Karl the data disk. "Can my Gompers clipboard read this?"

"It should," Karl replied.

Sarah opened up her clipboard and fed the disk into the universal input slot. She looked it over for a second, then said, "This was before my time. Just a moment. The file's matching something in our database. You might want to call Dragon."

Karl took her clipboard from her. "He's arriving in a few hours for the party tomorrow. Your new friend just gave us one heck of a present."

"I'll say, but those coordinates bother me," Sarah said. She took back her clipboard. "Yep." She handed the clipboard back to Karl. "I was afraid of that. It's deep inside Earth territory. Way deep."

"That, it is," Karl agreed. "I'll see what Dragon wants to do. It is, after all, his money."

Sarah relaxed in the biggest bath tub she'd ever seen. She had two hours before she and Karl were having supper with Dragon. The warm water swirled around her and she just wanted to stay there forever.

~ * ~

Forever turned out to be about an hour. In an astronomical oddity, the world she was on and Mars had days that were exactly the same length, even though the Tau world was bigger. The chimes starting ringing way too soon. They had a timer in the bathroom. She must not be the only person to ever drift off. She reluctantly climbed out of the tub and got dressed.

Sarah had to walk with Karl a short distance to the place Dragon was staying at. It seemed like a private residence.

One of Karl's countrymen opened the door. He seemed confused as to what to do next. "I'm not the king here," Karl reminded him. "I'm just some guy from Chiron. Dragon is expecting us."

They were taken into a large room with lots of plants. "Ah, right on time," Dragon greeted them. "Sarah, do you like Almerian wine?"

"I've never had any." She sat next to Karl on a couch near the window. "Hope it's better than the local variety."

"The Tau have a great many talents," Dragon said. "Making wine is not one of them, though they seem to like their version." The servant handed her and Karl each a glass of red wine. "This is made from berries on my estate back home. I brought it with me."

Sarah took a sip. This product, she liked.

"So, Sarah, your friends have given us an unexpected gift. Have you looked over the policy settlement?" Dragon asked.

"Yes."

"Then, you see why I'm interested in a cargo we long ago wrote off," he said.

"Yes?"

"Good, then, it's all settled," Dragon said.

"What's all settled?" Sarah asked.

"Our supper is ready." Dragon led them into the dining room.

The servant placed a meat dish in front of her. It smelled wonderful.

"What is this?" she asked. "It doesn't look familiar."

"No, I don't suppose Martian Hydroponics does steak. At least, not properly," Karl said. "Steak, Sarah, must be cooked over an outdoor fire. That sort of cooking is banned on Mars."

Sarah cut off a slice and tried it. It was quite good. She tried another slice.

12
CELEBRATE

Talbot's had made choosing what to wear a snap. But there was one item they couldn't help her with. Sarah had no idea what the protocol was for wearing the medal they'd given her. She didn't even really know what the medal was for. She put it over her neck. It glistened in the light and matched her golden dress beautifully.

The door buzzer sounded. Karl was right on time. A more comfortable conveyance whisked them to the palace. Soldiers in garish colors of differing types were everywhere. Strangely, when they noticed her medal, they all snapped to attention. Two large doors were opened for them and they entered a large ballroom. Sarah could hear some chatter, though her translator remained silent—that pesky second dialect again.

They entered the ballroom. Her translator didn't have much of a problem with what was said then. His Royal Majesty, King Karl Phillip Geste III of Chiron and Miss Sarah Meadows of Mars.

Next came a receiving line. They had to be greeted by various Tau. Females of the species looked pretty much like the males she'd dealt with. Females did not serve in the military in Tau society. Sarah had no idea why. Females had crimson eyes. The males had green ones. Sarah realized someone, a Chironese, was walking right behind her.

"Empress Soudan," he whispered to her.

Sarah bowed. "Your Highness."

Soudan nodded, then turned her attention to Karl. "Welcome, your majesty."

"It is a pleasure to finally meet you. You have done so much for my people," Karl said.

She nodded.

Sarah didn't need to be told who the next one in the line was.

The Chironese told her anyway. "Marshal Zuto, Supreme Commander of the Army of the Tau."

Sarah again bowed. "A pleasure to see you again."

"The pleasure is mine," Zuto said.

Then there was the Foreign Minister. Then there was some guy with a title she didn't understand, then another familiar Tau who needed no introduction.

"Emperor Sing," the Chironese shadow whispered.

Sarah again bowed. "Your majesty."

"I am glad you could come," Sing said.

"As am I," Sarah replied.

The Chironese fellow escorted Sarah and Karl to a table that was near a large head table. Dragon was already there. She had no idea what she was eating, but she liked it. She had no idea what she was drinking, but she liked that as well—especially after the fourth glass.

Sarah woke in her hotel room. She was on top of a crate marked GOMPERS INSURANCE on the side of it. "How did I get here?" She sat up. "Oh, I hope I didn't make an ass out of myself."

She opened the case. It contained one MDF space suit, color brown. She didn't take much comfort in a second label which read SURPLUS. "Dragon spares no expense."

Sarah staggered to the bathroom. "What the heck was I drinking?" she asked the disheveled face looking back at her in the mirror.

The door buzzer was sounding. She staggered to the door and opened it. Two Tau soldiers stood there. "Yes?" She fumbled around for the translator. "Yes?"

"We are here to take you to the spaceport," the one with the most colorful insignia explained.

She pointed at the crate in the middle of the room. "We're taking that. I need a few minutes."

The soldier held out a small vial of liquid. "Emperor Sing said this will help."

"Oh no, I did make an ass out of myself." She took the vial and slugged it down, not even caring if it was, in fact, some sort of poison. At least poison would put her out of her misery.

13
SALVAGE

After two days without saying a single word, Commander Goth asked, "Why us?"

"Excuse me?" Sarah replied. She turned off the notebook. The book she'd been reading was boring, anyway.

"Why us? Why us for this mission?" Goth asked. "It is not Tau problem."

"Well, that's true. It's like this. The new chancellor of the Martian Republic is afraid of offending Earth. Really afraid. A Martian ship going this deep into Earth territory could cause a major diplomatic incident. You lot, on the other hand, are already at war with Earth. They can't get much madder than they already are. Besides, it was a Tau probe that found it."

"Looking for secret Earth base, not derelict ship. This ship is no match for an Earthforce cruiser."

"They haven't caught us, yet," Sarah pointed out.

"We still have to get home."

"If we're able to salvage the *Lisa Marie*, you guys are going to be very wealthy," Sarah said.

"We have to share it with our emperor," Goth countered.

"Well, it is his ship," Sarah said.

"It is Earth ship? Why not have them come out here?" Goth asked.

"It's an Earth cargo ship, but it's a Martian cargo. My company insured the cargo, not the ship. If we could recover some of the cargo, the Gompers Insurance Company will recoup some of its losses, even after paying you guys a salvage fee," Sarah explained. "Earthforce would simply seize everything and keep it all for themselves. At least, that's been our experience. So, turning it over to them would be the same as staying home."

Most people on Mars called the Tau "lizards." They certainly didn't always approach things the way a human would. "We can turn around and go back home if you like?" Sarah continued. "If you're afraid of mixing it up with Earthforce, I understand."

"Too late for that," Goth said. "We are here." He said something else in the second dialect that Sarah couldn't pick up.

"By golly, there it is. Target bearing twenty degrees," Sarah reported. "Range: one kilometer." She was getting so she could actually read some of the instruments. There was no portable pocket translator for their written language.

"Slow to one quarter," Goth ordered.

"One quarter speed," Topo, the helmsman, answered.

"Go to maneuvering thrusters," Goth ordered.

"Maneuvering thrusters," Topo replied.

"Docking sequence in five seconds," Goth ordered.

Sarah was amazed at the detail of the scanning beams on her console. "Hull appears intact. I've got a clear hatch on top of it. Two of them, actually. Let's grab the aft one."

Goth nodded, then said something in that annoying second dialect.

Topo gently landed the patrol ship on top of the *Lisa Marie*. "Magnetic seal in place." The scout ship was tiny, compared to the large freighter. It only took up a small part of the space on top of the hull.

"It is possible life support and power may still work," Goth said. He handed Sarah a handheld unit. "No sign of structural damage."

Sarah was reading the instruments. "It looks pretty darn cold down there." Sarah looked at Goth, then Topo, then Ting, the third member of the three-person crew. They were all looking expectantly back at her. *Warm blooded reptiles, bah. These guys were afraid of the cold.*

The procedure, according to the manual, was to send one person, and only one person, to board a derelict ship to determine if it was safe. If a bulkhead collapsed or there turned out to be booby traps, this greatly reduced casualties—unless you're the idiot who went on board. Goth could not order Sarah to do anything. Sarah was not military. She wasn't even Tau. She was human. And this ship had been sitting out in the icy cold of space for over ten years. "How about I go have a look at the power systems," Sarah offered.

She opened up the bag that contained her Martian Defense Force military surplus pressure suit. No, the Gompers Insurance

Company would not provide a new space suit if they could get a surplus one somewhere at half the cost. And they always seemed to find everything at off price venues. Someday, if she was still alive, she was going to have to meet their purchasing agent–maybe cook him something made with surplus rations or take him for a ride in a surplus surface skimmer.

At least the suit fit fairly well. Ting looked over the connections and pronounced her ready to go. She entered the airlock and waited for it to seal behind her. Then, she tried the handle on the hatch. It wouldn't budge. That seemed to be why Ting gave her a hammer. Hammers were Ting's solution to nearly everything. He was an engineer, they kept telling her.

Sarah gave the handle a whack. Then another. In no time, she had the hatch to the *Lisa Marie* open. The interior was cold, dark and foreboding. It was no wonder the reptiles didn't want to go. No matter how hard her helmet lights struggled, it was like their energy could only get a little bit beyond her before succumbing to the darkness of the derelict space ship.

The sensor in her hand confirmed what she suspected. The power generators had been charging everything for years. The ship's systems showed active on the life support panel. She turned them on, first the lights, then the heat, then the air filtration. Whatever happened to the ship, lack of environmental systems did not seem to have been the cause.

Still, everything was eerie. As the interior began to warm, moisture that had long been frozen began to form into a sort of fog. She also discovered the lights she'd found were little more than red glow plugs. It was becoming obvious this was the backup system she'd activated, not the primary. As they warmed, the glow plugs gave off a dim red light that may have been energy efficient, but it was hardly pleasing.

As the ship tried to wake up, Sarah made her way to the bridge. She turned on the primary computer. To her amazement, it came on. "Wow!"

"You have found something?" Goth asked.

She didn't realize she'd been transmitting. "I've got basic life support warming up the ship. The main computer's even working."

"Have you located the cargo?" Goth asked.

"In time, good sir. One thing at a time." Sarah made sure the radio in her helmet was off. What she'd feared was still strapped in a seat at the engineering console. She didn't want to let out a screech like a girl. Of course, she was a girl. Of course, the Tau didn't know the difference. *She* was their only reference point for human behavior. And they weren't going to catch her screaming just because there were a few frozen bodies lying around on the bridge. Frozen bodies that were certain to thaw soon.

She bit down on her tongue when the dead guy at the engineering station's arm dropped. No screaming. No running away. The body was simply thawing. Of course, it couldn't possibly have thawed that fast. She went over and touched it. Frozen solid. Then, she felt the air blowing through a vent below the panel and relaxed a little.

The handheld meter said there was enough air pressure and it was now slightly warmer than freezing. She unsnapped her helmet and took it off. The air was cold and clammy, but at least she was free from the claustrophobic tyranny of the helmet. She told the computer to play back the log.

Sarah found a recreation area after leaving the bridge. It had the usual games and comfy chairs and such. There was even a keyboard in the corner. It was still turned on. The keyboard had been on for ten years. She ran her fingers down the keys, then headed for the corridor to connect back to the scout ship. As she left the room, she heard the keyboard play back the notes she'd just played. She looked back into room and wondered why it would have such a playback feature.

Something did not just touch me. Something did not just touch my neck, she told herself. This ship was too darn creepy. She started back to the scout ship, trying just to walk and not run. Every few minutes, she found herself jerking her head one way or another. It always seemed that there was something moving, just out of the corner of her eye. She knew that wasn't possible and the crummy lighting from the glow plugs made everything look odd and distorted. The fog didn't help things. Even her breath was fogging. She figured the fog would go away if the ship got a little warmer and the air kept circulating.

It was time for some reptiles to earn their pay. She climbed up the ladder and through the hatch that went back into the scout ship. "I'm back." Sarah started taking off her space suit. "I found out what happened to this ship," Sarah explained. "You guys ever hear of Argomite reactors?"

The three of them stared blankly.

"Well, the Argomite Company built these defective reactors and put them in mostly merchant ships. They were defective. They weren't shielded properly. Sometimes a ship would be buzzing along in hyperspace under heavy power load and they'd suddenly flood a ship with radiation without warning. Worse thing was, the company knew about it but was too cheap to fix the problem. The poor crew had no idea. It only affected a small number of ships. Word got out. There was a big hullabaloo. Gompers didn't know about the reactors or they'd never have underwritten a policy. I played back the computer. That's what happened. The ship shut down and just drifted around for ten years. The crew was dead, but there wasn't any real damage. We could fly this baby home right now, though I'm not sure I'd jump into hyperspace without a radiation suit on."

She noticed Ting was checking their ship's sensors. "Relax, it was gamma radiation that leaked out. It's long gone. I scanned and there's less radiation down there than there is in here."

"You found cargo?" Goth asked.

"Well, not yet. You guys can go check it out. I can't do everything," Sarah said. "Down the corridor to the end, then two decks down the stairs. There's probably more carenthium than we can carry."

"We will see if they have a pump," Goth said.

"Good idea," Sarah agreed.

As her companions climbed down the ladder, Sarah finished getting out of her space suit. She was going to warm up for a few minutes before going back down to explore. The computer hadn't given up the location of the purser's office, amongst other things.

The ship's sensors suddenly started going off in alarm mode. Sarah scrambled over to the controls, then fumbled around to figure what they were trying to tell her. The visuals were mostly gibberish, as she still only had a rudimentary understanding of the Tau language in written form.

Energy was being discharged. It appeared the Tau were shooting at something or somebody. Then, she noticed yet another problem as well.

The three reptiles really zipped up the stairs and back into the scout ship. Ting was the last one up. He closed the hatch in record time.

"Guys, were you shooting at anything in particular?" Sarah asked.

Goth looked at her for just an instant, then said, "Invisible people."

"Uh, okay," Sarah replied. She waited for more explanation. When none came she said, "We've got another problem, too." She pointed upward.

Goth went to a window. "Oh no." An Earthforce cruiser had docked with the other hatch of the *Lisa Marie*. It was so big its tail extended over the top of their scout ship. They were boxed in. They couldn't leave if they wanted to. "This is why I did not want to come here."

"Well, I think it's an odd coincidence that they just show up a few minutes after we do, on a derelict ship that's been adrift for a decade," Sarah said.

There was a sort of sizzling noise for a few seconds, then the hatch from the *Lisa Marie* popped open. Goth yelled something in that second dialect Sarah couldn't pick up. All three Tau fell to the floor. Sarah joined them. A flash grenade came up through the hatch and exploded. Seconds later, a helmeted head popped up and aimed a laser rifle around the cabin.

"We surrender!" Sarah yelled.

~ * ~

The handcuffs were awfully tight. It was still miserably cold and damp in the *Lisa Marie*, but at least Sarah had finally found the purser's office. She had no idea how long they'd been there. There weren't any clocks or any other way to measure the passage of time. There was just silence, a cold clammy silence in a dark little room lit by one pathetic glow plug that barely worked. "I hope they take this thing into hyperspace so they can all die," Sarah said.

"That would include us," Goth pointed out.

"Who cares? They'll kill me anyway."

"It seems someone has lost her sunny disposition," Goth

said.

"What!"

"I make joke," Goth said.

The Tau had no sense of humor. She was certain of it. Things were getting weird. "Who were these invisible people you were shooting at?"

"Down by cargo area," Goth said. "They pushed Ting to the floor, then tried to take his knife."

"Lasers don't work on them," Ting added. "Don't understand that." He looked expectantly at her.

"Don't look at me. I wasn't there. I don't know what you guys got into." It was a lie, of course. She knew, or at least suspected, what might have happened. Stories of strange things abounded on derelict vessels with dead crews, though there were usually more skeptics than believers in such phenomena.

The hatch burst open. Two men in black Earthforce uniforms came into the purser's office. The tall, bald one was a commander. The second man wore no insignia. He was shorter, with red hair and a goatee, though it was his eyes that Sarah would remember. They were cold, gray eyes that seemed to look right through a person.

"I'm Commander Kent, XO of the Earthforce cruiser *Hawaii.*" He looked at Goth. "You are a long way from home, commander."

Goth stared back at him, but said nothing.

"You have a name?" Kent asked.

"I am Goth. This is Engineer Ting and Helmsman Topo," Goth replied.

The commander scratched his chin for a moment. "And you just up and went all the way out here to salvage a ship no one's seen or heard from in ten years?"

"Obviously," Goth said.

"You'll be taken to the prisoner of war facility on Minion Prime. That's an Earth colony that, ironically, was the destination of the *Lisa Marie.*" Commander Kent seated himself behind the purser's desk. "Although the ship is in good shape, I'm puzzled why you'd bother for a load of carenthium."

"Have you seen the price of carenthium lately?" The other man finally joined into the conversation. He sat himself on the purser's desk top and crossed his arms in front of himself. Without looking at Sarah, he asked, "Why did Gompers Insurance want this ship?"

Sarah glared at the unnamed man, but said nothing.

"A load of carenthium is valuable. It helps fuel space ships and all. But, perhaps there is something else afoot here." He unfolded his arms. "No matter. We'll figure it out."

"My friend here is from Military Intelligence," Commander Kent said.

"Who'd have thought it," Sarah answered.

"Miss Meadows, we have quite a file on you. I doubt your friends here know as much about you as I do," the intelligence officer said. "When I've finished your interrogation, you'll be taken back to Earth where you will be tried, then executed for espionage."

"What a surprise," Sarah said. "I'm a Martian citizen. This is a derelict vessel subject to salvage under the Law of Space Treaty. How can I possibly be a spy? What is there to spy on?"

"It's right above you," the intelligence officer said. "Not that I need a reason. Our military courts are far more efficient than your Martian Criminal Tribunal. We don't let facts get in the way of a good trial."

The two men both stood. "Guards will move you all onto our ship in a few minutes," the intelligence officer said. "The brig of the *Hawaii* is a better place for you than tied up in here." They both marched out of the purser's office.

"Sarah Meadows, I think these men do not like you," Goth said.

Somehow, the way Goth said it seemed funny. Sarah let out a brief snicker of a laugh. The odd thing was, there was another laugh at the same time and the three Tau soldiers weren't saying or doing anything. The sound, she began to think, had emitted from her translator, which was still active and in her pocket.

"Is there someone here with us?" Sarah asked.

The empty chair behind the purser's desk moved so it pointed directly at Sarah.

"Invisible people," Goth said.

"My translating device that I use to talk to my Tau friends here may pick you up as well. Who are you?" Sarah asked.

"Why have you come? You are not welcome," a voice said. It sounded feminine. "Leave us alone."

"Are you Captain Mercer?" Sarah asked.

"Why have you come?" It repeated.

There were only two women on the crew and the other was the cook. "Are you Barbara Mercer?" Sarah repeated. "I'm from Gompers Insurance. That's why we're here. We insured your cargo."

"You brought *them* on board," the voice said.

"The Tau are the least of your worries," Sarah said.

"Leave us. Leave us be."

"I can't. We're prisoners. Captain Mercer, we just were trying to recover some of the insured cargo. We'll gladly go. It's Earthforce you should fear. They'll tow this ship to Mercer Prime and dismantle it for scrap. Is that what you want?" Sarah asked. "Is that what you want?"

"No. Not now. Just leave us alone. Just let us be," the voice said.

"Fine with us. Help us get out of here. I can get rid of Earthforce. It will be just as it was," Sarah promised. "But, we need your help." There was no answer or response, though Sarah suspected there was no one in the room anymore.

The three Tau started talking in that annoying second dialect again. It seemed baffling the translator couldn't pick it up, especially in light of what had just happened.

More time went by. It was hard to tell how much. Then, the door burst open and three marines came in—two corporals and a sergeant. "We're taking you back to our brig," the sergeant said. Apparently, there was one guard for each Tau soldier. A strawberry blonde girl from Mars didn't need her own guard, evidently.

The funny thing about Earth marines was almost all of them carried an obsolete weapon in a sheath that went into their boots. The black nylon knives never break or react to metal or conduct electricity, supposedly. And they never had to be sharpened. And, the manufacturers of these knives probably never envisioned they would all float out of their sheaths and stab their owners at the same exact time. Then, those same knives pulled out of their victims. Everyone knows you always pull the knife back out to hasten blood loss and kill the victim. A knife still in the wound blocks the blood from escaping.

The two corporals both collapsed to the floor, each screaming as their limbs lost strength and blood surged from their bodies. Their screams only lasted a few moments, then the corporals were silent. Their eyes still stared pleadingly toward their sergeant, still showing the disbelief at what had just happened to them.

But not the sergeant. He snatched his knife back from his unseen assailant and held it in front of his face as it dripped his own blood over his right hand. A strange, twisted grin appeared on his face. It was an almost satisfied look as he stared at the knife–his knife. Then, he started laughing. It was a maniacal, hideous laugh. As he laughed, his blood gushed up from his chest and showered his throat and vocal cords, making it the most horrid, gurgling laugh Sarah would ever hear. Then, finally, mercifully, the laugh stopped and the sergeant fell onto the already lifeless bodies of his two fallen comrades.

Unseen hands quickly took the electronic key off the sergeant's belt and all of them were free.

"Leave us," the voice Sarah attributed to Captain Mercer said.

"Sure thing, but I came here to try and recover something we insured. Until I saw the ship was intact, I didn't even know if it was on board." She pointed at the purser's safe behind the desk. "It wasn't on the manifest, but it was on the insurance policy. Give me the combination to the safe, captain."

"No," the voice said. "Just go."

"It's brought misery everywhere it's gone. As long as it's on board, others will come. If I take it back to Mars, there won't be any reason for anyone to ever disturb you again," Sarah said.

The lights flickered on the number pad on the front of the safe, then it clicked. Sarah quickly opened the safe. A green velvet bag sat on the middle shelf. She grabbed it. "Thank you, captain."

They found no resistance getting back to their ship. The Earthforce crew seemed preoccupied with offloading the carenthium and not with guarding a small scout ship that had little value or purpose.

"Earth guys damage hatch. I fix." Ting held up a hammer.

As Ting sealed the hatch, Topo and Goth took the seats at

the control stations. "There is a large ship above us. It is blocking our escape. You do have a plan?" Goth asked Sarah.

She was only half paying attention as she climbed into the turret that housed the laser cannon. "Carenthium is marvelous stuff. They love it for thrusters 'cause it burns in space. It's got its own oxygen, they tell me. And our Earthforce pals are pumping it through that big hose into their cargo tank." The laser canon would not arm. The target was too close, if she understood the Tau writing correctly. She flipped off the safety, pushed the override button and fired.

Scout ships were patrol craft, to monitor a large area with a small crew and flee and summon assistance if an enemy approached. But, they did have some fire power for when they got in a pinch. Sarah doubted the designers of the ship had their particular predicament in mind when they designed the craft. Crimson energy blasted all the 20 meters across the top of the *Lisa Marie* to the hose feeding into the *Hawaii*, right at the junction where it fed into the storage hold. An explosion ripped a hole out the side of the *Hawaii* a few seconds later.

The Earthforce ship seemed to be turning sideways. They'd only used a single magnetic seal to dock on top of the *Lisa Marie*, just as the scout ship had done. They'd lost that seal when the explosion went off. The *Hawaii*'s thruster's opened up. Whoever was on their bridge probably thought the problem was on the *Lisa Marie* and was trying to get some distance from a burning ship. A bright flash a few seconds later was the last of the *Hawaii*.

"Commander Goth, can you get us out of here?" Sarah asked. "I didn't think it would blow up quite so fast. Good thing it moved away."

Their own thrusters kicked on and the scout ship pulled away from the top of the *Lisa Marie*. Sarah fired a shot at the derelict freighter. She noticed Goth was standing behind her as she climbed down from the turret. "I shot their engines. No one's going to bother them anymore. That ship will never fly anywhere. With no cargo, it's now worthless."

Goth asked, "Why do the invisible people want to be left out here?"

"I can only imagine what they've been through. I guess they no longer belong anyplace else," Sarah explained.

"Make sure we get paid for the diamond in your bag," Goth said.

"You knew about the Parkside Diamond, the biggest natural diamond ever found on Mars?" Sarah asked.

"Of course. Had to be worthwhile for us to come out here. Our ships don't use much carenthium," Goth said.

"This thing's caused a lot of trouble." Sarah took the diamond out of the bag. "Surprised the Earthforce goons didn't figure out to look in the safe. Gompers insured this little rock for a lot of money."

Goth looked confused, even more than normal. "The invisible people killed the Earth marines to help us escape?"

Sarah shrugged. "They probably don't view death the way you or I do. I can't figure it. It was an Earth crew, they tell me, yet the invisible people liked us best. Take me home," Sarah asked. She put the diamond back in the bag and zipped it up.

14
REALLY GOOD STUFF

Sarah approached the customs guys at Fremont Station. The Tau took off and left, the station being just a little too close to Earth for their liking.

"Do you have anything to declare?" the customs agent asked.

"Yes, I do," Sarah said. She placed the bag on the counter. "There's a diamond in there."

The customs agent entered something at his terminal. "Estimated value?"

"Thirty million doubloons," Sarah said.

He looked up from his terminal. "Excuse me? I thought you said thirty million?"

"I did," Sarah replied.

"Uh?"

She unzipped the bag. "It's a Martian diamond. They're exempt from duty."

"Oh?"

"Have a good one." She closed up the bag and headed into the station. Her next stop was the station's branch of the Bank of Mars.

"Hello. I need to access my safe deposit box, please," Sarah told the lady wearing an eyepatch.

Her name tag read "Gwen." Gwen slid over a small box with a blue glowing screen. "Right thumb, please."

Sarah did as instructed. "Access code Footloose."

"Access code?" Gwen asked.

"Footloose. I have box three-ninety-one," Sarah said.

"Which box do you have?" Gwen asked.

"Box three-ninety-one," Sarah said.

"Right this way," Gwen said.

Sarah followed her to the box vault. She placed her thumb on a small panel. The box opened. Sarah placed the little bag she'd been guarding inside the box and closed the door. "I'm through."

"Are you through?" Gwen asked.

"Yes, I'm through," Sarah said.

"Right this way." Gwen escorted her back out to the lobby. The Bank of Mars was the only bank that had a branch on Fremont Station.

Sarah went down an elevator to level twenty-two, then approached the desk clerk behind the counter of the Andromeda Hotel. "Hi."

"We're full madam. I'm afraid we have no rooms available," the desk clerk said.

Unfazed, Sarah asked, "Is the Gompers deluxe room we have here in use?"

"What Gompers deluxe room?" the desk clerk asked.

"The one we have here at this hotel."

"There is no such thing," he insisted.

"Room forty-one, to be precise. It's permanently reserved for the Gompers Insurance Company," Sarah said. "I use it all the time."

"No, it's not. That's just a regular room."

"You are mistaken," Sarah said. "May I speak to a manager?"

A tall man with a bald head that glistened under the lights approached. "Is there a problem?"

"I am Sarah Meadows with the Gompers Insurance Company. I am trying to find out if the room we permanently maintain here is available."

"There is no such room," he insisted.

"I've stayed in it," she insisted.

"Well, we decided to rent it out because there's a big conference for the next few days. Gompers hardly ever uses it," the so-called manager stated.

Sarah struggled to remain calm. "Even though you send us a bill for it every month?"

"Precisely," he replied.

"This is outrageous."

"Take it up with our competitor. No, wait, we don't have a competitor. We're the only hotel on this station," the so-called manager said.

Sarah turned and walked away. She was most dangerous when she stopped talking and walked away. She noticed a gentleman was approaching the guest elevator. "Sir, excuse me?"

"Yes?" he cautiously asked.

"Are you staying at this hotel?" Sarah inquired.

"Yes?"

She asked, "Well, I was wondering, if I had sex with you could I sleep in your room with you?"

"Uh, sure," he answered.

Love that high male-to-female ratio, she thought. "Okay then." *I've got the most valuable diamond in the world and I have to be a whore to get a place to sleep. What a country.* She followed him into the elevator.

"Do you do this often?" he asked.

"Well, I don't like sleeping on the floor very much," Sarah said.

The elevator door opened. "I see. It's just down the hall, here." The man waved his room key and the door slid open.

Sarah finally found out what the economy rooms were like. She was not particularly impressed. "What's your name?"

"Max."

"I'm Sarah." She sat down on the only chair in the room. "I need to make a quick call before we get down to business."

"I knew it."

"What?" Sarah opened up her clipboard.

"Oh, I thought you were going to make a call to the surface and bill it to my room," Max said.

Sarah shook her head. "Don't be silly. Do you know what hotels charge for that?"

"Yes, I do know," he replied.

The bald lady appeared on the screen. "May I please speak with Don Don?" Sarah asked.

"I'll see if he's available."

Don Don soon appeared. "So, you're back. Where are you, exactly?"

"Fremont Station. I missed the last shuttle," Sarah explained.

"Oh well, no problem. We'll see you tomorrow then," Don Don said.

"Yeah. Those clowns who run the Andromeda Hotel have me a bit miffed, though," Sarah said.

"How's that?" Don Don asked.

"Well, they rented out the Gompers room for some conference and I can't have it. I'm having to prostitute myself with some stranger to have a place to sleep," Sarah nonchalantly reported.

"You're what?"

"Some guy agreed that if I had sex with him he'd share his room with me. At least I can get a hot shower and some sleep. I'm so tired." She wondered if she could even fit in the shower stall.

"What? They sent a bill. They billed us. They can't do that," Don Don said. "They sent me a bill."

"I've got to go now," Sarah said. She closed her clipboard.

"I knew it. You work for Gompers," he accused.

"You knew what, Max?" Sarah asked.

"This is some deal to trick me into buying insurance."

"Did you need some insurance?" she asked.

"No!"

"Fine, because I didn't want to sell you any," she said. "I'm real tired. Well, let's get you laid so I can get some sleep."

"I'm not so sure about this," Max said.

There was a knock at the door. A puzzled Max went over and opened it. "Yes?"

"Is there a Sarah Meadows here?" It was the bald manager person.

Sarah went over to the door. "Yes?"

"Uh, Miss Meadows, I just got a call from the president of our company. Uh, well, the Andromeda Hotel sincerely apologizes for the mix-up," he said.

"Mix-up was it?"

"The Gompers room is, unfortunately, in disposed, so I've been instructed to offer you the Presidential Suite, at no charge, of course," he said.

"How nice," Sarah said. "Well, Max, some other time." She followed the manager down the hall. He waved a key and the door opened. She wouldn't be hitting her head inside this place. "Uh, president of what?"

"Pardon?"

"Mars has a chancellor, not a president. Who is the Presidential Suite for, exactly?" Sarah asked.

"The president of Andromeda Hotels, of course," he said.

"Ah." There was a large bath tub. It was calling to her.

15
REWARDS

"Martian Red in a tall glass," Sarah ordered.

"Right away," the waiter replied.

She wondered what had become of the cute waiter. This guy was okay, but looked too much like Don Don for her liking. Sarah noticed she was no longer alone. Becky was holding two glasses of Martian Red. She placed one in front of Sarah, then took the vacant chair across the table from her.

Sarah took a sip of beer. "They have this stuff on the Tau world, I can't remember what they call it, but it's distilled, not brewed like this beer." Sarah took another sip. "Stuff's really strong." And another sip. "Boy, I hope I didn't make an ass out of myself."

"Apparently," Becky said, "you danced with the emperor and were the hit of the party."

"How'd you know that?" Sarah asked.

"I am the foreign minister. I know everything," she replied.

"Wish I could remember. I woke up on a shipping crate." Sarah chugged down the rest of her beer. "What can I do for you, Minister?"

"Nothing. I just thought I'd say hello," Becky said. She took a drink of beer. "And how is your friend, Karl?"

"Beats me. I've spent the last couple of weeks on a Tau scout ship getting threatened with execution and eating Earthforce nutrition bars, while Dragon and Karl hobnob with dignitaries on the Tau world and eat gourmet food. I don't think they're even back, yet." Sarah was pleased the waiter brought her another glass of Martian Red.

"Well, they're on their way back, as I understand it," Becky replied.

"Wonderful." Sarah struggled to suppress a belch coming on.

"Well, nice seeing you again," Becky said. She trotted over to the escalator and was gone.

Sarah finished her second beer. She wasn't really surprised

when the check arrived and she was being charged for three beers. Becky's glass was still almost full. "What the heck." Sarah slammed down that one as well.

It was late in the day when she finally showed up at the office. Sarah plopped down the bag containing the diamond on the bald lady's desk. "You might put this in the safe."

"What is it?"

"A diamond worth thirty million doubloons," Sarah said.

The bald lady's eyes seemed to get bigger. "You're just walking around with something like that? By yourself?"

"Yep. I'm pretty tough," Sarah said.

"Have you been drinking?"

"Yep."

"With a thirty million doubloon diamond? Just carrying it around?" The bald lady disappeared toward the back room where the safe was at.

Sarah made it to her desk at the bullpen. She hadn't been there two minutes when a familiar customer arrived. "Phillip Phillips, how the heck are you?"

"Well, me mother died last night," he said.

"I'm sorry to hear that," Sarah said. She took a small box out of a drawer and placed it on top of her desk. "Put your thumb on this for a second, Phillip."

He did as instructed.

"The machine wants to make sure that you're you. I never knew my mother. I'm an orphan," Sarah said as she entered a code into her terminal.

"No family?"

"None whatsoever," Sarah said.

"I guess I don't have anyone, either. Not no more," Phillip said. "Me pa died a long time ago. No brothers or sisters. No one, really. There was just me and me mother."

Sarah nodded. "Mom had a life insurance policy naming you as beneficiary."

"I know that. That's why I'm here," Phillip said.

"The public registrar has not issued a death certificate, yet. As soon as they do, we'll transfer the proceeds." Sarah leaned back in her chair.

"How long will that take?" Phillip asked.

"A couple of days, usually."

"Okay. Maybe I can quit my job at the sewage plant."

Sarah looked at Phillip for a moment. "I thought you liked that job."

"It's the best job I ever had," Phillip said.

"Well, don't do anything hasty," Sarah said. "Work, it's what makes us who we are."

"Uh, how much do I get?" Phillip asked.

"Uh, you don't know?"

Phillip looked down at the floor. "No. Not really. Mom never said, exactly. She just said to be sure and come here if she died."

Sarah went into another drawer of her desk and took out a small white card. "Phillip, this is the name of a financial advisor. He's pretty good. Go and see him. People, well they may try and talk you into things. Having money can be a burden for some people."

"How much do I get?" Phillip asked again.

"Five million doubloons," Sarah said.

"How much?"

"Five million doubloons," Sarah repeated. "You're now one of the richest men on Mars, Phillip."

He started staring at the ceiling. "How'd mom afford so much insurance?"

"She reinvested the proceeds from her husband's life insurance in a new policy, one of our products that reinvests its dividends. Over time, well, five million doubloons, Phillip."

"Are you sure I shouldn't quit my job at the sewage plant?"

"Well, that's up to you," Sarah said.

"Of course, I wouldn't know what to do with myself if I didn't have work. Heck, I don't even have a girlfriend."

"I suspect, Phillip, that may change."

After Phillip was gone, Don Don asked, "Why were you handling a death claim? That's not the job of special ops. We've got agents sitting around doing nothing."

"I sold him the policy," Sarah said. "And I was also sitting around doing nothing. And I still have an all lines insurance license. Just renewed it, in fact."

Don Don went over to the other side of the office to try and listen in on someone else's conversation. He fumbled around straightening a desk no one was currently using.

Sarah noticed she had an encrypted message waiting. The source seemed odd. She opened it and stared dumbfounded at the screen for quite some time. Finally, as Don Don walked by her desk, she said, "I should've worked at the sewage treatment plant."

"How was that?" Don Don asked.

"Sewage. Nobody makes you jump out of APC's if you work at the sewage plant," Sarah said.

"What are you talking about?" Don Don asked.

"The Honorable Becky Hudson, Foreign Minister of the Republic of Mars, has granted me a new travel waiver," Sarah said. "She could at least pay for her beer."

"Travel waiver?" Don Don asked. "Beer?"

"A Martian citizen is now required to get a travel waiver if they knowingly travel into a war zone involving the Tau-Earth conflict, or the Earth-Chiron conflict. It just went into effect," Sarah said. "Got to keep track of what our citizens are doing."

"We don't have you scheduled for any trips right now, Sarah," Don Don insisted.

"Then who in the heck does?" Sarah asked.

16
HONORABLE WORK

It took a few hours to get her answer. Somehow, she was not very surprised when three Tau soldiers arrived at the office. They all snapped to attention in front of her desk. Tau soldiers, walking around Mars City was unheard of. The Earth Embassy would go ballistic. She liked it. She noticed a lack of garish color on these guy's uniforms. They were fairly low in rank. "Gentlemen, what a pleasant surprise. Did you want to buy some insurance?"

They all stared blankly at her.

"It was a joke," Sarah said.

"Never understand human humor," the one who seemed in charge said. He stood there for a moment, then announced, "Ambassador Kuhl requests the presence of Sarah Meadows at the Embassy of the Tau people, forthwith."

"I didn't know the Tau had an embassy," Sarah said.

"We do now," the soldier replied.

"Uh, how long has this been going on?"

"We opened an hour ago," he answered.

"I see." Sarah grabbed her clipboard. "Lead on." As they passed by the bald lady's desk, Sarah said, "I'm going out."

"You just got here," the bald lady replied.

"I know that."

The embassy turned out to be in a part of Mars City called South Dome. It required going on an underground mini version of Mag Lev to get there. They got off the train and proceeded down a corridor. Standing in front of two large doors were two more Tau Soldiers. These guys were armed. A gold sign was on the door that read EMBASSY OF THE TAU PEOPLE.

The soldier opened the door and Sarah followed them inside. Two female Tau were working on some terminal. Then, a male Tau emerged from an inner office. "Miss Meadows, good of you to come." The guy looked like one of the dignitaries at the party.

She really hoped she hadn't made an ass out of herself. "My pleasure. I was a bit surprised you opened an embassy on Mars."

"Our emperor felt if Earth can have an embassy here, perhaps we should as well. I am Kuhl."

"I have a feeling the Mars City Marshal just got a little nervous," Sarah said.

"Perhaps." he pointed toward the inner office.

Sarah followed him inside.

"We still have some decorating to do. These walls are quite plain." He pointed at a human sized chair, then plopped down on one of the bench-like seats the reptiles seemed to prefer. "Few Martians have ever seen one of our people. Our emperor believes it is time to change that."

"Well, ambassador, this was an unexpected surprise. What, precisely, do you want from me?" Sarah asked. "I doubt you want to buy insurance somehow."

"We want to offer you a job," he said.

"I have a job, ambassador," Sarah replied.

"We know. But, we were interested in section Eleven-A of the Gompers Insurance Company's employee manual."

Sarah opened up her clipboard. "I don't recall that, offhand." She brought up the page and read the section. "Ambassador, I'm not sure I understand?"

He handed her a document. "This commission is signed by Sing, Emperor of the Tau People. It is written in our language, then yours."

The document was on a heavy sort of paper with a very fancy type font. There was an official seal at the bottom.

"Also signed by Marshal Zuto. It was his idea, they say." The ambassador looked at her expectantly.

"If I understand this, what, precisely, is it you want me to do for you?" she anxiously asked.

"Win our war against Earth."

"I'm an insurance adjustor," she protested.

"Then adjust our war," he said. "Marshal Zuto say you are the greatest military strategist he has ever seen."

"Uh, well, uh." At least she knew why she had a new travel waiver.

~ * ~

Don Don noticed a new message had appeared at his office

terminal. Then he read it. Then he stormed out of his office and ran over to Sarah's desk. "Is this some kind of joke?"

"Not hardly, Don Don," she replied.

He seemed to be changing color, more red than usual. "It says military leave? You're not military?"

"Under section Eleven-A of the employee manual, reservists in the armed forces shall be granted leave when required to serve," Sarah stated. "So, I need military leave."

"But, this can't be. How? Are you telling me you're in the MDF?"

"No, heavens no, I'm not in the MDF," Sarah said.

"Then why do you need military leave?" Don Don demanded. His face was turning purple.

"The employee manual doesn't say which military you have to belong to, just that you have to be in the military," Sarah pointed out.

"I don't understand. Where, precisely, are you a reservist, then?" Don Don asked. The thought of Sarah joining Earthforce seemed preposterous. There weren't any other military options that he could think of.

"The Army of the Tau," Sarah said.

"What? The lizards? They don't even have a reserve?"

Sarah handed him her new military commission. "They do now."

"How many soldiers do they have in their reserve?" he asked as he tried to make sense of the document he was reading.

"Just me," she said.

"They created a reserve of Sarah Meadows?"

"Yep."

"Where are they sending you?" Don Don asked.

"Tartarus."

"Are you insane?"

"Yep. It sure looks that way."

The next morning, Sarah found herself back at the embassy. One of the female Tau kept looking at her as she sat in the lobby, waiting for the ambassador to complete a call to someplace. "They've been wondering what to do with you."

"Excuse me?" Sarah said.

"They're not used to dealing with humans. Our uniforms,

they won't fit you."

"Oh."

She brought Sarah a bag labeled Earthforce. "The flight mechanic uniform for Earthforce doesn't look that different than our army uniforms."

"Where did you get this?" Sarah asked.

"You probably would rather not know."

"Okay." Sarah found a laser pistol, model T-53, in the bag, along with a holster.

"The weapons designed for Tau are probably heavier than you want to carry around."

Sarah examined the T-53. "Gompers has a few of these. I've trained with them. They're actually a copy of a Martian design."

"Excellent."

They were highly effective, but had one major drawback. They did not run on continuous power. Before firing, you had to hit the power switch. They emitted an annoying high pitched beep, then it took 2.4 seconds to power up before you could fire them.

Sarah found a black nylon knife with boot sheath. She wondered if she was going anywhere with cranky ghosts around. "This could work. I'll try it on."

When the ambassador came for her, Sarah was outfitted and ready for action. She followed the ambassador into his office.

The ambassador opened a box and removed something that looked like rocks. He placed them on her shoulders. They were very colorful. Very colorful.

"I still don't really understand what my role is supposed to be," Sarah said.

"Zuto will brief you when you get on site. A ship will take you there right now. Oh, you might keep that weapon in the bag until you get onboard. The agreement we have with the foreign office is no weapons outside of the embassy."

"Makes sense," Sarah agreed.

The ambassador opened the door. Two soldiers snapped to attention. "They will escort you to the spaceport."

"I know the way," Sarah said.

"They will escort you to the space port," he insisted.

"Lead on," Sarah said.

Nothing much was said on the way out on Mag Lev. Then again, the Tau weren't all that chatty anyway. "What do you guys think of Mars?" she finally asked.

"We are here. Until they send us someplace else."

"Do you like it here?" Sarah asked.

"It does not matter."

"Well, try the cream pie at the Garden Spot. Some of your countrymen fell in love with the cream pie on Fremont Station. The garden spot's better," Sarah said. "If I had more time, I'd take you there myself."

"Socializing with senior officers is not encouraged," the Tau soldier said.

"I meant no disrespect," Sarah said. "I guess I didn't know you were senior officers."

The two Tau looked at each other. They seemed very confused. Finally, the response came. "We're not senior officers. You are."

"Well, I'm not entirely used to your way of doing things, guys. But I'll get up to speed." Mag Lev was slowing into the spaceport station. "Uh," Sarah looked at the rocklike things on her shoulder, "I know this may seem like an odd question, but what rank do you guys think I am?"

As the doors slid open, the answer came. "You are a general."

17
WAR

The Tau transport was docked at Fremont Station. Two women were looking out the window at it. "Aren't those those lizard people?" one of the women asked.

"Are you sure?" the other one asked.

"I think so," her friend insisted.

"I wonder what they want?"

"What if they come inside the station?"

"Maybe we should go back upstairs." They both marched past Sarah, paying her little notice.

Sarah decided to head down to the airlock. Her escorts from the embassy had seen her off on the shuttle up from Mars City. Interstellar transports seldom landed on the Martian surface, even though Martian gravity and atmosphere were so light. Specialized shuttles were the norm.

Ting and Topo were just inside the airlock. They were talking in that annoying second dialect her translator still could not pick up. Suddenly they snapped to attention.

"Hi guys," Sarah said. "Are you my ride?"

"We are ready to go," Ting said. He was holding one of his hammers. "Everything fixed now."

That was more information than she really wanted to know. "Tell the captain to get underway as soon as possible."

Ting nodded, then went up to the flight deck.

Topo looked over at a seat that was clearly too small for a Tau. He seemed unsure exactly what he was supposed to do.

"Secure the airlock, helmsman," Sarah ordered. "Prepare for departure." She went up to the flight deck. This was going to take a different mindset than she was used to. She looked over the four seats on the flight deck. They were all too big for her. She sat down in the one that didn't seem to have an instrument panel.

She noticed Goth was looking at her. "Commander Goth, nice to see you again. By now, I'm sure Earthforce is wondering what we're up to. I doubt they'll attack us in Martian space, but you never know." She started trying to figure out how to strap herself in. It was not lining up well and was way too loose. It would have to do.

Goth was still looking at her.

"Whenever you're ready to depart commander?" Sarah said.

Goth was still looking at her.

"Sometime today would be fine," she added.

Goth said, "We received orders to come here and transport a Tau general. So, here we are?"

"Surprise," Sarah said. "I've been given a direct commission by the emperor. I'll bet that doesn't happen every day."

Goth said something in that second dialect. Tupo took his position. The ship began to pull away of the station.

Ting said something in that second dialect, then strapped into the remaining seat. He held up his hammer. "Fixed now."

Sarah was not sure what it was he'd so proudly fixed. She decided she'd rather not know.

Tupo fired thrusters and adjusted their heading as the ship picked up speed. Then he looked at his instruments and it was obvious he did not like what he saw.

"Unfortunately, we're not hooked into the Martian grid," Sarah said. "I wouldn't be too alarmed. That's probably a Martian APC approaching. Hail them, commander."

"Our translator not as good as yours," Goth replied.

"Of course not. I don't need a translator. Hail them," Sarah said. She instantly recognized Nick Tanager when his faced popped up on the screen. "Commander why are you coming so close to us?"

He seemed confused. "What are you doing on board that ship?"

"That is none of your concern, commander. Why are you approaching our ship?" she asked.

"Orders to escort you out of Martian space," came the answer.

"We did not request any such escort, commander," Sarah said. "We thank you, but please withdraw."

"Your funeral," he said.

"Precisely, commander," Sarah said. She leaned back in the chair. After a few moments, she said, "Commander Goth, take us into hyperspace immediately."

"Not allowed to fly in hyperspace this close to Mars," Goth said.

"Commander Goth, take us into hyperspace immediately," Sarah repeated.

Goth nodded. The ship lurched as it picked up speed. Then the hyperdrive kicked in and the stars were replaced by streaks of light.

"I don't know if anything from Earthforce was lurking out there, but they have spies all over. While the commander's intentions were honorable, I believe it makes us look weak to require an escort. We are a Tau warship and we do not cower in fear of anyone from Earth," Sarah said.

"If there was an Earth ship waiting out there, then they've surely notified their forces on Gentara that we are coming," Goth said. "Earthforce does not like you."

"Yes, that seems likely." She wondered why her translator called the place Gentara instead of Tartarus. Gentara was the Tau name for the moon they were going to. The Martians used the Earth name.

"Gentlemen, if they're waiting for us when we arrive, what would you suggest?" Sarah asked.

"Not go," Ting said.

"Well, that's where my orders are. Let's try and figure something out before we get there," Sarah suggested. "Although I've always thought dying in a ball of fire careening out of the sky might be a cool way to die."

The three reptiles looked at each other, then back at her.

"That was a joke. Let's avoid dying if at all possible," Sarah said.

The three reptiles looked at each other, then back at her.

"We come out of hyperspace as low as we can without burning up, then get down as fast as possible," Garth said. "No one can hold in orbit for long without attack from other side."

"And I take it Earthforce gets to their bases using the same tactics?" Sarah asked. She activated her clipboard which she somehow forgot to return to Don Don and drew out the scenario. She showed it to Goth. "This sort of approach then?"

"Yes," Goth agreed.

"Interesting." She changed her little map slightly. "Perhaps we could try coming out here?"

"That's where Earthforce comes out," Goth said.

"I know, commander," she said.

He stared at the clipboard for a moment, then showed it to his helmsman. Then he handed it back. "They may not expect that."

The surreal nothingness of hyperspace vanished with the abrupt force and resistance as Tartarus's atmosphere tried to resist another spaceship violating its sensibilities. After the initial jolt, the ride quickly settled down to a smooth descent as Topo headed the ship toward the Tau help part of this world. They were out of Earthforce controlled airspace before anyone on that side realized what had just happened. Ting fired the landing thrusters and they plopped down on the surface with nobody getting a single shot off at them.

I have just come to a total hell hole to fight in some war I have no real stake in. Why couldn't I stay on Mars? Sarah thought as the blast of hot dry air hit her in the face and gave her a jolt of reality.

A handful of Tau maintenance workers looked at her suspiciously. She followed Goth down a walkway that went underground. At least the cavern was a little cooler. They turned a corner, then Goth suddenly snapped to attention. Sarah decided she better do likewise. Zuto emerged from the shadows. She hadn't even seen him. Night vision, advantage Tau.

"Commander, that was an interesting approach in you took. We almost mistook you for an Earthforce attack," Zuto said.

"We were concerned our departure may have been transmitted to Earthforce," Goth said.

Zuto looked Goth over for a moment. "So, you decided to come in right over Earth held territory?"

"No, sir," Goth replied.

"You did not decide to come in that way? Was navigation off, commander?"

"Our navigation was perfect," Goth said.

Sarah decided to end Goth's misery. "I decided to come out of hyperspace there, sir."

"I see," Zuto said. "Commander, you are dismissed. General, come with me."

Sarah followed him deeper into the cavern. They went inside an ante room. The lights automatically came on. The room was stuffed with military equipment. One half of the room was filled with Earthforce meal kits.

"You may not like our food," Zuto said. "We have this. Many varieties. I do not care for Earth food, though I admit the banana pudding is tolerable."

"Compared to some of the wonders Martian Hydroponics comes up with, Earthforce rations will be fine, sir." They even had strawberries.

She noticed Zuto was walking toward another part of the cavern. She hurried to catch up to him. They went in a meeting room. There were a few maps on the wall and a large oval conference table that looked like it was made out of stone. There was a portable field communication unit and the Tau version of an access terminal. A little underground stream ran against one side of the room, then disappeared underground.

"You can read up on what troops are available. We have five Marten class attack ships ready. You can start with them." He pointed at a clock on the wall. "We use same time as our home world, everywhere." The clock read 11.00. "Staff meeting at fourteen hundred. You can brief commanders on your plan."

Then, Sarah noticed he was gone. So much for getting a chance to observe the operation. She couldn't tell much about her new boss, other than he was not very chatty. She didn't even know if he was mad or impressed with their approach over Earth held territory when they came out of hyperspace. She hoped, over time, she'd have a better take on him. Her first concern was the five Tau commanders who were not likely to like taking orders from some human woman who no military experience. *Why didn't I just stick to selling insurance?* She asked herself.

Down to business. She knew the Marten class was a newer class of ship similar to what she'd been riding around in with Goth and his crew. Small, fast attack ships. They were kind of like a more sophisticated version of the pirate raiders Johnson LeClark used. Apparently, they were hers to command. She hoped her clipboard could break down the Tau written language so she could figure out who she was commanding. And she was very anxious to see what they had in the way of intelligence reports.

But first, she ventured back to the supply room to grab a few pouches of rations. She selected strawberries, banana pudding and a self-heating coffee cup. It was not a balanced meal, but it would do for the time being.

The strawberries were dehydrated. They somehow reconstituted when she opened the package. It even came with its own spoon. MDF field rations were not nearly this good. And there was whole room full of them just for her. She did wonder how the Tau had so many Earthforce supplies.

18
STRATEGY

The instant coffee was actually better than the stuff people drank on Mars. She put away the empty container for the banana pudding, then waited expectantly. Precisely on time five Tau officers entered the room. Sarah remained seated. A few moments later Marshal Zuto entered. She stood to attention. So much to get right. Being a civilian had been so much easier.

"This is General Meadows," Zuto introduced her. "Commanders Bercy, Moth, Dinka, and Pence. General Meadows is taking command of Task Force Five."

"Nice to meet all of you," Sarah said. She knew immediately who she was going to have trouble with. She'd had enough dealings with the Tau she was starting to understand their mannerisms.

"Human! No!" Bercy yelled. "This cannot be!"

"Commander do you have something to say?" Sarah asked.

He pointed at her. "I no work with that."

"I see," Sarah calmly replied. *Gompers training don't fail me now*, she thought. She'd been expecting this reaction since she'd arrived. It was one thing to see someone like her riding on a ship. It was another matter to take orders from them. Since he'd entered the room, Sarah noticed Bercy had a tendency to sway backwards on his legs. He probably wasn't even aware of it. But Sarah was.

Sarah took a leap and kicked Bercy in the chest just as he was off balance. He went tumbling backward into the little creek that ran through the cavern. As he flopped around Sarah pressed her new Earth Marines knife against his throat. He stopped moving. She slid the knife back in the holster and went back over to the table. "Next time, I will not be so forgiving." She picked up the portable field communicator. "I was appointed directly by the Emperor. If any of you have a problem with my being here," she threw the device as hard as she could straight at Bercy, who somehow caught it as he climbed out of the water, "then I suggest you call the Emperor and take it up with him."

She noticed Bercy was heading for the door. "Commander, you have not been dismissed."

Bercy stopped. He looked very bewildered.

"Sit down gentlemen. This is the plan I've come up with." She looked over at Zuto. She had absolutely no idea what he was thinking. He showed no reaction at all. Everyone, including the dripping wet Bercy, sat down.

"This is the Earthforce maintenance facility at Minion Prime. It is one of two used to repair Earthforce ships. While it is deep inside Earth's territory, there are no other bases anywhere near it. We will attack it and destroy it, or at least inflict enough damage to put it out of service." Sarah noticed there didn't seem to be much enthusiasm.

"Who wants to attack a repair base?" Moth asked. "It's a low value target."

"Low value because there's little glory in it?" Sarah asked. She did not wait for an answer. "Look at it this way. Earthforce is seriously overextended. Between their war with us and their occupation of Chiron, they do not have enough ships and troops. As it is, they have been deferring maintenance whenever possible. Frankly, most of their fleet needs repairs of one sort or another. Now, if we cut their repair capacity in half, they will have a number of ships that will be unable to fight. They will be waiting for repairs."

She took a sip of coffee. "With the ships we will be using, should we attack an Earthforce cruiser, we would likely fail. At a minimum, we'd take a lot of casualties. By making it impossible to get repaired, or forcing it to go all the way back to Earth for repairs, we have taken that vessel out of action without ever actually firing a shot at it."

She finished her coffee. "The duty board says all of your ships are ready for deployment. Is that correct?"

No one said anything.

"Is that correct?" Sarah repeated.

"Yes," Moth said.

She looked at each one of them until she got a "yes" out of each of them. She finally came to Bercy.

"Yes," he said.

"We'll deploy in two hours," Sarah said. "'I'm transmitting the coordinates and specs of the station to each of your ship's electronic systems. Dismissed."

"We'll see you when we return," Moth said.

"Commander, I think you misunderstood me. I'm coming with you–you specifically. You will be in command of your ship. I will command the overall mission. Prepare your men."

When no one remained but Sarah and Zuto, she looked over at him. She had no idea what he was thinking. She stood. "I'll try and bring back your ships." She looked at the door. "With your permission?"

He gave the slightest of nods.

She took that as her leave and headed out.

19
MAINTENANCE

Minion prime was a pretty little place. It had about 80% of the size and gravity of Earth. Unfortunately, it lacked anything near Earth's land mass. It was 90% water. Earth was determined to prove that colonization was the way of the future. Once interstellar travel became possible, they were determined to make a go of colonization. After the disastrous strikes and problems with the Martian Colony, and a feeble president granting Martian independence, things were going to be different this time. They were going to have their economy dependent on Earth. They would not survive on their own. There would not be another Mars.

An orbiting space dock and accompanying facilities were built. They would maintain Earth's vast fleet of spaceships. For industry, Earth built prisons that floated on the ocean. Most workers were in some way employed in the penal system, space dock, or supporting positions such as food production. Thus far, it had worked—economically.

From a military standpoint, the place was a disaster. To even get parts replaced, a warship had to be taken out of service for days. The colony was too remote. Now that the war continued, the facility could not even keep up with the demand. There was a serious and growing backlog of maintenance problems that could not get repaired, fleet wide.

The colonists were benefitting beyond anyone's expectations. There was now a labor shortage and people were living in unprecedented prosperity. And it was costing Earthforce twice what maintenance of its fleet would cost if it had repair facilities closer to its operating areas.

The Admiralty dearly wanted to take the fight to the Tau home world. That was impossible. They did not have the ships. There were times when Earth was so poorly defended due to its fleet maintenance problems that even the Martian Defense Force could have taken the planet with little resistance. It was a constant tug of war between differing commanders over the working ships. Some factions wanted more vessels held back to protect Earth, while others argued for stepped up military action against the Tau.

Then there was the Chiron occupation. The plan had been to loot that world's natural resources. The reality was that program was way behind schedule. For all their effort, Earth had an unruly indigenous population and an empty space station that no one wanted to travel to for their efforts.

The space station near Chiron, which they controlled, was equipped for maintenance overhauls. They did not dare use the Chironese workers to repair ships. And there were no human workers to be spared for the task. That would mean constant exposure to sabotage, though it had been discussed.

So, at least Minion Prime was populated with human beings from Earth. At least alien sabotage had never been a concern at the maintenance facility. Just the never ending backlog.

~ * ~

"General Meadows, you said you wanted to be woken," Moth said.

She stretched a bit. She noticed Moth was holding a small plastic box.

"It is a tradition, right before we go into battle, we eat Guama grubs. They are a great delicacy," Moth said. He held out the box. "I just thawed them out." They were moving. They were thawed all right. Little yellow grubs, about the size of her thumb, each with one red eye, were wiggling around in the box.

She'd been looking forward to an Earthforce omelet with ham and cheese for breakfast. They wanted her to eat grubs. She grabbed one and popped it in her mouth. She bit down on it. It squished around the inside of her mouth. She managed to swallow. She struggled to keep it down. It was the vilest thing she had ever tasted. It tasted like the dirt Billy Hawkins made her eat in the first grade, mixed with rotten vinegar and that sewage mixture she'd pulled Karl out of–all in one squirming little squishy package. There were not enough coffee packs in the entire universe to make that taste go away.

"Would you like more?" he offered.

"No, not right now," Sarah said. What a wonderful thing to

wake up to. She desperately waited for the coffee to heat itself. She needed to try and wash away that horrible taste. Sarah made a mental note to herself to be sure and bring back some of those grubs for Don Don when the war was over. "Commander, while the other ships are attacking the repair facility itself, I'd like your crew to attack any ships parked in the outlying areas. We don't have to destroy them, just inflict enough damage to keep them out of action."

The ship carried a crew of six, not counting her. There was the commander, the helmsman, an engineer, two gunners, and a rocketman. The gunners manned laser turrets. The ship also had a battery of small rockets for the rocketman to fire. The engineer could take over any firing position if somebody went down. She, of course, was completely useless. She had no real function on this ship. They were not used to someone of her rank being aboard.

"Can these ships go dark, with minimal electronic emissions and generic transponder signals that look like harmless Earth transports?"

"Yes, General," Moth replied. "Already done."

"Excellent, commander," Sarah said.

"That reminds me," Moth said. He then said something in that second dialect she still could not pick up or understand. "We're reconfiguring our color to solid black. What works on Gentara does not work in deep space."

The Tau really loved camouflage. They not only tried to mask the visual appearance of everything from ships to tanks to water towers, but things like heat released to the surrounding area as well. Supposedly, they themselves could change color, though she had not yet seen this done.

After significant fiddling around, Sarah had the reserve console configured so she could make sense out of it. She hoped, in a few minutes, she'd be able to monitor all of the ships in the task force.

The surreal look of hyperspace gave way to normal space. The planet Minion Prime was off to their right. It looked like a greenish blue gem glistening in space. The General Maintenance Facility, the largest space maintenance facility in the known galaxy, was directly ahead of them.

There was no sign of any activity concerning their arrival.

Sarah had a hard time believing they were that lax in wartime. Even the MDF would be challenging five unscheduled ships popping up out of nowhere. There was nothing. "Any communications? Weapons locks?" Sarah asked.

"None, General," the engineer said. "None at all."

"Signal the attack," Sarah ordered. "Take this ship on a heading of one-eighty. What's that big dark thing floating over there?" Her gut tightened. She was pretty sure what it was. And it was her worst nightmare. She answered aloud her own question. "Earthforce heavy cruiser." But it was just sitting there, totally dark. It didn't even have running lights on, which was crazy in a congested area with so many ships around. "I can't believe they're that careless. Haven't you guys ever attacked here before?"

"It wasn't considered important," Moth said.

"Fire on their targeting sensors, then aft engines on our first pass," Sarah ordered.

There was a bright flash as something exploded in the main space dock. Another flash followed a few seconds later. Sarah noticed on her board all of the Tau ships were still there. The explosions were not her guys.

The rocketman let loose with a volley into the engine area of the cruiser. There were a series of smaller flashes as various things exploded.

"Earthforce interceptors," Moth said. He gave an order in that second dialect and the ship veered away from the cruiser. The lasers streaked out into the darkness after the interceptors.

Sarah noticed more interceptors were showing up from somewhere. "I think we've outstayed our welcome. Let's get out of here."

Something blasted through the hull. Some of the electronics exploded. Commander Moth slumped over. A fire started behind the main instrument panel and air was streaming out of the cabin. In a few seconds the air leak stopped thanks to the self-sealing hull. Sarah pulled Moth away from the panel and stretched him out on the floor while the engineer put the fire out with an extinguisher.

It looked like shrapnel had hit him in the head and abdomen. Sarah opened one of the emergency kits and put the self-adhesive pressure bandages over the wounds. Then she looked around. All the crewmen were still there. Sarah went back over to her visual monitor. She counted all the ships they'd come with.

20
DECISIONS

"I'm Marge Kelso and this is the evening news," the pretty raven haired woman with piercing sapphire blue eyes told her audience. An image was presented of what looked like a star in the sky. "People are wondering what this bright light in the sky is. Some think it's a comet. Others speculate it's simply the asteroid Titus." She pressed her hand against her right ear. "Oh my god! The light in the sky is the space repair facility. It's just been attacked by a massive fleet of lizard people. The carenthium storage barge is apparently burning in space. People are urged to go to their shelter assignments at once. The lizard people are believed to be landing all over the planet in a massive invasion." The broadcast was turned off.

All of the curious faces in the auditorium looked completely bewildered. Sarah put down her can of Earthforce grape juice. "That is your enemy at work," she announced to the gathered crowd. "Even I can't explain that broadcast and I'm supposed to understand these people. A probe is on the way to try and do a damage assessment. One thing I am certain about is the leaders of Earthforce are going to feel obligated to do something about our attack. Stay vigilant. Some type of counter attack is all but certain."

Zuto dismissed the troops. Sarah started for the little cubbyhole which had become her quarters. It was right next to the room packed with Earthforce supplies. She noticed someone moving slowly.

"Commander Moth, how are you feeling?" Sarah asked.

Moth turned toward her. He was fairly bandaged up. "They say I'll live."

"Good to hear it," Sarah said.

"They say you saved me after I was hit," Moth said.

"It was nothing."

"Hardly nothing."

"I've got just the thing for you. Follow me." Sarah led him down to her quarters. She had a pile of rations stacked neatly on a table. She picked up one of the black Earthforce pouches, looked it over, then handed it to him. "Try some of this."

"It will make me heal better?" Moth asked.

"Not hardly. I think you'll like this. Give it a try," she suggested.

He looked suspiciously at the package. "It's Earth food."

"Try it. I'll see you later," Sarah said. She watched him walk off with his packet of banana pudding. "After those grubs I should have given you straight mayonnaise," she said after he was gone. Now, for that bed. It was a flat stone bed. That may work okay for the lizard people. It was not going to do for Sarah. She continued her quest through the Earthforce supplies. Then, hiding near the back of the room, was total bliss. An hour later, she had her Earthforce hammock all set up just to her liking.

She was about to hop up on it when she sensed she was not alone. She turned toward the open door of her room. Zuto was standing there. "Sir?"

"The data has come back from the probe. The repair base sustained massive damage. They have one space dock bay still working. A large cruiser is now in there. It has sustained massive damage."

"All in all, not a bad day's work," Sarah said. She immediately regretted it. Zuto was much more reserved than the other Tau she'd known. She had absolutely no idea if he was even pleased with the news.

"You will need to select another commander for the fifth ship. Moth will not be able to serve for some time," Zuto said.

"I'll get on that," Sarah said.

"He believes he would have died if you had not stopped his bleeding so quickly," Zuto said.

"I'm sure the rest of the crew would have helped him if I had not been there," Sarah said.

"That is what I told him." Zuto walked off without any further comment.

She started to get back on the hammock to try it out. She heard someone else at the door. It was a low ranking Tau. He seemed nervous. "Yes?"

"I am Kurt."

When no further explanation came, she asked, "What can I

do for you, Kurt?"

"An officer of your rank is entitled to an aide," he said. "Two, actually."

She had wondered about that, but had been preoccupied with getting her bearings and such. "Yes?"

"The quartermaster said I could have the job, if you approved." He stood there expectantly.

"I see." She went over to the table and picked up another ration pack. She tossed it over to Kurt. "Eat this."

"It is Earth food," he said.

"I know that."

Very reluctantly, he opened it. He did not seem pleased with the sight of the yellow goo. He tasted it. Then he took some more. In no time, he had devoured the contents.

"Well, Kurt, my first order of business tomorrow is to find another commander. Moth is seriously injured. But that is for tomorrow. I need to get some sleep. You are dismissed."

Kurt seemed bewildered. "I do not understand why I had to eat the yellow goo?"

"Did you like the yellow goo?" she asked.

"Yes."

"Well, so do I. There is no more of it. I don't know how they keep coming up with so many Earthforce supplies, but if you see any of this, I want it. Good night, Kurt." She closed the door. Her hammock awaited.

~ * ~

It had become time to deal with an issue she had been struggling with. Splashing water on her face was not getting things done. The Tau were bathing in the hot spring farther down the cavern. Sarah had conflicting views on how to deal with this problem. There no showers or bathtubs here. Bathing with the Tau bothered her. Logically, they wouldn't be that interested in her whether she was in uniform or not. But, she did not want to display any weakness or vulnerability in front of them. Her experience with Commander Bercy reinforced that view.

They had latrines that were not all that difficult than what she was used to. It was bathing that worried her. She climbed off her hammock and set out in exploration of the cavern. She hoped, in the middle of the night, few others would be around.

She went past the hot springs. She noticed, at certain points, some chemical glowed on the rocks. This meant she was not completely dependent on her flashlight. The place was huge. It might even be bigger than the Barsoom Caverns back home. There were tunnels and rooms leading off all over the place. She kept listening for water.

It wasn't long before she found some. A little trickle of a stream was flowing down into the bigger underground river that flowed out of the caverns. She followed the stream, looking for the source. It didn't take long. She found a spring. Little clouds of steam wafted off the surface. Now, was it going to be scalding hot? She stuck a finger in. It wasn't that bad. In seconds she peeled off her uniform and slid underneath the water. When she ran out of air, she reluctantly sat upright. Sarah Meadows had just found heaven. And it was all hers.

21
ADMINISTRATION

She slept very well after her bath. The hammock was quite agreeable. The Earthforce waffles were also quite agreeable. She headed for the briefing rooms, wondering what calamity could ruin her remarkably good day.

The first contender sat at the conference table. "Good morning Commander Bercy," Sarah said.

He snapped to attention. That was an improvement.

"Be seated, commander." She sat down. "What can I do for you?" Sarah asked.

"I request transfer to another unit."

"I see." She paused. "The reason for your request?" Sarah leaned back in her chair.

"I do not like you."

"I see." She thought for a moment. "There are times, commander, when we have to deal with things we do not always like. There are plenty of Tau who have good reason to be suspicious of humans. But, keep in mind, I am Martian. I have never even been to Earth."

"All humans same," he snarled.

"When I was little more than a baby, my parents were killed by Earthforce troops in what was called the Deimos incident. Earthforce boarded Fremont Station, a Martian space station, and started killing everyone who moved. The reason: They claimed someone on the Martian moon Deimos had fired a missile at their ship. Deimos is uninhabited. There was no one on Deimos. After they killed a hundred and twenty people, they returned to Earth and were never punished in any way. The cowards running the Martian government did nothing. And people wonder why I hate Earth."

He just sort of stared at her.

"My question to you is: Is it because I'm human or because I embarrassed you the other day? I may be a little tougher than you thought." Sarah stared at him for bit. "Is it customary to challenge the authority of an officer on her first day?"

"No. But I could not believe they wanted me to obey human."

"I realized that. You made that quite clear. My problem is, well, there was this boy named Billy Hawkins. When I was in school he and some other boys pinned me down on the ground and made me eat dirt."

He looked completely baffled.

"Well, after they let me up, I beat the snot out of that boy. He ran away crying. Kids all over the school laughed at him. He had committed the greatest sin in the world. He got beat up by a girl." Sarah reached over and activated one of her remaining coffee packs. "So, commander, my pondry is, do you want to be reassigned because you hate humans, or because you got beat up by a girl?" She took a sip of her coffee.

"I was wrong to challenge you."

It wasn't really an answer but it would have to do. "Yes you were. We have mission briefing at thirteen hundred. I'll see you then."

Kurt entered the room carrying a stack of food pouches. "I found some more."

"Ah, Kurt, give the commander one," Sarah said.

Bercy looked at the pouch. "Human food?"

"We'll see you later, commander," Sarah said. She took a sip of coffee. "Now, let's get down to business."

"I don't think he likes you," Kurt said.

"No, I don't think he does either. But I told him about Billy Hawkins and he's so confused right now he doesn't know what he thinks."

"Who is Billy Hawkins?" Kurt asked.

"Some other time," Sarah said. She noticed a disk was on the table. She put it in her clipboard. It took a moment for the translation. "So, these are the available officers then?"

"Yes, just three."

"Commander Goth, I already know. These other two, well I'll read up. What exactly does an aide do?" Sarah asked. "I've never had one."

"I don't know," Kurt said. "I've never been one."

"I guess we'll go with Commander Chalk," Sarah decided.

"See if he can be here for the mission briefing."

After her aide had left, Sarah looked back at the files one more time. She'd dearly wanted Goth, but was afraid her fondness of him would cloud her judgment. As she read his file, she wondered why he kept getting passed over for promotion. It did not say.

She had time to kill before the mission briefing. She wandered out into the main cavern area where one entered the underground complex. There was a lot of activity. She went over to a group of soldiers who were busily trying to get a manifold to go back in place over the air intake of a hover tank. They were all pushing. She doubted her contribution would help much, but she gave it a push. The manifold locked into place.

The soldiers suddenly realized she was there and seemed greatly distressed. They finally stood at attention. "Relax gentlemen. At ease. Carry on." She wondered over to another tank. The crew there were putting away welding equipment. She noticed the label on the case read Earthforce Official Property.

Like the first crew, this crew snapped to attention and seemed bewildered at what they should do. This surprised her a little. "Tank Commander Tink, how the heck are you?"

The commander stared back at her. "Who?"

"Commander Tink?"

"Who. We all look alike," the Tau commander replied.

"Oh?"

"That was joke," he finally said.

Kush and Pepo seemed to like it. They were bobbing their heads. "I should have you flogged for such insolence!" Sarah yelled.

All three of the tank crew snapped to rigid attention. "Yes sir!" Tink said.

"That was joke, too," Sarah said.

It took a moment, then they all three started bobbing their heads.

"Good to see you again," Sarah said.

"Word has gotten around about the human general. We thought it was just a rumor. Then we heard about the attack on the maintenance base. They say you saved entire crew from dying."

"It was one guy. I just put a pressure bandage on. That's all." Sarah said. She noticed Kurt was looking around on the other side of the cavern. She climbed up on the tank and went down inside.

Tink poked his head through the hatch. He seemed confused.

"That's my aide, Kurt," she whispered. "I'm hiding." To her calculation, she sat in the tank for about five minutes.

Tink stuck his head back in the hatch. "He is gone now."

She climbed out of the tank. "He probably wants me to do something or sign something."

"I hide from people all the time," Tink said.

"I've got a mission briefing. It was nice seeing you guys. Be safe." She headed back to the conference room.

At the exact time for the meeting Sarah entered the meeting room. She counted four commanders plus Kurt. "Be seated."

"General, Commander Chalk is missing. He may have been captured," Kurt reported.

"Well, that is not good news. I guess we'll have to proceed with four ships. No, actually I have another idea." She turned on the footage of the maintenance facility they had just been to. "You'll notice massive damage. This attack exceeded my expectations. However, this is a massive facility, as you all know. We are going back to inflict even more damage. I know this was not viewed as a glamorous target. But ships in disrepair, ships that can't get parts, are to our advantage and I am convinced Earth has cut far too many corners and this will lead to our victory."

She took a sip of Earthforce instant tea. "Would you like some of this Earth tea? You lot don't always like the same things I do, but you can have some." No one expressed any desire, so she continued. "Notice that defenseless cruiser. More importantly, it is in the one remaining space dock. Let's put that out of business. This large structure away from the others was thought to be a warehouse. Obviously, that's where the interceptors came from. The traffic control structure is here," she pointed it out with the highlighter. "And, if you look below the space dock, you'll see this complex. Marshal Zuto and his staff believe it's a parts facility. If we can knock out all of their spare parts, they are going to have a hard time flying anything." She held up a small bowl. "I've placed the targets in this bowl. Each can draw one out. The fifth assignment is overlook, taking targets of opportunity while watching out for incoming ships."

She passed the bowl around. When it came back, Sarah removed the one remaining piece of paper.

"We have five commanders?" Bercy asked. "Who commands the fifth ship? Moth is hurt. Chalk is missing?"

"I will the command the ship myself," Sarah said. "We deploy in two hours. Unless anyone has questions, dismissed."

"I will see about finding another officer while you are gone," Kurt said.

"No, you are coming with me," Sarah said.

"I, uh, have never been in combat. I worked for the quartermaster," Kurt said.

"Then this is your lucky day. What finer honor than dying with your general in battle?" Sarah finished her tea. "Let's go, Kurt."

As they headed for the launch area, Sarah noticed someone was suddenly walking along with them. "Tank Commander Tink, what can we do for you?"

"May I walk with you a moment, General?"

"You already are," Sarah pointed out.

"So I am."

"We are about to go and give our lives in battle for our glorious emperor," Sarah said.

"Well, if you come back alive, I've noticed something interesting," Tink explained.

"Interesting how?"

"We were out in the western sector, near the inland sea. There is an abandoned Earth settlement. Humans all died before the war. I don't know why. Some disease they say. There were Earth men driving around. Quite a few of them. We had to withdraw. Jump Jets showed up. Place has no military value, my superiors say. They are not interested."

"I find that very interesting," Sarah said. "I would think it's at least worth a little reconnaissance. You have the coordinates?"

"I do." Tink pointed his handheld map unit at her clipboard and they both blinked.

"I'll look into this if we make it back," Sarah said.

Tink veered off toward the tank area.

"Going to another commander is frowned upon," Kurt

pointed out.

"So, it is," Sarah agreed. "This is our ship."

Engineer Moe closed an access panel. Then he snapped to attention. "Sir?"

Sarah was not entirely thrilled with the sirs she kept getting, but there was a language problem. In the context of military service, there simply was no feminine context to anything in the Tau language. "What is the status of the ship?"

"Fueled and ready for action. I just finished repairing the hull damage," Moe reported.

"This is my aide, Kurt. He will be going with us. Although Commander Moth is recovering, he is not able to join us today. I will be in command of the ship. Inform the crew to prepare for takeoff."

"Yes, sir." Moe climbed inside the ship.

"After you, Kurt," Sarah said. She waited for him to go in, then went in herself. "Seal the hatch and start preflight checklist."

Sarah hoped that all of her time tramping around the galaxy with the Tau and the MDF would pay off. She now understood most ships systems fairly well. But she still struggled with the written language, though she recognized most symbols on the controls. Regulations required this class of ship be commanded by a certified pilot. Either no one had noticed she was not one, or no one had the guts to say anything. She struggled to strap into a seat that was never designed for her.

There was a two-tone beeping, followed by a flashing on the communications console. "Incoming message," Moe reported.

"Is this a secure channel?" she asked.

"Yes, General."

Sarah nodded. "Put it on."

Marshal Zuto appeared on the console. "Our base on the western continent is under heavy bombardment by Earthforce," Zuto said. "Ground units are also moving in."

"Do you want us to divert to the western area and render aid?" Sarah asked.

"No," Zuto said. "Now is the perfect time to attack them, General."

Sarah nodded. She touched the console for ship to ship. "Task force launch!"

As they zipped along toward their destination, there was little to do in hyperspace flight. Sarah couldn't even see the other ships. She knew they were out there, but she still would feel better if she could see them. All she could do was eat her banana pudding and wait.

When Sarah had been a child she had nightmares of bees. Bees would swarm out of hives and attack her. She had recurring nightmares about it. This was puzzling to the adults as there were no bees on Mars. For just an instant, their target reminded her of a beehive. It was sort of shaped that way. And the interceptor shooting out of the launch tube reminded her of the bees.

"Rocketman, seal up the hive," Sarah ordered.

Though he seemed confused, he sent a volley of rockets into the launch bay. The flashes from a series of explosions followed a moment later.

Seconds after that, there was an explosion off their port side. The bright flash was followed by debris that bounced off their ship, but did no real damage. Her starboard laser gunner seemed real pleased with himself. "Moe, get some distance from these structures so we can see what's going on." Her position board was not picking up two of their ships. She hoped it was because the debris was blocking her system from picking them up.

As they moved away from the structure, her heart skipped a beat. An Earthforce cruiser was bearing down on them. "Holy crap. We're a sitting duck."

"No weapons lock," Moe said.

"Them or us?" Sarah asked.

"They have no weapons lock on us or anyone else," Moe said. "There's not even an energy reading in their weapons array."

"Deferred maintenance strikes again. Let 'em have it! Task force, converge on that cruiser. All weapons!" Sarah had a better view of her task force now that they were clear. She still only counted four ships, but that was better than three. The three ships converged and started pounding the cruiser with rockets and laser fire. After two bright explosions blew out the right side of the cruiser, Sarah ordered, "That cruiser will never fly again. Let's get out of here." Her ships were not built for protracted firefights and she didn't know who else was in the neighborhood.

She counted ships again. They were definitely missing one.

She flipped the scope switch to a broader range. That made them stick out like a beacon, but Sarah figured the enemy already knew they were there. Near the atmosphere, way removed from the battle, was the missing ship. "Commander Bercy what are you doing?"

"Earth cowards flee to planet. We chased them."

"Time to leave. Withdraw," Sarah ordered.

And all five Tau ships went off into hyperspace.

~ * ~

"This is an urgent bulletin. The Earthforce repair facility is again under attack for the second time this week. An invasion fleet of over one hundred ships has overrun our defenses," the announcer said. "Citizens are urged to be on the lookout for a possible invasion of cities here on the surface. Stay tuned for more developments."

~ * ~

Sarah entered a command into the console. "Helmsman, please confirm this course adjustment. I want to change where we come out of hyperspace."

"Course confirmed," the helmsman answered back. "Do you want me to advise the other ships?"

"No. Just us."

The ship jolted violently as it emerged into normal space and immediately struck air. It made some horrible noises like it was an animal in the death grip of a tiger.

"Surface to air rockets are being fired. Should we start evasive maneuvers?" Moe asked.

"Full throttle. Head for home. I think we're out of range for those missiles." She hoped she was right. Nothing hit them.

22
TARGETS

Sarah exhaled as the switches were flipped to off on the ship's systems. They'd made it back without a single casualty. And the base was still intact. She wondered how the western base had fared. She had never been there. It was just a dot on a map. She climbed out of the ship. It was always good to stand on land.

The ship next to them looked pretty torn up. "Commander Bercy, what have you done to this ship?" Sarah asked.

"Earth scum fired some sort of shrapnel at us." He looked for the first time at the hull. "On inside it did not look so bad." There were large sections of shredded metal where the hull was supposed to be.

Sarah pulled a piece of metal off of the hull. "This one won't be flying for a while. Take command of my ship. See that it and the other ships are refueled and ready to go back out. Mission briefing in one hour."

She turned and looked around for Kurt. He was gawking at the damage to Bercy's ship. "Kurt, find Tank Commander Tink. Get him and every single tank commander you can find to the briefing room in one hour. I'm going to try and find Marshal Zuto."

Earthforce prune juice was not really to her liking, but it was handy and Sarah really wanted some quick energy since she didn't have time for a meal. Zuto was in a small office talking to two officers she did not know. Sarah patiently waited outside. Finally, the two officers left. She went door. "May I have a word, sir?"

Zuto sort of nodded.

"How bad was the damage to our western base?" Sarah asked.

"It was minimal."

"One of my ships was badly damaged, but we inflicted major damage on our target. We even took out another cruiser," Sarah reported.

"I have a feeling that was not the main reason you are here,"

Zuto said.

"No sir," she admitted. "I want to take the ships back out. I've ordered them refueled."

"You do not have to win the war in a single day," Zuto pointed out. "You can take a few more days to do it."

Sarah explained, "There is an abandoned settlement that has suddenly seen a lot of activity."

"We do not feel this is an important target," Zuto said. "Although I know Commander Tink is convinced otherwise."

This would be where naive Martian girl should slink off and let the real soldiers do what they knew best. There was a reason they kept Tink out in the desert. They were tired of him. Sarah nodded. "It's not just Commander Tink's opinion. If the site is so unimportant, why have they moved in an anti-aircraft battery?"

Zuto was quiet for what Sarah thought was an inordinately long time. He then pressed his intercom. "Get my advisors back in here." He looked at Sarah. "You have a mission to prepare for."

The four ship commanders looked curiously as the ten tank commanders poured out of the briefing room. They then entered.

Sarah opened another self-heating cup of coffee. It was her third one that day. Earth coffee was incredibly expensive on Mars. She couldn't help indulging herself a little, though she was starting to get some caffeine jitters. "If you'll look at the diagram, we're going to come down single file out of space. That will give them a minimal aspect to lock on to. And, if the intelligence report is correct, we will look like one ship coming down instead of four, at least at first. The downside is that first ship is vulnerable. We'll take electronic countermeasures and try to blind their targeting system with laser fire. As we get close to landing, attack anything that looks like a threat. Our ships are not intended for surface combat. Your gunners are not used to this type of targeting." She took a sip of her coffee.

"Will our targeting locks even work on ground targets?" Bercy asked.

"Don't know," Sarah said. "Tell your gunners they may have to switch off and just fire manually. We are a diversion. The tank force will be attacking from the east. Unlike our ships, they definitely have the firepower to take on ground targets. We'll land and initiate ground fighting. My one big worry is we're not sure how much anti-aircraft capacity they have. Load up boys."

Sarah looked at her aide, who seemed to be trying to slink off back into the cavern. "Come on Kurt. This will be a great opportunity to die in battle." Flying off with Bercy in command would likely fulfill her prophecy if anything would. Strangely, since their first encounter, she'd had remarkably little trouble with him. She was sure she'd have to kill him, but that never happened.

The plan was to go up like they were heading off for another attack on some poor helpless Earthforce facility, then swing around and come straight in on the so-called abandoned site Tank Commander Tink had grown obsessed with. Bercy gave an order to the crew in that annoying second dialect. Sarah wondered if the Tau had figured out she could not understand it. Regardless, they were underway. It didn't take very long to swing around Tartarus and they were soon re-entering the atmosphere.

"Begin countermeasures," Sarah ordered. "Move into single file position. Hopefully we'll look like just one ship instead of four ships bearing down on them."

"Unless they have multiple sites monitoring us," Moe pointed out.

"Just keep them as confused as possible," Sarah said.

One rocket fired off from the surface and went between the first two ships. Most of their fire was directed toward the tanks that were approaching the settlement on the ground. As she looked downward, she could see movement, but it was hard to tell the tanks because of their camouflage. They made a hard landing at the edge of the compound. The hatch popped open and the emergency escape ramp dropped into place.

"Come on Kurt. You want to live forever?" It was obvious to Sarah that Kurt lacked a certain enthusiasm for combat. She had dragged him along more because he didn't want to go than any real military usefulness. She worried he might get killed. This was a real battle with real shooting. She tossed him the Tau basic field rifle. It wasn't a rifle at all, but that was how it translated. They fired an energy burst–little blue streaks that would penetrate most types of armor. "Guard these ships. Don't let Earthforce get their hands on them."

Kurt seemed suddenly relieved. "Yes, General."

She picked up another field rifle for herself. Her sidearm was not meant for a heavy exchange of fire.

And the heavy exchange of fire had already started. Earthforce ground troops mainly used two types of weapons. There was a projectile weapon that really was a rifle. It had a laser targeting ability. The filed glasses she was putting on not only helped with the glare of the all-too-bright sun, but she could see the thin little red beams. If the gunner forgot to suppress that laser, it could be followed back to the shooter.

The second weapon in use was a true laser rifle. It fired a thick laser beam that could cut somebody in half really fast. The drawback with these was they used a huge amount of power and had to be recharged constantly or the soldier had to carry lots of bulky replacement power packs. Even though they were somewhat inferior, most troops used the rifles.

Sarah stayed low to the ground and advanced on the first row of buildings. She heard a few shots, but couldn't tell where they were coming from. The hover tanks were now well within range were opening up on positions she really could not see from her location. She hoped her guys didn't end up in a crossfire. "Tank commanders, all four ships are landed on the south side."

"Acknowledged," somebody replied.

Sarah looked to both sides. This would be an odd arrangement for an Earth squad. Four ship commanders and a general on the ground with a handful of ship's gunners and helmsmen. But, if they wanted orthodox military, they shouldn't have hired Sarah Meadows. She was an insurance agent. She pointed forward. There was a row of quonset huts that had her attention. Next to them was the portable anti-aircraft battery. Tink and his fellow tank crews had already obliterated that location. "There should be more troops than what we've seen." She noticed some soldiers were running off into the desert, away from the hover tanks. "If nobody's home, what the heck is going on here?"

They advanced on one of the huts. The door was not locked. They quickly cleared it and moved on to the next one. There didn't seem to be anyone there, either. As they left that hut, a bullet whizzed right over Sarah's head. She could hear it go by. Immediately, two of the ship's gunners returned fire. An Earthforce soldier slumped over and there was no more gunfire.

The third hut brought small arms fire from inside when they

tried to open the door. A grenade lobbed inside settled that argument.

The fourth hut seemed deserted. As they cleared it, Sarah noticed it had a closet at one end, which the others had not had. Sarah nodded at Moe and raised her own basic rifle. Moe opened the door. Sarah aimed at a man sitting on the floor. "Hands on top of your head!" She trained the rifle's targeting laser on his head.

He slowly complied.

"Stand up, slowly!" Sarah ordered.

As he got up, Sarah noticed his uniform. He was wearing the gray and black camouflage that Earthforce wore on Tartarus. But he had three black stars on his collar. "Search him for weapons."

Moe patted him down, then nodded. "Nothing."

"Well, General Hudson, looks like you'll be a prisoner of war," Sarah said.

"How'd you know my name?" he asked.

"Your name is embroidered on your uniform," Sarah replied.

He looked down at his shirt. "Oh." Then he looked at her. "You're that Martian bitch!"

"General Meadows."

Tank Commander Tink entered the hut. "The compound is secure." He noticed Sarah's prisoner.

"How many casualties?" Sarah asked.

"One wounded on our side," Tink said. "Eight humans dead, twenty-seven are prisoner."

"That's odd, General, don't you think? This nice facility out here in the middle of nowhere. This nice facility without enough troops to even guard it properly?" she slung the standard rifle over her shoulder.

Sarah turned off her translator. "Who was the wounded Tau?" she asked Tink in her best effort at standard Tau language.

"Assistant Quartermaster Kurt," Tink replied. "A group of five humans rushed the parked ships. He fought it out with them. He killed them all. He is not badly hurt."

"Very good. Return to your unit. Well done commander." She refocused her attention on the prisoner. "And an awfully high ranking officer for such a rinky-dink outpost? Why are you here, General?"

"It was supposed to be better. We can't hold ground. We don't have enough troops to hold an area. Everything's razzle dazzle technology, then the lizards simply move back in those blasted invisible tanks and it's like nothing happened. I finally got Earth to commit more troops. This was going to be one of our forward bases. But the troops never come. There aren't enough ships to transport them. They're still sitting on Minion Prime playing cards all day."

Sarah seemed very pleased with herself all of a sudden. "Well, we'll be relocating you to a prisoner area." She noticed a stool and kicked it over to him. "Or did you come for the peace conference?"

"Peace conference?" the bewildered man asked.

She sat down on one of the chairs. "Yep, the peace conference." She told one of the tank troops that had remained, in Tau, to go and fetch her clipboard from the ship. Then, to the general she said, "Let's end this war, right here, today, General."

23
CEASE FIRE

The Tau soldiers stood around, mostly bewildered at why no orders were coming from anyone as to what they should be doing. Tink had ordered the tanks into a perimeter around the outpost. They were told to be on the lookout for any approaching Earthforce. And the general who had brought them all there was just sitting inside a hut.

One Earth jump jet did a high flyover, but made no effort to attack. It was obviously a reconnaissance flight. That didn't bode well for later, though as fears of a counter attack grew.

After what seemed like an eternity, Sarah emerged from the hut with an Earth officer who was not restrained or tied up. The Earth officer was left alone in a small building that contained communications equipment.

General Meadows returned to her ship. The ship's crew had all returned. Perimeter duties had been essentially taken over by the tank crews. Sarah opened a packet of banana pudding. "I need a secure channel to Marshal Zuto. I do not want to speak to one of his aides. It must be him. If he's asleep, wake him. If he's in a meeting, interrupt him."

"At once, General."

It did not take long for him to appear on the screen. "Your report is late, General."

She turned back on her translator. This message had to be given right. "I know and I regret that, sir. In fact, I think you will be most disappointed with me," Sarah said. She glanced at her clipboard. "My clipboard has finished translating into Tau. I'm sending you an agreement. I know you did not want me to end the war in one day and that I was to take a few more days to accomplish this. And I'm deeply sorry if I have disappointed you in this regard. However, I have just negotiated a cease fire agreement with General Hamilton of Earthforce." She paused for just a moment then continued, "In fact, the agreement I just sent you is the framework for a peace treaty. If Congress will ratify it and the Emperor is willing to sign it, then the war will be over. Earth will withdraw completely and we will go forward with a shared arrangement for the minerals mined on Gentara. As we speak, General Hamilton is sending the same agreement to his superiors as well."

"What is your situation there?" Zuto asked.

"We took the outpost with little resistance. One wounded on our side, no fatalities. We have a tank perimeter. So far, there is no sign of any counter attack."

Zuto appeared to be looking over the agreement. "Return to the base at once."

"Yes sir," Sarah said. She finished her banana pudding. "Someone go and find Tank Commander Tink."

It did not take long for Tink to arrive. "You wanted to see me, General?"

"A couple of things. First, an unarmed Earthforce transport will be arriving to take General Hamilton back to their headquarters. I have been ordered to return to base for consultations with Marshal Zuto. Commander, we have negotiated a cease fire with Earthforce. If this holds, then your troops will be relieved in two days. Until then, you are in command," Sarah ordered. "The three other space ships will remain here. Their crews can supplement yours to guard prisoners and perform sentry duty."

Tink seemed instantly uncomfortable to hear this. "Uh, spaceship commanders outrank me."

"I know that. They remain in command of their ships. You are in command of the outpost. And, should this all fall apart and Earth attack, kill the human prisoners, burn this place to the ground and get the heck out of here."

"Understood, General."

"Now, fly me back to our base," she instructed Commander Bercy.

It was a short flight back to the base. Sarah found Zuto sitting quietly in his office. She stood at attention.

After quite some time, Zuto said, "Be seated." After another pause, he said, "I have reviewed the agreement you reached with Earth. I can find no objection to it. I await a response from the Emperor."

Sarah sat there quietly.

"You have nothing to say?" Zuto asked.

"No sir. You have not asked me anything," Sarah answered.

"Most officers would be wanting to tell of their great victory against the enemy?"

"I sent you my report. I can think of nothing to add," Sarah said. "In spite of my commission, I am not Tau. I am not military. I have simply done the job I was hired to do."

"So you have. What do you wish to do now?" Zuto asked her.

"I could use some rest. We'll see if this cease fire works out. We could be back at war tomorrow. I, for one, do not trust Earth any farther than I can spit," Sarah said.

"Dismissed," Zuto said.

Sarah wandered back to her quarters. Would it be Earthforce stir fry chicken or Earthforce lasagna with bread sticks? She selected the lasagna. The packet heated up instantly and she gobbled it down with the supplied biodegradable plastic spoon made from cornstarch, according to the information printed on the back side of the packet.

Then, she headed off in search of her little hot spring. She needed a relaxing soak in hot water. She deserved a relaxing soak in hot water. She took off her uniform and slid into the steaming pool. They could use a few hot springs on Mars. A private hot spring did not exist. There was a public bath in Mars City. Public basically meant a bunch of horny old men. She had not been there since she was a student at the Martian School of Economics. She doubted she would ever go back.

Mars had a water shortage and a cavern like this one with water running through it had yet to be discovered. The Barsoom Caverns were actually bigger than this one, but dry as a bone.

When she ran out of air, she poked her head above the water. There were boots next to water's edge. They were not her boots. As she wiped the water from her eyes she struggled to identify the occupant of those boots in the minimal lighting. "Commander Goth?"

"I am sorry to disturb you, General. Marshal Zuto wants to see you," he said.

"Very well. Uh, how did you know where I was?"

"I asked Kurt."

"Oh." That begged the question of how did he know. "I was going to visit him after I got out of here, actually." She noticed he was still standing there. "Was there something else?"

"No."

"Dismissed," Sarah said. She waited for him to leave before climbing out and getting dressed.

She got another surprise as she walked back toward the compound. Bercy was standing there. Even though she'd had no further trouble from him since their first encounter, seeing him there on an unlit trail with no one else around made her nervous. She didn't even have her Earth Marines boot knife with her. "Commander?"

"May I speak with you?" he asked.

Sarah pointed out, "You already are."

"Marshal Zuto says you have recommended me for promotion to captain."

"I did?" She turned on her translator. She was getting comfortable enough with Tau basic that she didn't want to depend on it when she did not have to. But she had no recollection of recommending him for any promotion. "Well, you have served your emperor with distinction."

"I am ashamed of my first response toward you. You are a brilliant strategist and have shown you are not afraid to die in battle," Bercy said. "It is difficult for commanders of smaller ships to reach this rank."

"Well, I'm sure you will do me proud. I'm late for a meeting, but congratulations," Sarah said. She was feeling a little guilty about the thoughts she'd had about being unarmed around him. And why did everybody know about her secret bathing spot?

She found Zuto in his office. She stood at attention. "You wanted to see me, sir?"

"Yes. So far, the cease fire is holding. Things are moving very quickly with the peace treaty. I need to bring you current on a few matters. First, we are taking a new look at your use of smaller ships. Until now, they've mainly been used to patrol remote areas. I've placed Bercy in command of the task force." He handed her some insignia that was less colorful than her own, but more colorful than a commander. "By tradition, you should place these on his uniform as you are still his commanding officer. He will carry the rank of captain."

Sarah took the insignia. Of course, she already knew about the promotion.

"Second, we have no direct diplomatic relations with Earth. The only place where we even have close-by embassies is Mars City. We have found the Foreign Office there less than cooperative. They have discouraged having the president of Earth and our Emperor come for a treaty signing, citing security reasons."

Zuto looked through some papers. "So, it has been decided the ambassadors will sign on behalf of the Emperor and the President. I would like for you to attend the signing ceremony on behalf of the Army. To not have a high-ranking officer there might be interpreted that the military does not back the agreement, even though nothing could be farther from the truth."

"I would be most honored. The Martian Foreign Office has benefitted from the war and from Earth's occupation of Chiron. These events have distracted Earth to some degree. Earth has a long history of bullying Mars over everything from trade to access to the asteroids in the solar system. Their fear is, with peace comes an increased risk of problems with Earth. So, I'm not surprised at their response. I can suggest a venue for the signing ceremony that I think would be acceptable to both sides and is a place where the Foreign Office has no influence."

"Excellent. Convey your suggestion to the embassy. Third, Commander Goth will be returning you to Mars. You leave tomorrow. I have instructed him to land directly at Mars City Space Terminal. In the past, we have always preferred Fremont Station and the shuttle to the surface because of the fuel savings. I think, this time, it will be warranted to purchase the extra fuel."

Zuto held up a simple envelope, though it had an orange seal on the edge. "This is an official diplomatic note. It bears the seal of the emperor. His Highness requests that you deliver it to his Majesty, the King of Chiron." He handed her the envelope.

"It will be my pleasure, sir," Sarah said.

"Dismissed."

Sarah nodded, pivoted and marched out of the office. Before getting some sleep, she went by the infirmary. Kurt was the only patient there. His leg was bandaged heavily. Otherwise, he looked fine. "I'm sorry you were unable to die in battle," Sarah said.

"They say you are returning to Mars," Kurt said.

"It's true. I leave tomorrow."

Sarah did not sleep well on her hammock, even though she was quite tired. Eventually, morning arrived.

Sarah approached the parked ship. The crew all snapped to attention. The crew of the next ship over also snapped to attention. "Commander Bercy, step forward."

Bercy moved out and stood to attention.

"By order of the Emperor of the Tau People, you are hereby ordered to take command of this task force and accordingly shall be henceforth known as Captain Bercy." Sarah peeled the backing off of the new insignia and placed it on his uniform. "Congratulations, Captain. Step back."

Sarah was fighting hard not to get choked up. "It has been a great privilege and honor to serve in battle with all of you. May victory and honor be with you now and for always." She paused for just a moment. "Dismissed." All said without the translator. She hoped she hadn't insulted somebody's heritage.

24
DIPLOMACY

Ting was holding one of his hammers. "Good morning, General," he greeted her. "We are ready to depart."

"Very good." Sarah climbed up the ladder and into the ship. "Commander, I would like to make a course adjustment. It may actually save a little fuel. When we take off, fly directly over the main Earth base–transponder on, no countermeasures, no camouflage. We'll either be marking the start of a new era, or we will be a giant fireball in the sky."

Topo and Goth did not seem overjoyed with the instructions.

"Launch when ready," Sarah said as she struggled to strap into a seat that was not designed for her.

It was only a few minutes before they were flying over Earth held territory. The anti-aircraft capabilities of their headquarters were vastly greater than the feeble setup at the recent battle for the poorly defended outpost. "They are tracking us," Topo reported.

"Tracking okay, weapons lock not so good. We're high enough we shouldn't be seen as a threat to them. But, if they're not going to honor the cease fire, we might as well know right now," Sarah said.

"We are leaving atmosphere and are out of range," Topo advised everyone.

Sarah felt a little relieved. "Guys, I am so tired. Unless we're going to crash and die or the Emperor calls, let me sleep. Please?"

"Yes, General," Goth said. "Which Emperor?"

"Which Emperor?" Sarah asked. "There's more than one?"

"The emperor of the Tau or the emperor of Mars?" came the clarification.

Of course there was no emperor of Mars. Mars had a democratically elected chancellor. Apparently Goth did not make any distinction. "Well any emperor would be okay, I guess." It was hard to reach a ship in hyperspace, in any event.

When the ship came out of hyperspace, they were still some

distance from Mars, which was right where they were supposed to be. Goth was fumbling around with the ship's new translator module.

"Commander, would you prefer I do it?" Sarah asked.

"Yes."

"Martian Approach Control this is Tau vessel two-two-four-nine," Sarah said.

"Uh, could you repeat?" came the reply.

"Tau vessel two-two-four-nine requesting a vector and approach clearance for Mars City," Sarah asked. She was certain somebody was looking things up. She told Goth, "It's not like before. We have diplomatic relations and everything now."

"Tau two-two-four-nine you are clear for approach. We are transmitting approach vectors for Mars City." The voice was different from the first one. The prescribed course popped up on the new Lydar navigation system.

"There you go, commander." She pondered something for a moment. "If we just reached an agreement, how come this ship has Lydar and onboard translation?"

"We were the designated transport to Mars since the new embassy opened," Goth explained. "That is what we do now. We fly people around."

"I guess that makes sense," Sarah agreed.

Mars was considered any easy landing by most shuttle pilots. Its thin atmosphere was easy for most ships to slice right through. Most landings on Mars itself were cargo ships. Those carrying humans preferred to dump off at Fremont Station and let specialized shuttles take things the rest of the way. A Tau ship was still a new experience for the controllers and customs people. This was only the second time one had ever landed on Mars. The first one was when the embassy opened.

"Have you guys actually been on Mars before?" Sarah asked.

"No, just to Fremont Station," Goth replied.

She noticed Goth was carrying a black case. It was not really the case, it was the orange seal on it that caught her attention. Sarah was not surprised to see a few extra customs officers in their white uniforms standing at the station, trying to figure out what the lizard people were up to.

"Welcome to Mars City," a tall man said. "What is the nature of your visit?"

"Diplomatic," Sarah replied. "We are part of the official delegation for the Tau embassy to attend a treaty signing tomorrow at the Martian School of Economics campus."

"Ma'am, could you please place you hand on this pad for just a moment?" another customs officer asked.

"Certainly." Sarah did as instructed.

"Our computer identifies you as Sarah Meadows, a Martian citizen," a third customs officer said.

"Yes?"

"But you said you represent the Tau?" a fourth customs officer asked.

"They are not mutually exclusive," Sarah replied. She held up the envelope Zuto had given her, then pointed at the case Goth carried. "I am General Sarah Meadows of the Tau Army. This is an official diplomatic note bearing the seal of the emperor. The case my commander is carrying also has a diplomatic seal." If she had not been with them the encounter might have been easier.

The presence of the Martian girl was confusing them. Very confusing.

"I will be leaving the army following the ceremony tomorrow, gentlemen. But, today, I am still an officer of the Tau Army." There was little else to say.

"She's got a travel waiver signed by the Foreign Office," the fifth customs officer said. "I've never seen one of those."

The little gate next to the customs booth opened. "Enjoy your stay."

As they got on board Mag Lev Sarah said, "I guess we should go directly to the embassy. Where the heck are you guys staying?"

"We were told we would have to stay on the ship," Goth explained.

"Too bad. My place is so small there's no room there." An idea popped in her head. "I know where you guys can stay. You'll like it." She pressed a local call on her clipboard.

"Sarah, how goes the war?" Karl answered.

"We won," she said. "I just arrived back on Mars."

"Splendid. The office has been so boring of late. It's no fun harassing Don Don when no one there appreciates my efforts," Karl said.

"Could do me a little favor?" Sarah asked.

"Name it."

"Could my crew bunk at your place tonight? They have to go to some ceremony tomorrow and I don't have anywhere to put them tonight. There's just three of them," Sarah explained.

"I think we can manage that," Karl agreed.

"We'll be over later," Sarah said. "Guys, Karl's place is really nice. He's from Chiron. Maybe he'll even cook you something. He's a great cook. A really great cook."

Ting asked, "Isn't Chiron…"

"Yep, still occupied by Earth. That's why Karl lives here," Sarah said.

Mag Lev quickly whisked them into the city. The drop off was only down an escalator to reach the embassy. As they approached, the two Tau soldiers standing outside the doors snapped to attention. "General Meadows, Commander Goth and crew to see the ambassador."

They opened the door and went inside. There was more art and decor since her last visit, though it was still basically the same. One of the staff approached Goth. "Commander, I can take your sealed case."

Goth seemed very glad to get rid of it.

Ambassador Kuhl came out from an interior office. "Welcome." He ushered Sarah and Goth inside. "I'll be glad when we can get this ceremony over with. There is always the fear something could go wrong."

"Well, we'll have to hope for the best," Sarah said.

"I'm glad you both are here. Believe it or not, you two are the ranking officers," the ambassador said.

Goth added, "We're the only officers."

"That's true," Kuhl agreed. "Of my small contingent of soldiers, none of them are officers."

"Isn't it customary to have a military attaché?" Sarah asked.

"It is. And I haven't got one. I've asked for one, but there have been no takers," Kuhl said.

"I'd be happy to do it," Goth offered.

"Commander Goth, I'm sure you would do an excellent job. But it is a captain's billet and I do not have the power to promote you," Kuhl explained. "General Meadows, our Foreign Office opposed opening this embassy. They are distrustful of humans. We have it only on the direct orders of the emperor. The emperor feels we have to deal with humans moving toward the future. I believe we may soon have an embassy on Earth itself, with the foreign minister delaying it every step of the way."

"I would agree with that," Sarah said. "But why doesn't the emperor simply replace him?"

"It's a her, actually. Our society is complicated. Traditionally, there are no females in the military. But, the foreign office is ninety percent female. I am a rare exception because I'll take the posts no one else wants. And no one wanted this one."

The ambassador's color changed to orange. "Oh, I meant no offense. Your situation is unique. Since you are the only human most Tau have ever seen, your gender was not really a concern."

"I figured as much, already. But there is a lot about the Tau I still do not understand," Sarah said.

"I notice you both are carrying side arms?" Kuhl seemed puzzled. "We sort of have agreed to a no weapons policy around the city."

"We walked right by customs. They never said a thing. Frankly, with our diplomatic pouch, I think they didn't know what to do with us." Sarah patted her T-53. "I suppose I could leave this home tomorrow."

"That might be best," the ambassador agreed.

Sarah asked, "Well, what is it we have to do during this ceremony?"

"Not much, really. I'll show you what we have planned," Kuhl said.

25
CEREMONY

Karl answered the door. He gave Sarah a quick hug, then ushered everyone inside.

Sarah introduced her companions. "This is Commander Goth, Topo and Ting. There's a ceremony tomorrow out at the MSE campus and the ambassador wants us all there."

"Splendid," Karl said. "I don't know what you boys eat, but I just baked a cake out of some of the local ingredients. Perhaps you'd like to try some?" Karl ventured off into his kitchen.

"He's a really good cook," Sarah said. "Trust me on this."

Karl promptly returned with four small plates, each bearing a slice of cake. "Don't take her word for it." He handed everyone a plate.

Sarah took a bite. It struck her as something they'd fix her if she died and went to heaven. "Oh my."

Goth took a bite. His crew looked at their plates, then at him to see if he was choking or showing signs of dying. They noticed Goth's plate was already clear. They each tried some of the cake.

"The guys aren't all that crazy about what my kind eat. Still, they seem to have a weakness for sweets." Sarah finished her serving. "What the heck is it?"

"It's a cake variation on my fungus bread. I need to come up with a better name for that," Karl said. "Sit down everyone. Do you guys like beer?"

"What is beer?" Topo asked.

"It's a drink that makes you do stupid things, then it makes you feel really bad," Sarah said. "Actually, I have no idea how it affects you lot."

"Perhaps some water?" Goth asked.

"Coming right up," Karl said. "I gave my housekeeper the night off. It's just me, but I don't mind." He quickly returned with three glasses of water and one of Martian Red Ale.

Sarah reached inside her pocket and took out an envelope. "That reminds me, this is for you."

Karl took the envelope, looked it over, then opened it. He read it. It was only one sentence long. He seemed kind of depressed.

"Something wrong?" Sarah asked.

"Well, not really." Karl handed her the note.

It simply read "I'm sorry." with the emperor's name as well. "Sing." Sarah looked at it a moment, then handed it back. "I'm not sure I understand?"

"Some time ago, I met with Sing. We were going to hold out for a unified settlement for both our worlds," Karl explained.

Sarah took a sip of beer. "I guess I mucked that up. I had a lot to do with the peace treaty. The emperor suddenly had a treaty agreement dumped in his lap out of the blue. That's awfully hard to turn down."

"I don't blame anyone," Karl said. "He had to do what's best for his people. Unfortunately, I think Earth will become even more oppressive against mine."

"Uh, Karl, we're a bit confused," Goth said. "Sarah told us you were a cook."

"No, I said he was a good cook. The cake we just had bears witness to that. Karl is the King of Chiron, living in exile here on Mars," Sarah said.

"Oh."

"Yes, these days I cook now and then and I sell insurance," Karl said.

"Hah!" Sarah took a sip of beer. "When was the last time you sold a policy?"

"Today, actually," Karl replied. "One of your old customers."

"One of mine?" Sarah was skeptical.

"Yes. Phillip Phillips came in. He just got married. He wanted to buy some insurance for himself and his bride. A lovely girl. They seem quite happy. He asked about you. I told him you were on leave for a while and signed him up."

"Is he still working at the sewage plant?" Sarah asked.

"Yes he is," Karl said.

"That's interesting." Sarah gulped down the rest of her beer. "Karl, old buddy, you haven't sold a single policy since I've known you. You're listed in the directory as senior claims adjustor. Why would you, all of a sudden, go and sell a policy?"

"I do have an insurance license," Karl pointed out. "And all of the agents were in some stupid meeting with Don Don. I was the only one out in the bullpen."

"That makes sense, somehow," Sarah agreed.

At that moment the front door exploded. Five masked men emerged from the smoke. They probably expected there might be a servant. It was unlikely they expected three Tau soldiers standing there.

Sarah hit the button on her T-53 and her hand kept on going. Her Earth Marines boot knife came up with one quick motion and she rammed it right through the throat of the closest attacker. They were so concerned about the big reptilian soldiers they'd completely ignored the strawberry blonde girl wearing a similar uniform. Before the 2.4 seconds were even up she'd drawn her sidearm and the targeting laser was targeted on a second assailant. His head sort of exploded when she fired the instant it came up to shooting power.

People often did not realize how fast the Tau could move. Many an Earthforce soldier had died making that mistake. Topo lunged forward and hit one of the assassins so hard he went flying right through the wall. At the same time, Ting threw his favorite hammer. It struck one of the assailants, knocking him out cold.

The one remaining assailant took off running. "Topo, Ting stay here in case there are more of these guys. Goth, you're with me," Sarah ordered. She ran out into the public corridors. This guy was pretty fast. He was just rounding a corner and disappearing from sight.

"Can we find him?" Goth asked.

"Don't have to. I know where he's going," Sarah said. "Follow me."

The waiters of Ling Fung Restaurant were somewhat surprised when Sarah and Goth ran through the kitchen. They then ran through a service area which was a junction for pipes leading out to the sewage area. They ran by a sleeping maintenance worker who never even noticed them. Then they ran up two flights of stairs.

The masked man came around the corner just as they came up the stairs. Sarah destroyed a public trash can as she fired at the assailant and missed. Their quarry raced through the double doors of the Earth embassy and was gone.

The targeting lasers from four T-53's danced over Sarah's chest. She looked back down the beams to four Earth marines, each with a sidearm identical to her own and each one of them was trained on her. Sarah switched off the power button and lowered her weapon. "Stand down Commander."

"We can take them," Goth insisted,

"Stand down, Commander," Sarah repeated. "We can't win this one."

There were a bunch of Mars City marshals milling around by the time they got back to Karl's residence. Most of them were eating cake. There were some maintenance guys Sarah recognized from Gompers first response team. They were measuring the doorway, though they all had cake in their hands as well.

"I know I said Earth would get more aggressive, but I didn't think it would happen that fast," Karl said.

"Were they going to kidnap you?" Goth asked.

"No, my good fellow, I think it was more likely they were assassins. I have little ransom value, but my demise would strengthen their puppet government," Karl said.

"Uh, Karl, I've been wondering something?" Sarah asked.

"What's that?"

Sarah hesitated a moment, then asked, "Do you have any heirs?"

"Yes I do. My daughter, the princess has been staying on Almeria, at Dragon's home," Karl said.

"How come you never mention her?"

"It just never came up. Frankly, I didn't want Earth's hired goons to know where she was, or even be sure she existed. Want some more cake?"

"Yes, please," Topo said.

Sarah was glad to finally get home. It had been a long absence from her apartment. She looked forward to a little more familiar routine. But, first, the ceremony. She told her terminal what time to wake her, took off her clothes, then stretched out on the bed. It felt weird, lying on a bed instead of a hammock. She was asleep in a few minutes.

26
OLYMPUS

Sarah was up before she'd asked the terminal to wake her. The attack on Karl's house was unsettling. Karl, as usual, brushed it off. From Sarah's point of view, this was a major escalation of things with such a brazen attack right in Mars City–and one of the attackers openly fleeing into the embassy of the great planet Earth. And, those same wonderful Earth people were going to go and sign a treaty with the Tau in just a few hours. All because of her.

She was eating banana pudding, at least the Martian hydroponics version of it. Bananas did not grow on Mars–efforts to import them had always failed. Some plants adapted to cultivation on Mars while other ones did not. She had no idea how they made what she was eating or what it really contained. Sarah was going to miss all of those Earthforce rations. This version of banana pudding was white, instead of yellow. Since she'd never actually seen a banana, she was not really sure which was the correct color for them.

The door buzzer was beeping. She wondered who it could be at such an early time. She looked through the peep hole. It was Becky Hudson. Sarah opened the door. She was stark naked and had pudding all over her face. "Minister?"

Becky did not seem very happy. "You, my dear, cause trouble for me everywhere you go."

"What now?" Sarah asked. "Surely you can't blame me for the attack on Karl's house."

"I don't blame you for the attack. You turned it into a fiasco," she said. "With the war over with the lizards, Earth is more militant than ever. They want things."

"So, you agreed to look the other way while they conduct a brazen attack right here in the city?" It seemed incredible to Sarah. It seemed preposterous. "I can't believe you."

"Unlike you, I have to look at the overall picture before acting. I warned him the government could no longer guarantee his safety. I begged him to relocate to another planet. He refused,"

Becky said. "The attack last night was inevitable and he knew it."

"Minister, I can't believe you are telling me all of this?" Sarah licked the pudding away from her lips. She suspected it might be mistaken for something else around her mouth. She noticed there was some on her tits as well, but thought licking them might cast a different angle on the conversation. "The war would have ended whether I had fought in it or not. I just helped it along to its inevitable conclusion."

"And now you want the signing ceremony right here on Mars?"

"It was not what I wanted. It was worked out before I even knew about it. They wanted to do it here in the city. I merely suggested the venue," Sarah said.

"You are very naive," Becky said. "I should have sent them to your house, but I didn't know you were back."

"The assassins or the ceremony?" Sarah asked, though it was a rhetorical question. "The new law required me to have a travel waiver. How come you let me go if my actions were so awful?"

"With the Tau ambassador standing right there? On what basis could I refuse? All my best laid plans to give Earth the minerals it needs are in ruins thanks to you," Becky snarled. "You've ruined everything."

"At what cost, Minister?" Sarah asked.

"You think I care about lizard people? You think I care about those purple idiots on Chiron? Earth can kill them all. God I hate you!"

"Well, Becky, thanks for sharing that with me." Sarah slammed the door shut. Nothing better to start off the day than some irrational tirade. It was time for a shower. She couldn't go around with pudding on her tits.

The news broadcast filled in a little more light on the situation. The Chancellor of Mars was facing a no confidence vote in the legislature later that day. The Foreign Minister, Becky Hudson, had just been sacked. Sarah was starting to miss the simplicity of living with the Tau. All of the bizarre conspiracy theories about the Martian government being in cahoots with Earth, apparently, were true after all.

It was time to get dressed. She had a signing ceremony to go to.

The Tau delegation all boarded Mag Lev and were on their way to the campus of the Martian School of Economics. The school sat just at the base of Olympus Mon, an extinct volcano that was the tallest mountain anywhere in the entire solar system. Sarah often wondered if they'd built the school there simply so they could put the mountain on their official documents and recruiting materials. It wasn't as if the students could frolic on it during breaks from class. Since Mars had no breathable air, it required considerable equipment to climb around on the mountain. Still, Sarah had recommended it because of the majestic backdrop and the fact the school would relish the chance for free publicity that comes with hosting such events.

Dr. Thornton was hovering around the atrium, making sure the bunting on the tables was straight–each table decorated in the school's colors of gold and blue. Sarah wondered why so many academic administrators were bald. They'd made a lot of strides in hair replacement over the years. He looked over at her and smiled.

Sarah approached, slightly in front of the delegation. "Good morning, Dr. Thornton."

"Hello Miss Meadows," he greeted. "It is still Miss?"

"Yes, well, not exactly. For the ceremony anyway, General Meadows would be preferred."

"But of course," he replied. He suddenly seemed to realize she was wearing a uniform.

Sarah turned toward the delegation. "Dr. Thornton, the president of the Martian School of Economics, may I present Ambassador Kuhl, Chief of Staff Kronda, and Commander Goth." Kronda had been the Tau who had outfitted Sarah before her deployment, though Sarah had not known her name then.

The Tau all nodded in acknowledgment. Ting and Topo did not rate an introduction for such occasions. Two of the embassy soldiers who had come along were ignored as well.

The Earth delegation marched into the atrium. There were twice as many of them as representing the Tau. A brigadier general approached Dr. Thornton. She was a rather attractive redhead. "Dr. Thornton, I am General Margaret Bane, Military Attaché. May I present Ambassador Robert Smith, Chargé d' affaires Ethan Howard, and our embassy staff."

"She was listed yesterday as Lieutenant Colonel on embassy

roster," Goth whispered to Sarah.

"Of course," Sarah whispered back. "A sudden promotion? She has to appear to be of comparable rank to me."

"You still outrank her," Goth whispered.

"I know," Sarah said.

Sarah noticed some of the faculty and even a few students were pouring into the atrium area. She whispered to Kuhl, "It won't be long now and they'll be recruiting at Okemedon for new students."

"They already are," the ambassador replied.

"Welcome everyone," Dr. Thornton announced. "It is a truly great honor for us here at the Martian School of Economics to host this noteworthy event."

And so Sarah struggled to remain awake for the following hour of speeches extolling what a wonderful place the MSE was and how delighted everybody was to be there. Then came the actual treaty signing. That lasted about a minute. And it was all over. Some people left to return to whatever it was they did. Others milled about for small talk.

General Margaret Bane made her way over to Sarah. "So, will you be returning to Okemodon, General Meadows?"

"The capital?" Sarah asked. "No, I'm a reservist. My duty is done. I'll be staying here on Mars."

"Must be a letdown to go back to selling insurance," Margaret said.

"Not really," Sarah replied. "I love the insurance business. I was born to sell insurance."

"Really? Well, perhaps we should have lunch some time," Margaret suggested.

"Certainly," Sarah agreed. "So nice meeting you." She nodded to Goth, who in turn nodded to his crew. They all slid out of the crowd and went to the Mag Lev station. Sarah was so glad when the train pulled away. "Well, that was fun."

Goth gave her a puzzled look. "It was?"

"That was a joke," Sarah explained.

"Oh."

She saw them off at the space terminal, then headed back to her apartment. She hung up her uniform and relaxed on the bed for a few moments. She'd been through a lot of late. It was nice not having anybody want anything, not having to make any decisions. She looked at the clock. It was still only midday. Sleeping all day was not really her style.

She put on that green dress she had not worn in years. She hated that dress. Boys seemed to like it. It was very low cut, especially for a casual dress. It showed a lot of cleavage. It was not appropriate for a business. And it was kind of tight. It had always been tight. It was not the pudding, though she decided she might lay off deserts for a while, unless Karl baked them. But, the dress was the opposite of her military uniform and there was always the chance it might annoy Don Don.

"Hello," Sarah greeted the bald lady at reception.

"Good afternoon," the bald lady replied, with a certain emphasis on afternoon in her voice.

Sarah opened up a small plastic box she was carrying. Martian Customs had not even asked about having anything to declare. She held the box out. "These are Tau grubs. They are considered a rare delicacy by the Tau. Would you like one?"

The bald lady looked at them suspiciously. "They don't look too good."

"Suit yourself," Sarah said.

"Well, I guess I could try one," the bald lady decided.

"Excellent," Sarah said.

Sarah made her way to the bullpen and plopped down at her desk. "Ah, it's good to be back."

"Are those Tau grubs?" Karl asked.

"Yes, they are Tau grubs," Sarah said. "Would you like one?"

"Madam, you seem to forget I have been to Okemodon," Karl said. "I've been offered them before."

Sarah could just hear the bald lady blurt out "Oh my god!" as she seemed to be racing off toward the restroom.

"Oh yes, so you have," Sarah replied. Don Don marched by her desk. "Oh, Don Don," she held out the box, "these are a rare delicacy for the Tau. They're quite expensive. Would you like to try one?"

Don Don looked them over. "Uh, I don't know. Has anyone else had one?"

"Rachel up at reception just had one, actually," Sarah said.

Don Don shrugged, took two of them from the box, then

ventured off to his office. "Uh, thanks."

"You are most welcome," Sarah said.

"Who is Rachel?" Karl asked.

"The bald lady up at reception," Sarah replied.

"But she doesn't give out her name," Karl pointed out.

"I know that, but that doesn't mean I don't know it," Sarah said. "I can be very resourceful."

Don Don came rushing out of his office. His hands covered his mouth as he raced for the restroom.

"You are positively evil," Karl said. He opened a drawer in his desk and took out a plastic box of his own. "I saved you some fungus bread."

"You are so wonderful," Sarah said with her mouth full as she devoured her treat.

27
GETTING DOWN TO BUSINESS

Sarah's terminal binged. There was a message from the Bank of Mars. A deposit had just been made into her account. She logged on to see what it was. She smiled.

"Good news?" Karl asked.

"The best." She pointed at the terminal. "The Tau pay better than I thought they did."

"I'll say," Karl agreed. He gave her a puzzled look. "You took a job without knowing what it paid or what you'd be doing?"

"Yep," Sarah agreed. "Heck, it was a miracle that I even survived."

Karl asked, "Is that what they teach at the MSE?"

"Not exactly." Sarah looked at the clock. "That reminds me; I agreed to be guest instructor tonight. Dr. Thornton asked me. Gotta run."

Karl seemed skeptical. "Dr. Thornton actually teaches?"

"One class a year," Sarah said.

"You're going in that dress?" Karl asked.

"Yes, daddy. The MSE student body is seventy-five percent male," Sarah pointed out.

"Well, even if your lecture stinks, I guess they'll still remember you."

"Let's hope so," Sarah agreed.

Mag Lev whisked her back out to the base of Olympus Mon. She headed out in search of room 427. She was surprised she couldn't remember where it was. Of course, she'd been away for some time. Then, suddenly, there it was. And she had a minute to spare.

"I'm Sarah Meadows. I'll be filling in for Dr. Thornton today." She looked at the blank faces filling the room. "So, what are your plans after graduation?" She got no response. "Do any of you have plans?" She still got no response.

Finally, some guy at the back raised his hand. "Is this going to be on the test?"

"Is what going to be on the test? We haven't done anything yet," Sarah pointed out.

The student answered, "I just wondered if this was worth sticking around for."

"I see." Sarah thought a moment. "No, it won't be on the test."

The student stood up and marched out of the room. He nodded as he passed by Sarah.

After he was gone, Sarah said, "Actually, Dr. Thornton asked for me to send him a memo so he could work some stuff into the next exam."

"But you told him it wasn't on the test," one of the girls complained.

"I lied," Sarah said.

"You can't do that," someone else insisted.

"I just did. What are you going to do about it?" Sarah waited a moment. "This is business ethics. Why shouldn't I lie to you? What reason do I have to be truthful?"

"Why would Dr. Thornton have you here if you're just going to lie to us?" another student asked.

"Why not? I don't see anything wrong with it. That student who just walked out on me was rather inconsiderate. Heck, maybe I'll tell Dr. Thornton we went over a bunch of stuff that we didn't." Sarah noticed her students seemed agitated.

"We should all leave," another student suggested.

"I'm the one who should leave," Sarah said. "I could be making money right now. Instead, I'm sitting here arguing with a bunch of lazy students."

"Who are you calling lazy?" someone asked.

"You don't seem to want to learn anything," Sarah pointed out.

"You aren't teaching anything," came the response.

"I see." She looked straight at the tall goofy looking student in the front row. "What's your name?"

"Eric."

"Well, Eric, you expect me to behave ethically. You expect me to teach you something. Don't you?" Sarah asked.

"Duh? This is Business Ethics."

"Yeah, but what you don't know is Dr. Thornton is going on

medical leave. I'll be teaching this class for the rest of the term. So, what do I get out of it? Eric?"

"They pay you," Eric replied.

"Yeah, but I want more. So, what's a good grade worth to you? I'm not going to give you one unless you make it worth my while," Sarah said.

"You can't do that. I'll tell the dean," Eric insisted.

"I can. I will. Next session, decide what it's worth to you. The top bidders get the best grades," Sarah said.

"Well, if I'm getting a suckie grade, I might as well leave," the short blonde girl announced.

"Yes, you might. Actually, I lied about Dr. Thornton. He's fine. He'll be back next time."

"What gives," Eric asked.

"You expected me to behave ethically. I was not. Why did you expect me to behave ethically?" Sarah asked.

"Because that's was instructors do," Eric insisted.

"That's what they do. I see. Now, I work for Gompers Insurance. Eric, if you came to me and wanted some insurance, say to protect your belongings, and I sold you a policy, are you with me?" Sarah asked.

"Policy, got it," Eric agreed.

"Well, say a few months from now, all of your belongings were destroyed by a meteor crashing into your room. What would you do?" Sarah asked.

"I'd file a claim."

Sarah nodded. "And when you file your claim, they would tell you Gompers doesn't insure property. In fact, they have no record of you. What would you do?"

"I'd whip it out," Eric said. That brought some laughter. "My policy."

"And the company says furthermore, they've never heard of Sarah Meadows?"

"I'd complain to the insurance department. People have to be licensed," Eric said.

"I see. And why do people have to be licensed, Eric?"

"Uh, to protect me from incompetent or unscrupulous insurance agents," Eric said.

"Exactly," Sarah agreed. "Anyone can write a policy. But, that company may not have the intention of honoring it, or they may be insolvent. Yet, they may still try and sell it to you. Why would they do that, Eric?"

"Greed."

"Anyone else have any other reason?" Sarah asked. The class was over in no time.

Sarah headed back over to the Mag Lev station. The down side was she now had to ride all the way back to Mars City. As she sat on the train, she counted six men. They were all looking at her like a piece of meat. She wondered what had possessed her to wear the stupid green dress. It was too short. It was too tight. A flirtatious admiring glance was one thing. That wasn't what she was picking up here. And her stupid short dress had nowhere to conceal an Earth Marine boot knife, let alone a T-53 laser. For the first time in ages, she felt vulnerable. It was a feeling she did not like. Then she had company. Some guy sat down right next to her on the nearly empty train.

"Hi," he said.

"Hello," Sarah replied.

"Heading back from Olympus Mon?" he asked.

"Something like that," Sarah answered.

"Live in Mars City?" the man asked.

That wasn't much of a pick-up line. "Doesn't everyone?"

"What do you do?" he asked.

An out. "I sell insurance," she said. "Have you had a coverage checkup recently? They say most people are dangerously under insured."

"You know, I've got to go find my wallet in the other car," the man said as he got up.

"Nice meeting you," Sarah said. Karl was right. She was evil. The insurance routine was probably a better defense than even a boot knife.

Sarah was so glad when Mag Lev finally pulled into Mars City. She wondered over to the escalator that would take her home. The first thing she was going to do was take the dress off. Then she was going to have some banana pudding, maybe even a banana milk shake. They didn't have cows on Mars. They didn't have bananas. Martian Hydroponics sold banana milkshakes in little packets that self-froze after adding water. And she had one waiting for her at home.

But she was being followed. It was the guy from the train. Apparently, the insurance pitch hadn't worked as well as she thought. Sarah said aloud, "Just once I wish I could go somewhere without having to kill somebody." She turned toward her unwanted suitor.

He was holding a badge and an id card. "Easy there. MBI."

28
OBLIGATIONS

Sarah was not too impressed with the cluttered office of the Martian Bureau of Investigation. She was even less impressed with Agent Steve Saunders. "Tell me, Steve, do you hit on all of the women you arrest?" She pulled on the hand restraints. Supposedly you couldn't slip out of them, no matter how nimble you were. So far, that seemed to be the case.

"I thought you'd made me. Better to let you think I was some guy looking for a girlfriend than a government agent who had you under surveillance," he explained. "Then, I was told to go ahead and take you into custody."

"But you have yet to tell me why I am in custody?" Sarah waited for an answer.

After several minutes came the reply, "We're waiting for the agent in charge."

"How nice." Sarah was going to burn that blasted green dress she was wearing. She felt like her tits were going to pop out of the darned thing. Of course, she could have put on some underwear. The damned thing was awfully darn short as well, especially when you're not wearing any underwear.

"Ah," Steve said. He stood up and motioned for her to do as well. He took Sarah into a dingy office and seated her on an identical uncomfortable chair to the one she'd just been sitting on.

Some bald guy was sitting behind a desk. "Miss Meadows, or can I call you Sarah?"

"I'd prefer Miss Meadows. Actually, I'd prefer General Meadows," Sarah replied. "And what do you like to be called?"

"Agent Lewis."

Sarah sat there quietly.

"No protestations of innocence? No mock indignation at being brought in?" Agent Lewis asked.

Sarah sat there quietly.

"Nothing to say?"

"Other than what I liked to be called, you have not asked me anything," she replied. "Steve here has not asked me anything. Nobody has asked me a blasted thing."

"Well, Agent Saunders was directed to take you into custody by me," Agent Lewis said. "Now then, there is a law here on Mars. It's called the Foreign Espionage Act."

Sarah sat there quietly.

"This law requires that people performing activities on behalf of foreign governments must register and declare themselves," Agent Lewis explained. "The outgoing foreign minister, Becky Hudson, told us you have been running around doing all sorts of things for the Tau Empire. Yesterday the Tau even transmitted funds to your bank."

Sarah sat there quietly.

"Nothing to say?" Agent Lewis asked.

Sarah pointed out, "You still have not asked me anything."

"Well, we believe you have met the requirements of the statute and should be held accountable," Agent Lewis said.

Sarah sat there quietly.

Agent Lewis apparently realized he still had not asked her anything. "Care to comment on that?"

Sarah smiled. "Well, Agent Lewis, I believe that I do, indeed, fall under the act. I was just sitting here thinking how fast any Tau soldier could tear you to pieces. Was there anything else you wanted to discuss?"

"You're awfully nonchalant for somebody facing a prison sentence," Steve said.

"I do not believe I'm facing a prison sentence," Sarah replied. "Frankly, since I haven't done anything unlawful, I just figured you guys liked my dress and were going to gang bang me on top of the desk. You two are idiots."

"And why is that, Miss Meadows? You just admitted your activities fall under the statute," Agent Lewis said.

"Gentlemen, have you nothing better to do than harass some poor girl who has had a long day? I am registered as an agent for the Tau Empire. I know all about the statute," Sarah said. "I graduated with honors from the Martian School of Economics. My honors thesis was on laws pertaining to foreign agency, and especially the Foreign Espionage Act."

Agent Lewis looked over at Steve. "Agent Sinclair, you said

you checked on this?"

"I called over there and they said no one ever registers, not ever," he insisted.

"I registered under the statute, using the form provided by the Public Recorder. I filed the form with them, as prescribed under the statute. And it sounds like neither of you two clowns even bothered to go over there and check on it. Sarah Audrey Meadows. One-thirty-one Mars City Mall West, in care of M. Ashcroft Burke, attorney at law, who I may be calling shortly."

Steve hastily went out to the main office area. He came back a few minutes later. He didn't look very happy. He reached in his pocket and pulled out a key button, which he pressed. The restraints let go of Sarah.

Sarah was actually glad neither agent ever apologized. She felt most apologies were meaningless and insincere anyway. But she was glad to get out of there.

She decided to stop at the Skylight Refectory before going home. After the server brought her glass of Martian Red Ale, she noticed a familiar face sitting at another table. She took her glass over. "Hi, I hope I'm not intruding. Remember me?"

The gentleman, who Sarah thought was about her age, although beards sometimes make people look older, thought a moment. "Ah, I arrested you once."

"You do remember."

He made a gesture toward the vacant other chair. "Hank Carver."

"Sarah Meadows," she said. "Did you transfer to Mars City from Fremont Station?"

"No, I just had a few days off," he said. "Last I saw of you was during a brawl at the cafeteria with some lizard people. You were fighting some guys from Earth."

"Then you stunned me," Sarah said.

"Yep. You went down like the proverbial sack of potatoes," Hank agreed. "How'd that turn out?"

"They dropped the charges. Boy, I had to fork over a month's pay to cover the damages," Sarah said.

"Was it worth it?" Hank asked.

"Heck yeah," Sarah said. "Seems every time you turn up I get arrested. Just got out of an interview with the MBI."

"Martian Blundering Incompetents?" Hanks offered. "Those of us in the Marshal's Service are not too impressed. They're mostly staffed by friends of political appointees. Who'd you kill?"

"No one. They thought I was a spy," Sarah said.

Hank took a sip of beer. "Oh. Who are you spying for?"

"The lizard people," Sarah said.

"I see."

"Not trying to change the subject, are you staying in Mars City?" Sarah took a sip of her beer as she waited for an answer.

"Yes. I'm at the Hilton, but I could only afford one night. Even with the government employees discount rate," he said.

"I sometimes forget how expensive it is to stay in hotels. Working for Gompers, they just pick it up," Sarah said.

Hank asked. "You know of a cheaper place?"

"Sure do," Sarah said. "You can stay at my place."

"Uh, okay," he decided. "I should go by and pick up my stuff from the hotel?"

"Okay."

"You aren't just trying to sell me some insurance are you?" he asked.

Sarah smiled, then drank the rest of her beer. "By the way, do you have any of those hand restraints?"

"Yep. They're in my luggage," he said.

"Ooh."

29
HONOR

There was absolutely no one at the office. Sarah pressed her index finger against the pad and waited for the security system to decide if she was her. There was a click and the door opened. The lights came on automatically. Sarah went to her desk and turned on her work station terminal. Her next stop was the coffee dispenser. The jolt from the hot liquid and caffeine helped clear her head. Not one, but two back to back call outs. "Join Gompers, the preferred employer of insomniacs everywhere." She took another sip of coffee and rubbed her eyes.

"Computer, call up the file for the Mars City Opera Hall." Sarah waited for the information to come up to the screen. "Note to claims: I am placing the status on hold pending fire inspector's report. One advantage to the Opera Hall is that it has atmospheric depletion fire suppression. If a fire is detected then part of the oxygen in the chamber is released causing the fire to extinguish. This system failed. Damage is extensive to the snack bar and box office with significant smoke damage to upholstery and carpet throughout the main theater. Preliminary loss estimate is one million doubloons. Send file." She took a sip of coffee.

"Bring up the file for Mars City Bank." The information came up on the screen. "An explosion from unknown explosive allowed entry into the safe deposit vault. Damage is substantial. A contractor's report will be required to assess damages. Computer, cross reference any individual policies for safe deposit box riders. Five policy numbers came up. Note to claims department, exposure is minimal. We do not cover individual losses from boxes, only damage to the bank and five boxes with individual coverage riders. Combine all claims to this master file. End summary." She leaned back in her chair and took another sip of coffee. "Sarah go sleepy now."

"Sleep on your own time," Don Don announced, "not on mine."

"Two call outs in one night. The Mars City Bank is a lot of

explosion damage but the actual losses are safe deposit boxes with little exposure. The opera is another matter. I'm waiting for the fire inspector's report, but I strongly suspect the fire suppression was sabotaged."

"Why would they do that?" Don Don asked.

"Could be some disgruntled employee who doesn't get enough sleep or missed a promotion. When accounting gets in, I'm going to see if they have someone who can do can do a quick look see of their finances. How best to get a remodel at our expense if you're low on funds?"

"Fires do that, get you new furniture, new carpet. Stay on it," Don Don said before he disappeared in his office.

"Sarah go sleepy now," she said again as she leaned back and closed her eyes.

She sensed a presence. She opened her eyes. "Smedley?"

"Hi."

"What brings you over here?" Sarah asked.

"You did? You wanted something about the Opera Hall?" He looked expectantly.

"Oh, I guess I did. How quick can you determine if the opera is in financial difficulty? They had a fire and I'm very suspicious about it," Sarah explained.

"I'll see what I can do," he said. "Where can I get started?"

Sarah pointed at Karl's station. He wasn't due in for another hour. "Start there, for the time being." Other salesmen were turning up for work.

"Okay." Smedley settled in at the station. "We have a contractual right to look at their credit history and, of course, the public records of a charitable corporation. I'll start with that."

"Good." Her coffee cup was empty. She wanted more, but was feeling too lazy to go and fetch some.

"Miss Meadows, please come to my office," Don Don said over the office intercom.

She let out a sigh. Her body did not want to get up, but she finally convinced it to obey. She went down the hall and into Don Don's office. "Yes?"

Don Don seemed even more uptight than usual. "Miss Meadows, why are you so tired? You can barely function."

Sarah agreed. "What else is new?"

"I'm a bit confused."

What else is new? Sarah thought.

"You weren't even on call last night?" He looked at his clipboard. "What happened to Ralph?"

"Central dispatch couldn't reach him. So, they called me. Then I got home and they called me back out," Sarah said.

"But where is Ralph? He hasn't reported to work? This is intolerable." Don Don put his clipboard down.

"I don't know where Ralph is. I just know that he's not here." Sarah wondered if there was anything other catastrophe. "Can I go now?"

"Go where?"

"That guy at Karl's desk is checking on the finances of the opera hall. I want to see if he's found anything," she said.

"Oh. Okay then," Don Don agreed. "Where is Karl?"

"He's coming in an hour late. He sent you a memo."

"Oh, I guess I saw that. Carry on."

Sarah went back out to the bull pen. "My dear Smedley, find anything yet?"

"Oh yes indeedy," Smedley said. "They're flat broke. They were going to be audited by the Department of Revenue today. They've requested a postponement because of the fire. Something's mighty funny, if you ask me."

"Thank you good sir," Sarah said.

"I'll see what else I can dig up," Smedley said.

Sarah closed her eyes. Her eyelids were no longer willing to obey her brain. She sensed a presence. Her eyes reluctantly opened.

"Who is that man at my station?" Karl asked.

"Smedley," Sarah said. She closed her eyes again.

"Why is he here?" Karl asked.

"He's working on something," Sarah said.

"I can see that. Why is he working on something at my station?"

"Move him over to Ralph's station," Sarah said. "It's Ralph's fault anyway."

"Why is it Ralph's fault?" Karl asked.

"Because he didn't answer the pages last night. I've been up all night dealing with fires and explosions and I was supposed to be off. One minute I'm getting tied up and having my clothes ripped off of me, the next minute I'm looking at a big hole in the side of a bank vault." She opened her eyes. Everybody in the bullpen area, including Smedley, was staring at her. "I didn't say that, did I?" She closed her eyes. When she had been a little girl she thought that when her eyes were closed other people could not see her. Maybe that was still true.

"Miss Meadows, please come to my office," Don Don said over the office intercom.

Sarah opened her eyes. The people were still there. They could still see her. She ventured down to the office.

Don Don looked up from something he was reading. "I need you to go over to Ralph's house. Try and see why he's not responding."

"Okay," Sarah agreed. She headed out and tried to remember where Ralph lived. She was thinking it was next to the market. That was it. The main city escalator would get her there in no time.

Ralph was an enigma. He'd taken early retirement from the Martian Defense Force. He'd been some sort of intelligence officer. Then he'd hired on with Gompers, figuring he'd spend a few years in the leisurely world of selling insurance. Like Sarah, he soon found himself doing other things. Unlike Sarah, he couldn't take the pressure and went back to selling insurance. Don Don had put him back in the line of fire when Sarah bugged out to go fight a war. So, Sarah was quite concerned about him, though her exhaustion had retarded some of her thought process. She would have eventually gone looking for him even if Don Don hadn't asked.

She found his place tucked in a space next to a market. She pressed the door buzzer. Nothing happened. She pressed it again. Sarah unfolded her clipboard and pressed a command function. The door popped open. "Hello! Ralph!" She poked her head inside. "Ralph, it's me, Sarah. Are you here?" She went farther inside. She found Ralph.

He was hanging by the neck from a light fixture. A stool lay on its side beneath him. "Oh Ralph." She pressed a command on her clipboard.

"Mars City Marshal's Office," a voice answered.

"I've found a dead body," Sarah said.

There were tons of questions. Sarah had few answers. She was glad when they finally let her go. It was late when she got back to the office. Only Karl remained.

"Where have you been all day?" Karl asked.

"Don Don sent me to look for Ralph," she said.

"Did you find him?"

"Yep." Sarah dropped into her chair and leaned back.

"Why didn't he come to work?" Karl asked.

"Because he's dead," Sarah said.

"Oh."

"Hung himself." Sarah got out of her chair. "I need to go home. I was beat before I came in. I'm just like a ship on autopilot. By rights, I should call Don Don. I was hoping to catch him before he left."

"Did he have any family?" Karl asked.

"He supposedly had a grown daughter. The marshals are going to try and get a hold of her."

"I'll call him. Go on home," Karl said.

Sarah headed for the door.

"Oh, Sarah, that Smedley fellow left you a report," Karl said.

"Fine. I'll read it tomorrow."

Sarah noticed Hank was heading down the escalator she was about to head up on. He had his orange duffle bag on a shoulder strap. "Hi there sailor."

"I was wondering whatever happened to you," Hank said. "You said you'd be right back?"

Sarah shrugged. "Welcome to my world. First an arson, then someone blows a hole in the wall of a bank. Then a coworker dies."

"I honestly don't know what to say," Hanks replied. "I've got to catch the shuttle."

"And people wonder why I'm not married." Sarah shrugged. "Maybe I'll see you again sometime, if I'm not off chasing after space pirates or something."

Hank reached over and kissed her. "And you didn't even sell me any insurance."

"I'm losing my touch," Sarah said. She ventured up the escalator and over to her apartment. At least Hank made the bed.

She liked people who were tidy.

It was time to get ready for work. She didn't remember falling asleep. She hopped in the shower, then put on some clean clothes. At least the Gompers gods had let her sleep. She missed sleeping. She'd once heard there were people who actually slept all night long.

The bald lady was at reception. Sarah ventured over to her work station. Karl was already in. There was a little brown cake with little crunchy things on the icing. Sarah took a bite. "Oh Karl, why don't you give up on insurance and open a restaurant or a bakery. Every woman on Mars would be in love with you and simultaneously hate you for making her fat."

"Ah, somebody from Earth would just blow it up," he replied.

"And they say I'm cynical," Sarah said with her mouth full of cake. "Damn this is good."

"Sorry to hear about Ralph," Karl said. "Any idea why?"

After she swallowed her cake, Sarah said, "Who knows what demons people have in their heads. I know people never seemed to leave him be. The MDF moved him into a job he hated from one he liked. I think Gompers may have done the same. But, people can quit. People can say no thanks. I don't have all the answers."

With her cake consumed, Sarah ventured down to Don Don's office. "It's officially a sabotaged fire system and arson on the opera hall," Sarah said. "I'd like to recluse payment on the policy."

"Accounting says they're in financial trouble," Don Don said. "Why do people always think a fire will solve their problems? We're pretty good at figuring this stuff out. I'll draft a notice this afternoon."

Sarah nodded her acknowledgment and returned to her work station. She could have easily drafted the notice herself for his signature, but why do work that Don Don can do himself?

A bewildered looking man in a blue and gold uniform was standing in the bullpen area. "May I help you?" Sarah asked.

"That bald lady said to come back here," he said. "I'm not sure I'm at the right place. I've got a letter that has to be hand delivered and signed for."

"Who are you with?" Sarah asked.

"Mighty Messenger Service." He looked at the packet's label. "Is there some Geste Two, King of Chiron here?"

"Yes indeed." Sarah pointed over at Karl. "That's him."

"Could you sign for this, sir?" he asked.

"As long as it's not from Earth," Karl agreed.

The messenger handed Karl a small electronic pad. "It says it's from the Prime Minister of Almeria. Boy, that's a long way away."

Karl signed for the packet. The messenger seemed glad to be rid of it and sashayed out of the office.

"Expecting anything" Sarah asked.

"Prime Minister's office? It doesn't mention Dragon or Gompers. I guess I'll open it and hope it doesn't explode." Karl pulled the little tab and opened it. The packet contained one single piece of paper. Karl read it. He then placed the piece of paper down and put his head on his desk. He seemed to be crying.

A very puzzled Sarah went over and picked up the piece of paper. It was indeed from the Prime Minister of Almeria, which also was the only place other than Earth that maintained an embassy on occupied Chiron. The other worlds, including Mars, had all closed their embassies after Earth's invasion. The ceremonial scepter and crown of the King of Chiron was now on public display at Margrave Space Station and were to be auctioned off to the highest bidder in one month. She gently touched his shoulder for just a moment, then let him be.

Sarah finished up her paperwork on the cases she had been working on. She noticed Karl was gazing off at the ceiling. She went over to his station. "How about I buy you lunch?"

"I'm not all that hungry," he said.

"How about I buy you lunch?" Sarah repeated.

"If I have to," Karl agreed.

30
TYRANNY

"Martian Red," Sarah told the waiter.

Karl asked, "Do you have Chiron bark whisky?"

"Never heard of it," the waiter informed him.

"Vodka with orange juice, then," Karl decided. "Don Don will be so happy with us drinking on company time."

Their drinks soon arrived. Sarah held up her glass. "To Don Don."

Karl tapped his glass to Sarah's. "To Don Don."

They were at the place next to Sarah's apartment. It had an open, outdoor feel, as much as any place in Mars City could convey the illusion of being outdoors. Sarah glanced at two older men who were playing chess at a nearby table. "Now there's an ancient game. It goes back to Egypt, Ancient Egypt. Chess is a lot like war. A lot of people think you win by having a better strategy and not making any mistakes, but that's not true."

Then lunch arrived. Norwegian Blue Stew. Sarah doubted any of the ingredients were from anywhere near Norway, but it really was blue, with chunks of white things in it. At least it came with fresh baked bread. It actually tasted better than it looked. Many of the products offered by Martian Hydroponics took on odd colors no one could really explain.

"How do you win at chess?" Karl asked after trying his food.

"You win by thinking three moves ahead of your opponent," Sarah said.

"Chess or war?" Karl asked.

"Both, actually. When I was in school, there was this boy named Billy Hawkins. He once made me eat dirt. Well, when we got a few years older, he asked me to play chess with him at recess. I beat him. He got beaten by a girl. He was teased relentlessly by the other kids for weeks. Then, the next year he asked me to play him again. I told him I'd let him kiss me if he could beat me. He asked me to play him nearly every day. He never got to kiss me. The poor boy never, ever beat me at chess, no matter how hard he tried. I thought about letting him win, once, but I just couldn't do it. And I beat him because I was thinking moves ahead of him and he was just reacting to me. Ever play?"

Karl replied, "No, though there's something similar on my world, but the board and pieces are a little different."

"I can't begin to understand what it must be like to have your planet taken away from you," Sarah said. "Changing the subject."

"It is not really something I can even describe," Karl said. "I always hoped, somehow, we would manage to get things back. Now, the puppet government has grown so bold they've put my scepter and crown on display. Worse yet, they're going to sell it. It is another in a long line of insults directed specifically at me."

"You shrugged off the hit squad the other day," Sarah pointed out.

"That was different. This is more demeaning—way more demeaning." Karl finished off his vodka and contemplated ordering another one. "They're looting my planet and doing everything they can think of to mock me as they do it."

"Well, then, you should stand up to these people," Sarah said.

"How should I do that?" he asked.

"I think you should go get on a ship and go over to that space station and demand your scepter back," Sarah said. "Make them give it back to you." She had barely touched her beer. It was not liquor talking. "Tell them to get the hell off of your planet, while you're at it."

"And, then they gun me down?" Karl asked. He held up his empty glass and waived to the waiter. He definitely wanted another drink.

"But, you'll die knowing you stood up to them," Sarah said. "That's what's important. And people all over your planet will say something like our king had some balls."

Karl took a big gulp of the fresh drink. "You want me to fight a battle I cannot possibly win?"

"Exactly," Sarah said. "That's exactly what I want you to do. Be Billy Hawkins. He kept at it even though he couldn't possible beat me. That kid never gave up."

"When my planet was overrun by Earthforce we did not have the means to stop them. I was off world. I had no way to even get back, not that my presence would have really mattered. I suspect my being on Mars was part of their plan. Strike while I'm gone. They'd have been better off if I was home. They could have killed me and been done with it."

"Historically, killing the king is the best way to take over," Sarah agreed. "But you're still around and that will be something they will regret."

"Hah. I know they regret it," Karl said.

"I meant you'll make them pay," Sarah explained.

"I'd sort of accepted a life in exile here on Mars. Then those assassins came. I'm obviously not even going to get that. And now, they mock me by putting my scepter up for sale. I feel so damn useless."

"That, my good sir, is why I want you to go back. Go back and end this. Make them tremble at the sound of your voice," Sarah said. She finally drank some of her beer. "Wouldn't you rather be a martyr than have to work for Don Don the rest of your life?"

"What the heck. You think they'll execute me or just gun me down the second they see me there?" Karl asked.

"Who knows? I'd give you a show trial, then execute you. But that's just me."

"You're really serious, aren't you?" Karl asked. "That I should go back?"

"You built that space station," Sarah said.

"Well, had it built," Karl said. "Now it sits there practically empty. No one wants to go there."

"Well, tell them you want your station back." Sarah decided to use her personal Gompers card to pay the check.

"Okay. I guess I will. Beats getting blown up here in Mars City, I suppose. Thanks for lunch. I guess I should see when the next ship goes that way," Karl said.

"In two days. There's an Almerian ship," Sarah said.

"How'd you know that?" Karl asked.

"I checked while you were crying at the office," she said. "You're already booked, though I slightly altered your name, in case anybody's checking. It's on me, pal."

Karl stared at her for a moment. "You booked me passage on a ship before you even knew if I wanted to go?"

"Yep. How's that for sales ability?"

Karl asked, "What should I tell Don Don?"

"Don't tell him anything," she suggested. "He'll figure it out, eventually. I guess we should head back to work." They sauntered back to the Gompers office.

"Where have you two been?" the bald lady demanded.

"We went to lunch," Sarah said. "Now we're back."

"Don Don was furious. He couldn't get a hold of either of you."

Sarah looked at Karl. "So that's who kept trying to call us."

"Because of you, Don Don had to go and meet the fire inspector at the opera house. It wasn't even his case." She looked really angry.

"He could've sent you," Karl said. He headed for his desk.

"I do not do that sort of thing," she stated.

"Oh, by the way, I need into the secure call room," Sarah said.

"What for?" the bald lady asked.

"Because I need to call somebody," Sarah replied. "And it needs to be secure."

"You'll have to wait for Don Don," the bald lady declared.

Sarah smiled at the bald lady. "Unlock the secure call room or I am going to shove your bald head in the toilet and flush it twenty-five times."

Sarah closed the door of the secure call room and frosted the windows. "Open line please, Meadows, Sarah, special operations, Gomers Mars City." She plopped herself down in the swivel chair and span around a few times while she waited for the security system to decide if she was, in fact, who she claimed to be.

"Destination of call?" the terminal asked.

"Okemodon Palace, we are calling His Imperial Majesty, Sing, Emperor of the Tau People," she instructed. "Inform the receiving end the call is incoming from Sarah Meadows, General Sarah Meadows." The terminal beeped a few times. Finally, her call started to go through.

After completing her call, she ventured over to the bullpen and looked at Karl. "Having any second thoughts?"

Karl nodded. "Lots of them. But, in spite of that, I kind of think you may be right. This is something I need to do. I've become too complacent, just sitting here and hoping somehow it will work out. It'll be good to die for my people."

"That's the spirit," Sarah said. "We don't even have to shuttle up to Fremont Station, either. We're actually booked on a freighter leaving right here from Mars City. How's that for luck?"

"We?" Karl asked. "What's this we?"

"I wouldn't miss this for the world," Sarah said.

"As I recall," Karl said, "Earth's people don't like you much better than me."

"Ah, that's ancient history. They were nice as could be at the treaty ceremony. I did them a favor by getting them out of a war they could never win."

"Why couldn't they win it?" Karl asked.

"Well, I could go on about overextended resources and stuff like that. Truth is, they couldn't win that war with the Tau because I was on the other side." She plopped herself down in her chair. "I'm me and Earth was Billy Hawkins."

Don Don walked by them. He glared at Sarah for a moment, but continued to his office.

Sarah said, "Don Don's back."

"I noticed," Karl agreed. "A shame we don't have some other work we could stick him with."

"Well, it's been sort of quiet, today." Sarah sensed a presence. It was the same messenger who had delivered Karl his bad news. "May I help you?"

"Hi, I'm with Mighty Messenger Service. I've got a packet for a General S. Meadows?" He looked at her expectantly. "Is he here somewhere?"

"I am General Meadows," Sarah explained.

"Sign here." He handed her the packet. "Funny, you don't look old enough to be a general?"

As she opened the packet, Sarah said, "That's okay. I'm retired now." She handed the messenger back his signature pad." It's from Almeria Freight and Commerce. It's some information on our trip. Why can't they just transmit it?"

The messenger started waving his hands. "Oh, I know."

"Will you enlighten the rest of us?" Sarah asked.

"They hate transmitting anything. They'll only use electronic communication if they have to. They're our biggest customer. If it weren't for them I wouldn't have a job." He sort of gave her a half-assed salute, then left.

Karl said, "What an odd fellow."

Sarah handed the paperwork over to Karl. "Just weight limits on baggage, what time to be there, that sort of thing. Nice of them to send it, I guess."

"They are a very thorough people," Karl observed. He handed back the material about their trip.

Sarah started to look it over in more detail. "How come they kept an embassy there and continue to trade? No one else will touch commerce with Chiron."

"It was Dragon's idea. If there wasn't someone not under Earth's thumb, I wouldn't know anything. As it is, the Almerians regularly manage to get information to me. Though, a note from the prime minister is unusual. But, thanks to them, I know they're selling my scepter," Karl explained. "It hasn't turned up in the *Martian Daily*."

"You sly dog, you."

31
DESTINY

They were greeted at the space terminal by an Almerian. Almerians were rather large, by human standards. In spite of Karl's history with them, the crew did not act like they had any idea who he was. The ship had a passenger cabin that was plain in terms of amenities, but the seats were configured for human sized bodies.

Riding on a freighter was different from a passenger ship. There would be no attendant. If you wanted a meal, you'd have to get it yourself. They were shown where to sit and where the bathroom was. That was about it for orientation. The passenger area was a round area between the crew compartment and the cargo area. There were four passengers booked on this trip. The other two were both humans. Sarah believed they were from Earth. Karl seemed a little agitated by this, though the passengers showed no sign of any recognition.

After they were underway, the two Earthers introduced themselves. "Hi, I'm Bill and this is Jeremy, we're from Lloyds of London. That's an insurance company on Earth. Are you two from Mars?"

"Yes, we are. Well I am anyway. Karl here, obviously, is from Chiron. He's heading home for a bit. Going to look up some people," Sarah said. "So, you sell insurance then?"

"Well, nothing for personal lines, so you can both relax about that. We insure commercial projects, and cargo. Heck, we even insure the space station we're going to," Bill said.

"Funny, such a small world. We both work for Gompers," Sarah said. "Insurance is everywhere."

"No kidding. Imagine that," Bill agreed. "What's Gompers doing going out in the boondocks?"

"Well, just kind of getting a feel for things. These boycotts can't last forever. Someday, trade has to pick up. When it does, we'll need to be there," Sarah said. It was a lie. Gompers wanted nothing to do with the place and she'd already been there before just to prove that hypothesis. Sarah didn't want them to know they were going there simply to stir up trouble. The Gompers line would do, as it had just a ring of credibility to it.

Jeremy finally joined in. "Looks like we may get some competition."

"I'm sure there's plenty of business to go around," Sarah said. "I wonder what they have to eat on this rust bucket." She did not particularly want to talk about insurance for the entire trip.

Bill was first to unbuckle. "Good idea." He floated over to the food storage area. "I hope they have ice cream."

They did, strawberry ice cream. It was from Earth, not something dreamed up by Martian Hydroponics. "Gimme," Sarah asked. She pulled back the lid and took the provided plastic spoon and took a bite. These guys from earth were so spoiled. They could get real ice cream easily. On Mars, there were no cows. You either got reconstituted ice cream from Earth or something Martian Hydroponics made out of who knows what.

Bill was not as adept at eating in a zero g environment. He had to go after his first bite of ice cream. He managed to gobble it out of the air, before the floating glob caused a nuisance.

Boredom soon set in. Freighters were not big on entertainment. In fact, there wasn't any. You either brought your own or you stared out the porthole window at the nothingness of hyperspace. Sarah soon wrapped herself in the courtesy blanket and drifted off to sleep. Sarah loved sleeping, perhaps because the dispatchers at Gompers so often deprived her of it.

Then, finally, the freighter was docking at Margrave Space Station. "Welcome to Margrave Space Station," some guy with an Earth accent greeted them as they cleared the airlock. This was the freight area, not the passenger arrival section—not that it mattered much with so few people traveling to the station or onto Chiron. The two men from Lloyds headed off to whatever they were going to do. Sarah and Karl headed for the hotel area. Nobody seemed to recognize Karl. Absence does not make the heart grow fonder, apparently.

"Why do we need a hotel room?" Karl asked. "Why not just go and get this over?"

"Because," Sarah paused just a moment, "I need to change. I don't have the right outfit on."

Karl shook his head in disbelief. "What difference does it make?"

"It makes all the difference in the world," Sarah insisted. They went to the guest check in desk. "I'm Sarah Meadows checking in."

The front desk agent looked at his screen. "We have you in a deluxe suite for just the one night. And we've received a funds transfer. It's always easier for our Martian guests since the Martian credit cards don't work here."

"That is correct."

He printed out a key and handed it to her. "Your room is just around the corner, to the right."

"Very good," she said. The room was right where he said it would be. She plopped her heavy duffle bag on the bed. "I'm sure glad they have so few people come here they don't even bother with customs inspections."

"Did you see it?" Karl asked. "Right out there on the promenade."

"Right where it's supposed to be," Sarah pointed out. "Well, give me just a minute to change and all hell breaks loose." She disappeared into the bedroom, but left the door open.

"I still don't see why you insisted on coming? I am quite capable of making a fool out of myself all by myself," Karl said. "I can just bust the case, grab my scepter, then run down to the life pods and hope I make it to the planet."

"Nonsense, you need my help. In fact, I am indispensable," Sarah said. She emerged from the bedroom, now dressed in her Tau army uniform. She had her T-53 holstered and slid her boot knife into its sheath. "Ready?"

"You're wearing that? Haven't you taken this general stuff a little too seriously?" Karl asked.

"Ready?" Sarah repeated, with an annoyed tone in her voice. They headed down the hall. The promenade was a simple few feet down a set of stairs from their room, which was no accident. The room she reserved was carefully selected. Most visitors to the area, which was built to host events and meetings, came up a wide ramp from the lower levels. Sarah held back a bit and let Karl take the lead.

Two human men stood by the display case, looking quite

bored. Though they wore no uniform, they were obviously guarding the case. They looked curiously at the approaching Chiron person. "May we help you?"

"I hope so," Karl said. "That crown and scepter belong to me and I'd like them back."

"Excuse me," one of the guards asked.

Karl repeated his demand, "That crown and scepter belong to me and I'd like them back. I am King Karl Phillip Geste III and I want my scepter out of the blasted case right now!"

One of the guards started talking into his wrist. The other one didn't seem to know what to do.

"Your majesty..." Sarah waved, trying to get Karl to move over to the side just a bit. She drew her T-53 from its holster and flipped the power up switch. She aimed at the case and waited the requisite 2.4 seconds for the weapon to come up to power. Then the display case sort of exploded. She'd aimed high, above the prized items.

Karl grabbed his crown and scepter and ran back toward Sarah while the two guards had no idea what to do, but neither of them wanted to move toward the woman holding the T-53 laser pistol. Suddenly there were all sorts of alarm horns sounding. People on the lower level were running around frantically, though they didn't seem to know where to go. "Shouldn't we be going?" Karl asked.

Sarah holstered her weapon. "What's the rush? Savor the moment."

"You have lost your mind," Karl said. "We've got to get out of here." He noticed the two guards had both fled the area.

"You need to relax more, Karl," Sarah calmly said. "Just relax." Sarah looked down the ramp. There seemed to be a whole lot of commotion going on. Then she noticed there were quite a few bodies coming up the ramp.

"Is there something you haven't told me?" Karl asked.

"Well, yes, sort of," Sarah admitted. "I thought it might be nice to invite a few friends to come along."

The bodies coming up the ramp were all dressed somewhat like Sarah was. "It's like playing chess," she said. "Stay a few moves ahead of the opponent."

One of the Tau had insignia with almost as garish set of

colors as hers were. She recognized the Tau officer from a picture, though she had never met him. She gave a slight nod of recognition. The Tau officer responded in kind with a nod of his own.

"Captain Gant, I am General Meadows," she said. "And may I introduce Karl Phillip Geste III, King of Chiron."

Captain Gant nodded toward Karl.

"How many ships did you bring me?" Sarah asked.

Gant seemed a little surprised by the question. "All of them."

"Excellent," Sarah replied. "Do you have a detachment of soldiers to help the king get this station under control?"

Gant nodded. Two mid-grade officers and about 100 soldiers moved forward.

"They should do nicely." Sarah turned toward Karl. "Well, the first part was easy enough. You've got your station back. The next part may be a little tougher."

She recognized someone else in the delegation. "Captain Bercy, I'd like you to take the task force of smaller ships and surround this station. I do not want Earthforce to come and take it back."

"Yes, General Meadows," Bercy replied. "They will not set foot here."

"General Gant, may I have the pleasure of dying in battle with you and your crew?" Sarah asked.

"We would be honored," Gant replied.

"Your Majesty, Captain Gant commands the newly commissioned cruiser *Tejshank-Sing*, named after the Emperor's father." Sarah turned on a small transmitter. "One final formality. This a repeater that will patch into the station's com system and reach the Earthforce fleet and the planet as well. Read this please?" She handed Karl a piece of paper.

"This is King Karl Phillip Geste the Third, to all Earthforce vessels and personnel in orbit and on the surface of Chiron. I hereby order your immediate and unconditional withdrawal from the planet Chiron. Those who defy this order do so under pain of death."

Sarah switched off the transmitter. "Thank you. And one more little formality." She unfolded her clipboard. "Sign here."

"What is it? You didn't tell me about any of this," Karl said.

"I thought I was making a final stand."

"Ain't I something? Sign it. Trust me, just sign it," Sarah said. Karl was so confused he just signed the document. Sarah folded up her clipboard. "Now that you've signed a mutual assistance pact with the Tau Empire, would you like some assistance in removing these Earth scum from your world?"

"Uh, that would be nice," Karl decided.

"These soldiers remaining are here to assist you. You can confine the Earth personnel or throw them out the closest hatch. It's up to you. You're the king. Captain Gant, lead on," Sarah said.

33
SHOWDOWN

Sarah took a seat no one seemed to be using. It also was curiously the right size for her. She wondered who to thank for that minor bit of comfort. Captain Gant was a highly regarded captain. She had not met him because she had not spent any time on the larger warships. She wasn't sure how this veteran was going to take to being ordered around by some human woman. It was her party and it was time to find out. She handed Gant a recorded disk. "This is the battle plan I drew up. Please transmit it to the fleet. And, if you could open a channel as well?"

Gant put the disk in a viewer next to the captain's chair. He nodded to one of the crew.

"This is General Meadows. By order of the Emperor, I assume command of this fleet. We are transmitting the attack plan now. All commanders move into position."

Gant nodded again. "Change the ship's color to space black." The Tau loved camouflage even though few enemy ships visually looked at their targets.

"How many Earthforce ships are in the area?" Sarah asked.

"Twelve," one of the crewmen replied.

"Tactical officer, isolate command and control signals from the Earthforce fleet. I want to know which ship is in charge," Sarah ordered.

"The cruiser ahead of us. It had a transponder signature of the *UES Enterprise*," the tactical officer reported.

"Very well. Captain Gant, have your helmsman keep us right in front of that ship. If they move, stay with them. We should be faster than they are." She waited a moment to see if they were following her orders. They seemed to be. "I suspect they're in a state of total confusion over there. I doubt, after all this time in occupation, they expected an invasion fleet to show up on their front door today. I'm hoping they may not be too eager to die fighting for a place few of them even want to be. Of course, I could be wrong. Hail them. Let's see what we're facing."

"No response, General."

"Do I have an open channel?" Sarah asked.

"Yes."

"United Earth Ship *Enterprise*, this is General Sarah Meadows of the Tau Army." She waited a moment. "Are they receiving?"

"Yes."

"United Earth Ship *Enterprise*, this is General Sarah Meadows of the Tau Army. We have a three to one superiority. I suggest you respond before I blow you out of the sky," Sarah said.

"So you admit hostile intentions." The screen came up with a man in an Earthforce uniform. "Commodore Richard Montgomery. What is the meaning of this?"

"The meaning is simple, Commodore Montgomery. We are here. You are leaving. The only decision you have is whether you go under your own power," Sarah said. "You heard the King's order. It is time for you to go back to Earth."

"I don't have that authority," he insisted. The screen went blank.

Sarah noticed Gant seemed more interested in her than their adversary. He probably wondered if she had what it takes. "Captain, have your helmsman move us straight ahead, straight for that cruiser. And lock all weapons on the *Enterprise*. Not just the weapons on this ship, all of the weapons from every ship in our fleet."

Gant nodded. "Interesting strategy."

"Earth likes to bully everyone. Bullies usually turn out to be cowards. I want them to be absolutely clear we are not in any way afraid of them."

"They are hailing us."

Commodore Montgomery reappeared on the screen. "Are the Tau declaring war on Earth?"

"No," Sarah replied. "The King has requested our help under a mutual assistance pact. We are assisting."

"That's a crock, after all this time," the commodore said. "A total bunch of bullshit. We have a treaty."

"A treaty I wrote, Commodore. It doesn't mention Chiron in any way, shape or form," Sarah replied. "This is not a debate, Commodore."

"What, precisely, is it you want us to do?" he asked.

"All Earthforce warships are to leave this sector immediately. The people on the surface will immediately load on cargo ships and leave by the end of the day, Chiron Mean Time."

"We've got too much equipment for all of that," he protested.

"I don't care. Leave what you can't carry. The important key word here is leave." Sarah waited a moment. "You are still here."

"Your demands are ridiculous," he protested.

"They are not negotiable. Withdraw now, right now, or my fleet will force you out. I have nothing else to say," Sarah demanded. "What's it going to be?"

"We need to consult Earth," he argued.

"More like stall for reinforcements," Sarah countered. "Captain, signal the fleet to attack."

"No. Wait." He appeared to be talking to another officer with his mute switch on. The other officer left from view. "The day is yours, General." The screen went dark.

"The Earth ships are moving," the tactical officer reported.

"Moving where?" Sarah asked.

"Away."

"Advise of any change. What are they doing on the surface?" Sarah asked.

"We should send a scout ship for a flyover," Gant suggested.

Sarah nodded her approval.

"Not much of a battle," Gant said. "Very disappointing."

"I know," Sarah agreed. "Once again, I did not get to die in battle. Maybe someday. Captain, return this ship to the space station. I need to confer with the King. Let's leave the other ships deployed out here for a bit longer."

After docking, Sarah walked back up to the promenade level. There was a lot of activity going on there. A couple of tables had been set up and Karl had turned the area into a command post. There were a few Tau milling around. Somehow, the local Chironese workers on the station had all been pressed into service and were trying to keep up with Karl's rapid fire orders.

Sarah said, "Well, for someone who didn't even want to come to this party, you look like you're enjoying yourself."

"It's amazing how fast things are moving," Karl said. "The puppet regime folded like a house of cards. There's some looting going on, but it's not out of hand. The Earth folks are scrambling to get out. The biggest fear is they won't get on a transport and will get stranded. As soon as the Earth transports take off, I'm heading down to the planet."

"Sounds like a plan," Sarah said.

There was suddenly a familiar high-pitched sound coming from her right side. She turned as the familiar crimson line of a targeting laser rolled over her face. There was a T-53 pointed at her and the 2.4 seconds were about up. Hers was still turned off and holstered. Sarah looked back down the laser to its source. Holding the weapon was a human. She'd never gotten a name, but she remembered those cold gray eyes. "I thought I killed you when I blew up the *Hawaii*."

"I managed to get to an escape pod, no thanks to you," the man from Earth's military intelligence said. "You damn Martian bitch! Die!"

Then, there was a blue flash from across the promenade area and Sarah's assailant's head sort of exploded. His body fell into a heap on the ground. One of the Tau soldiers picked up the T-53 and switched it off.

Sarah turned the other way to see who her savior was. She was very surprised to see an entourage of Tau soldiers coming up the ramp into the promenade area. Zuto was in the front of the group and was in the process of handing a standard rifle back to one of the soldiers. The Tau soldiers on the promenade all immediately snapped to formal attention. That included Sarah.

Zuto stopped near the table Karl was at and gave Karl a polite nod. "Congratulations on your return to power, your Majesty."

"Welcome to Chiron," Karl replied. He noticed the locals seemed confused. "Everyone from my world, we are honored by a visit from Marshal Zuto, Supreme Commander of the Tau Army."

Captain Gant and some of his officers came charging up the ramp, probably even more surprised than Sarah was at Zuto's arrival. They all snapped to attention as well. Zuto gave Gant an ever so slight nod of recognition.

Then Zuto's attention turned to Sarah. "Report on our status."

"Earth's warships have withdrawn from the area. The

personnel on the ground are loading transports and have been ordered to leave by the end of the day," Sarah replied.

"How many casualties did we encounter?" Zuto asked.

"None, sir."

"And for Earthforce?"

Sarah pointed at the body of her would-be assassin. "Just him. He was an intelligence officer I encountered before."

"It seemed you made quite an impression," Zuto said.

"I do that to people," Sarah agreed.

"Satisfactory," Zuto said.

Karl tried to get back in the conversation. "There's going to be a big ceremony in the capital. Tell me you can come?"

"We are honored," Zuto said.

Karl started heading off the promenade. "I am told I have a call from Almeria that I need to take. Please excuse me."

Sarah moved over right next to Zuto. "His daughter has been living on Almeria." She stepped back to her original place.

Zuto turned toward Gant. "Captain Gant, when His Majesty returns, there are some details that need to be worked out. They may need security assistance on the planet for a while. We can be of help, but we do not want to be seen as replacing one alien occupying force for another. I would like you to coordinate this."

"Yes, Marshal Zuto," Gant replied.

"I guess my work is done here," Sarah announced. She wanted to go back to her room and looked to see if the stairs to that level were blocked by all of the Tau who standing around. She had never liked ceremonies and that was what was happening here.

"Stand at attention when I am addressing you, General," Zuto suddenly snapped.

Sarah immediately did just that.

Zuto moved over to where she was standing. "Some time ago, I gave you a medal. Do you still have it?"

"Yes, sir." She reached into her pocket and took it out, then handed it to him. She still, after all the events that had passed, did not really understand what the medal was for. No one had ever told her. She had translated the word friendship, but had not ever figured out the other two words on the medal.

Zuto held the medal up so everyone could see it. "I once gave this medal to Sarah Meadows. It is our friend medal. It is given out to those from other worlds the Tau consider our friends. This was a great mistake on my part. It never should have been given to her." He handed the medal to one of his aides. "There, it has been taken back."

Sarah was getting very confused, though she remained standing at attention.

"It was a mistake to give her a medal meant for an outworlder." The aide handed Zuto something that looked like a parchment. "This is a declaration signed by our Emperor. It declares Sarah Meadows to be a citizen of the Tau Empire. It was a mistake for her to have the medal because she is no friend of the Tau. She is Tau. She is a Tau warrior." He handed the parchment to her. "A mistake I now rectify."

Sarah dearly wanted to escape to her room. She was determined that no one see her cry like some silly human girl. But it was all she could do to keep from crying. And her knees were starting to shake as well.

"Return to duty," Zuto said. Something else followed in that second dialect, then everyone started to disburse.

Karl returned to the promenade area. "Did I miss anything?"

"No, your majesty. Just some Tau stuff," Sarah said. Her eyes were starting to water up. She had to get out of there. She would offer an excuse to withdraw. "I should make arrangements to return to Mars."

"Not so fast, General," Zuto said. "If I have to go to this ceremony and sit through speeches and flag waving and listening to people sing songs I don't understand, then so do you. You will join me on the planet for the ceremony."

So much for a graceful departure. "Yes, Marshal Zuto." There was no point in arguing about it. No one ever argued with Zuto about anything. His word was law, at least concerning the military. Except for the emperor, no one else in Tau society wielded more power.

"Splendid, you both can stay at the palace. I'm told it is in pretty good shape, overall," Karl said. "I cannot wait to see it again."

"Yes, your majesty," Sarah said. "A soldier had to be able to take orders as well as give them."

34
Moves

Sarah managed to finally make it to her room. It was still going to be a few hours before they went down to the planet, enough time to have a cool beverage and reflect on the days' activities. Earthforce had folded even more quickly than she'd envisioned. She knew most of them were not anxious to die defending some place they did not even want to be. Still, she thought they'd have to give at least some display of force. But the Tau brought way more ships than she'd expected, a good surprise. A Martian commander would have held some in reserve. But the Tau did not think like humans. And overwhelming force is an effective way to convince an enemy not to fight at all.

Then, she'd nearly been killed by an angry man from her past. There was no way she could have known the military intelligence guy from the *Lisa Marie* incident could still be alive, let alone on that very station on that very day. All things considered, it had been a good day. She looked over her parchment. At least it seemed like parchment. Whatever it was printed on, it looked very nice. She doubted many of these certificates existed. For a human to have one? The Tau had not had the best of experiences with humans. Yet, there she sat in a general's uniform holding a certificate signed by the Emperor.

How strange her life had become. She wondered if her parents would have been proud of her. They were blown to bits when she was six years old by an inexperienced tactical officer from Earthforce who mistook a plasma leak on an unarmed Martian shuttle for a weapons lock. No one from Earth had ever apologized for the incident or even seemed to care. Had that fueled her arguably reckless attacks on Earthforce? Who knew for certain? Yet the emperor of an alien race had seen some quality in her that earned her a direct commission into their army. And here she sat, in a chair, on a space station, drinking a very good beer from some place on Earth called Tsingtao. The door buzzer interrupted her thoughts. "Come in," she yelled, then she repeated the equivalent in Tau.

The door opened. Commander Goth was standing there. "Commander Goth, come in."

"How did you know it was me?" he asked.

"I don't understand? Why would I not know it was you?"

"We all look alike to humans," he said.

"No you don't."

"That was joke."

"Would you like a beer?" she asked.

"What is a beer?" he replied.

She poured him a glass. "Don't think about it. Just drink it."

He took a sip. He didn't seem very enthusiastic.

Sarah sat back in the chair. "What can I do for you?"

"We are ready to go to the planet," he reported. "Marshal Zuto said to come and get you."

She picked up the duffle bag and placed the strap over her shoulder. "Lead on my good fellow."

"The king has already gone to the planet. We are taking you and Marshal Zuto directly to the palace," Goth explained. "It is warm, with a light rain on the planet."

"Uh, okay," she replied. Weather. They never had weather on Mars, except for dust storms. Even Tartarus didn't have much weather–every day there was always horrible.

"It is not appropriate for you to carry your own bag," Goth said.

"Oh." She handed him the duffle.

Zuto was already on board. Sarah strapped in on the other side of Goth. After a quick systems check they were underway. "Is there any word on how the people of Chiron are taking things?"

"It is terrible," Goth said. "They say there is widespread dancing in the streets. I hope I don't have to dance in the streets."

"I'm sure they won't make you," Sarah assured him, although the thought of seeing Goth dancing in the streets amused her quite a bit. She wondered how the locals were going to take to her. She looked just like their oppressors. On the other hand, she did know the king.

Goth told the helmsman something in that annoying second dialect she still could not understand. The ship banked sharply, then started a sharp decent. "Not sure if all antiaircraft weapons are accounted for."

Sarah noticed Zuto made an ever so slight nod of approval. One thing about the Tau, they never talked your ear off.

Topo swung the ship back around and then they were landing on a large grassy area. Right next to the lawn was a huge building that sparkled in the sunlight. It looked like it was made of marble. "We are here," Topo announced.

Two Tau soldiers were loitering around the doors to the building. The moment they saw Zuto they immediately snapped to attention. A third soldier came charging out of the building. He told his two comrades, "Marshal Zuto is on the way down to the planet."

"Marshal Zuto is already here," Zuto said.

The soldier snapped to attention. "Sir."

Zuto sure made an impression. Sarah wondered how she could get that level of fear and devotion when she arrived someplace. It probably was never going to happen. She hadn't been in the army for 40 years cultivating an image.

"Go on inside," Zuto said. "I need to review security arrangements."

"Okay," Sarah said. Goth closely followed her. Topo and Ting followed even further back. Sarah decided to take advantage of the opportunity. "Goth, I need some advice. I don't always know the right thing to do with the Tau."

"Nothing," Goth said.

That seemed an odd reply to her. "I'm pretty sure Marshal Zuto himself saved my life up on the space station. I don't know how to acknowledge what he did. He was the one holding the rifle."

"Nothing," Goth repeated. "Do nothing."

"You sure?" It didn't seem right. Shooting the guy from Earth was no small favor. A second later and she would have been dead.

"Do nothing," Goth insisted. "Do you remember when you came to Gentara to do insurance study?"

"Yes, of course."

"Marshal Zuto himself met you. He was in tank. Right before you arrived, there was another tank crew. They came under ambush. A cadet from officer academy, on first day of field training, was out in open and hit by Earth sniper. Zuto, Supreme Commander of all the Tau Army, went out under fire and dragged cadet back to safety. He climbed in tank and went to meet you like nothing ever happened." They walked a few more steps. "That cadet is son of the Emperor. Tank commander filed report that he was not sure who saved the cadet. Much confusion on battlefield."

"Having the Emperor owe you one is something that, well…"

"Exactly. Tank commander obviously ordered not to mention it," Goth said. "Do nothing."

There were various doors and halls laid out in front of them. They were actually standing in what appeared to be an open and airy receiving area. Karl came running up to them. "I meant to greet you, but I've been so busy."

"Quite a place you have here," Sarah said.

"This is just the summer home," Karl said.

"Really?"

"Just kidding," Karl said. "Let me show you around." He opened a pair of double doors. "This is the Grand Ballroom. We used to have formal balls and such here." They went across the hall and he opened another set of doors. "This was the formal banquet room. The doors on the far side connect to a kitchen." They moved farther along and Karl pointed out the King's office and various other facilities.

He then opened the door to a very large room. It had enormous windows. There was a fireplace, a canopy bed. It also had an enormous bath tub. "This is one of the rooms some of our guests stay in. I hope you like it. Sarah, this is for you," Karl said. "I don't know if we'll actually dine this evening. We have no staff."

"Like it?" Sarah asked. She looked at the bath tub. It was bigger than her apartment on Mars. "Ooh."

"We'll go back out to the ship," Goth said.

"Nonsense." He turned toward Goth. "You guys saved me from the assassins. I've got a place for you."

Sarah noticed her duffle bag was on the floor. She had no idea where Goth and the crew had gone off to. She was all alone. Just a girl and an enormous bath tub.

She discovered a hidden refrigerator. It held an assortment of beverages she'd never heard of. She opened one of the bottles and tried it. It would do, though she wondered what it was. She peeled off her uniform. It looked like the bath tub was just about full of hot steamy soapy water. "No wonder Karl missed being the king."

Finally, when every part of her had that prune quality, she climbed out of the tub. Then reality set in. Her duffle bag, with her clothes inside, was gone. Her uniform was gone. And there weren't even any towels. "What kind of hotel are you running, Karl?" On the other hand, she popped open another bottle of the mysterious beverage, as long as she had this stuff to drink, did it matter? A little more of that stuff and she'd be dancing naked in the street anyway. She poured some in a glass. It was green. Green mysterious intoxicating beverage. She let out a belch as she stretched out on the bed. She may have been stark naked with no idea where her clothes were, but with a drink like that one, who the hell cared?

It was dark when she woke again. She had no idea how to turn on the lights. Sarah didn't know the Chiron language. She had no idea what to ask for, if that capability existed. Her translator was wherever her duffle bag was. She didn't remember seeing any obvious lights inside the bedroom. She tried clapping. She didn't know where that idea came from. It didn't work anyway. Sarah fumbled around and finally found the door. She cracked it open. There were lights on in the hall. She poked her head out the door. There didn't seem to be anyone wandering around. She closed the door and fumbled her way back to the bed. At least the bed was nice and comfy and she could always take another bath. All things considered, it wasn't really that bad.

35
STREET VENDING

It was light when her eyes opened. Since the windows had no curtains, the sun in the sky had a way of making a room all light. There was somebody in her room–somebody she did not know. Sarah's eyes slowly focused. Yep, the person looked like one of the locals. "Who the hell are you?"

The person stared blankly at Sarah. *Of course they don't speak your language here, Sarah.* She didn't know any of the local lingo. "You speak Earth?" Of course Earth spoke the same language she did.

The local person yelled out "Earth miagoulo," or something like that. Then that person ran out of the room. So much for that encounter.

"Where the hell are my clothes?" Sarah looked around the room in the morning light. "Where the hell are my clothes?" She started to get out of bed, then stopped as she heard voices right outside the door. People seemed to be arguing about something. The door burst open and the same person as before entered with two others. The others were both wearing maroon shirts. They seemed like males. She still wasn't sure about the other one. One of them was holding a rope with a noose tied on it. The other one had some sort of barrel weapon, which he pointed at her.

"Well, this day is starting off well," Sarah said.

They pulled back the bedding and started trying to grab her. She kicked one of them hard enough to knock him on his rear. The other one got her in a headlock and was dragging her out of the bed.

Then some others came into the room. They were Tau. Sarah yelled in Tau, "Get them off of me!"

There was some more yelling. Then the three locals moved away from her. Since she had no translator, she really didn't understand what was going on, though she thought the three Tau soldiers were the same ones who had been by the door when they arrived.

"She is the maid. She thinks you are from Earthforce," one of the soldiers finally explained. At least they had translators. "These guys in maroon are the local militia. They were going to take you out and hang you in front of the palace."

"Would you ask the maid where my clothes are?"

More words were exchanged. The maid went over to the wall. A panel slid open. It was a closet. Her duffle bag was there. Her uniform was hanging there as well. Sarah tried to let her breathing and pulse rate slow down a little. "Tell them I am a General in the Tau Army. If I ever see any of them again, I will be the one doing the execution."

More words were exchanged. Sarah recognized "Earthforce" a few times. Then the three locals left the room.

"Thank you," Sarah said.

The soldiers nodded, then departed as well. "Let's drag the naked Earth girl out of her bed kicking and screaming and string her up in front of the palace." She decided another bath would solve the problem. She kept the duffle bag and uniform with her this time and locked the door.

After her bath, when she felt presentable, she left the bedroom. She ventured outside. It was a pleasant day. The sun was shining. There were clouds in the sky. Mars didn't really have clouds. She wandered off the palace grounds and found herself walking on a sidewalk along a rather busy street. Two guys in maroon were across the street. They were eyeing her suspiciously.

Things were different now. She had a T-53 strapped to her hip and a boot knife as well. Let them try something now. Helpless human girl? Bring it on. Then she saw something truly odd. There was a small eatery, almost more of a shack. There were outdoor tables. The sign in the window, in her language, not Chiron, read Hamburger Heaven. But the truly odd part of the picture was Goth, Topo and Ting were sitting at one of those tables and they appeared to be eating hamburgers.

She hadn't eaten a hamburger in years. They weren't very popular on Mars. That was Earth food. Having a hamburger stand on Chiron, truly weird. Tau eating burgers, even more weird. "Hi guys."

"General Meadows," Goth said.

"How are the hamburgers?" Sarah asked.

"They are good. But we have never had one before. The man said we could try one for free," Goth explained.

"Can't beat free," Sarah agreed. "Maybe I'll get one." She went over to the window. "Hi, can I get a hamburger?"

"Sure." The very human man turned and looked at her. "I didn't think any humans were left here. I was hoping maybe the lizard men might like them. If they don't, I'm sunk." He had a Martian accent. His name tag read "Bill."

"Can I get onions on it?" Sarah loved onions. She'd put onions on everything when she was little.

"Sure." He started cooking her order, then looked at her again. "That's not an Earthforce uniform is it?"

"No, it is not. Believe or not, I'm one of the lizard people, well sort of anyway." This guy seemed oddly familiar. "I didn't expect to see some Martian guy selling hamburgers on Chiron."

He shrugged. "How'd you know I was Martian? Haven't lived on Mars in years."

"Your accent," Sarah said.

"I imported some cattle. Raise them on a farm near the city. The Earth folks couldn't buy 'em fast enough," Bill said.

"You seem familiar somehow?" Then she realized something. "I don't have any local currency."

"No one does," Bill said. "Earth dollars, no one wants them all of a sudden. The local money was retired after the invasion. I don't know how I'm going to get paid."

Sarah put two Martian doubloons on the counter. "I've got these."

"You really are Martian." The coins disappeared. He handed her the burger, wrapped in paper.

Sarah went over to the table Goth and crew were at. "Mind if I join you?"

"No."

Well, the Tau don't talk your ear off. She sat down. "These are Earth food, mostly. You can get them on Mars, but they're not really popular." She took a bite. "Not bad."

"If that man wants Tau to buy them, they're going to need to be bigger," Goth said.

"Good point," Sarah agreed. "Billy Hawkins." She turned toward the window.

The man was standing right behind her. "Sarah?"

"It's been like forever," Sarah said. She told Goth, "We knew each other as children."

"Nice to meet you," Goth said. He and his crew got up. "We need to park our space ship somewhere else. It's in the way of ceremony."

"Oh yeah, that's right," Sarah agreed. "We'll see you."

Then she looked at Billy Hawkins. "You were at St. Theresa's, then all of a sudden your aunt on Earth sent for you and you were gone."

"It wasn't really up to me," he said. "And you, how'd you end up here?"

"I went to the MSE. After graduation, I went to work for Gompers. Then, through a strange series of events, I find myself actually in the Tau Army."

"Wow. You just never know how life will turn out," he said. "My parents get hit by a meteor out prospecting. Then life at St. Theresa's. Then selling hamburgers on some alien world."

Sarah took the last bite of her hamburger. "That was pretty good. There's this ceremony I have to go to tomorrow. There will be lots of speeches and flag waving. It's going to be awful. Want to come?"

"You make it sound so inviting," Billy said. "Blow it off."

"Can't. I've been ordered to attend by the supreme commander of the Tau Army. You do not blow off something the supreme commander of the Tau Army has ordered you to do." Sarah thought a moment. "There's a banquet later. In the palace. Apparently, I can bring a guest. Free food?"

"Will there be anyone like me there?" he asked.

"Like me?"

"Human."

"Only me. I doubt there will be any others," she said.

"Can I think on it?" Billy asked.

Sarah decided, "Sure. I've gotten used to being the only human. In all of the Tau Empire, I am the only human in their army. Heck, I don't think there's any humans at all on their planet."

"That must be kind of weird," Billy said. "Hey, since I don't have any customers any longer, fancy a game of chess?"

"Okay," Sarah agreed. "Gosh, we used to play all the time."

Billy went back inside, then returned with a travel sized chess set. "Haven't played in years." He started setting up the board. "You once told me that if I ever beat you, you'd let me kiss you. And I never could beat you, not even once."

"I remember," Sarah said. "You want black or white?"

"White, I guess." He moved out a pawn.

She moved out a knight. "Hey, after I leave in a few days, if you're looking for somebody to play, the king plays chess."

"How do you know that?" Billy asked.

"He can't beat me either," she said.

Sarah quickly took his pawn, then one of his bishops. As she was annihilating his pieces, he thought back to their time at St. Theresa's Orphanage. He remembered having a big crush on her. Then, he moved to Earth. He also remembered another side to Sarah—the time she beat him up. He was ribbed by the other boys for months over getting beaten up by a girl. And he wasn't the only boy she beat up.

And there she sat, in an alien uniform with some weird nylon knife sticking out of her boot. She sort of scared him a little. But damn she looked good. He imagined if you put her in something beside that uniform, she'd dress up quite nice. It was obvious she would beat him in another move or two. What else was new?

Then, something unexpected happened. She turned her king over on its side. "I concede." Before he could figure out what happened, Sarah reached over, grabbed him and kissed him. And it wasn't a little peck. It was a deep, long kiss, with tongue. She finally let him come up for air.

"Alas, I really should get back to the palace," Sarah said.

"You really know the king?" Billy asked.

"Yep."

"How about I walk you back?" he asked.

"Okay."

They started walking back toward the palace. "What are you going to do with all the Earth folks gone?" Sarah asked.

"I don't know. I've never been able to get that fungus bread right. The locals love it. I guess I'll go back to Earth. There isn't much to hang around for. That's the problem with being an entrepreneur. Something unexpected can just come out of nowhere. I knew the occupation was wrong, so I knew that this could happen. I just figured there were folks from Earth who might like some comfort food," Billy said. "I don't really want to go back to Mars. I've been gone too long. I've gotten used to fresh air and stuff."

"That makes sense. I'm still finding the sunshine and fresh air a little weird," Sarah said.

Three guys in maroon shirts were across the street. Sarah had a bad feeling about them. The so-called militiamen suddenly started running toward them. Sarah immediately reached down and switched on her T-53. But she did not draw it. Instead, she pulled out her nylon boot knife.

One of the militiamen was wielding what looked like a large piece of a broken mirror. The other two carried clubs. "Death to Earth!" one of them yelled.

Sarah was so glad she had her translator back. Now she could understand what people were actually cursing at her.

"Run!" Billy yelled.

"No," Sarah said. "Go if you need to." She used the flat side of her knife and struck the mirror fragment the closest guy was carrying. It shattered into pieces and the militiaman suddenly was holding nothing. "Seven years bad luck for you."

That individual, looking at the knife wielding human, turned and ran away. Sarah suddenly grabbed one of the clubs from one of the other attackers and yanked it right out of his hands. The third assailant took a swing at her, but she managed to pull back and make him miss. Her Gompers training had taught her to use people's force and momentum against them and to look for people off balance, just as she had that first day with Bercy. A simple blow to his side sent him sprawling.

She went over to Billy and slid her arm around his elbow and sort of dragged him along toward the palace. "Now then, what were we talking about?"

"You're rather nonchalant about that?" Billy observed.

"They were no real threat. They're just caught up in the moment. If I were you, I'd be real careful walking around the next few days," Sarah said.

Billy said, "I'll admit that mirror was a stupid weapon, but those clubs could have busted you up pretty good."

Sarah drew her T-53. She switched the power back off. "We were never in any real danger." She returned the weapon to its holster. "There used to be a saying about bringing knives to gunfights. It applies to clubs as well, methinks. Those guys were no soldiers. In war, one of the most important skills a soldier can have is the ability to size up an opponent and determine his weaknesses."

"I guess that makes sense," Billy agreed. She definitely scared him. He certainly wasn't sure if he liked being saved by a girl in a fight, either.

"Well, we're here. Thanks for walking me back." Sarah grabbed him and kissed him. "Try and come to the banquet?"

"Okay," Billy agreed.

Sarah strolled across the lawn. The spaceship was now gone and chairs were being set up. As she walked up the steps to the palace she noticed Zuto was standing there. He must have seen the altercation. "It's such a nice day, sir," Sarah said as she passed by him and went inside.

Also standing outside was Karl. He was in the shadows and Sarah had not noticed him. Karl moved closer to Zuto. "I thought we should go and help her, but that fight was over so fast."

"The laser weapon she carried could have cut them down in seconds. She correctly realized they were no real threat to her," Zuto said.

"Apparently," Karl agreed.

"She has no fear," Zuto pointed out.

Karl asked, "No fear of the militia?"

Zuto shook his head. "No fear of anything."

36
POMP

Twice attacked by the so-called militia in one day. Karl had his work cut out to fill in for the power vacuum the departure of Earthforce had left. And smooching with Billy Hawkins. Who'd have thought it? All on some planet she never dreamed she'd ever actually go to. Sarah took another drink of the green beverage from the refrigerator as she soaked in the bath tub. She wondered what they made the stuff out of. They had nothing like it on Mars. Maybe she needed to get in the import business. "Buy this green stuff. Yummy good."

Then she heard somebody out in the room. She hoped it wasn't more militia. "Hello?"

Nothing.

"I can hear you," Sarah warned. No one answered. She climbed out of the tub. She had her nylon boot knife at her side, the perfect weapon for people with paranoid delusions. After being dragged out of bed, she felt better with it at close grasp. She went out into the bedroom. There was a loaf of fungus bread sitting on a table. She touched it and it was still warm. The nylon boot knife did a fair job of cutting bread. "Boy I'm going to miss Karl's cooking." Since no one was around, she started licking the plate to get the last few crumbs.

The ceremony began the next morning. They had a bunch of people in purple robes. There were people singing songs that made no sense. And Sarah found herself sitting next to Zuto, right near the front of the goings on. She had no idea what was going on and just kept hoping that, mercifully, it would end somehow. Then a parade of children carrying flags came in and lots of people starting clapping.

That was followed with somebody in a purple robe. He rattled on for quite some time. Sarah had her translator turned off. She found she enjoyed it better when she couldn't understand what the participants were saying. Then Karl went up to the guy in the purple robe. Karl knelt and the guy in purple put the crown on

Karl's head and gave him the scepter. Then Karl rose and everyone started clapping.

Then Karl stated giving a speech. The speech went on and on and on. Then, mercifully, as if somebody had just put a bullet in her brain, Karl sat down and people stood up and started leaving. Finally, it was over.

Sarah sat patiently until Zuto finally stood. *Alas, an opportunity to flee.* "General Meadows," Zuto asked, "what did you think of the ceremony?"

"Well, it's okay, I guess," she said.

"At least you didn't fall asleep," Zuto observed.

That's what you think, buddy. "Of course not," she replied.

"Will I see you at the banquet?" he asked.

"Count on it, sir," she said. *After putting me through this, they better feed me.*

Sarah wove through the crowds and made it back inside the palace. She started for her room, then she picked up an odd smell. She decided to follow it. The aroma took her to a room not too far from hers. The door was ajar. She poked her head in. Goth, Topo and Ting were sitting by a fire in their fireplace. They seemed to be roasting something on a stick. "What are you guys cooking?"

"Guama grubs," Goth said. "They are a delicacy on our world. Would like one?"

"Hell no, I mean, uh, I don't really care for them," Sarah said.

"That leaves more for us," Goth said.

Sarah asked. "Did you guys blow off the ceremony?"

"No one told us we had to go," Goth replied.

"Are you going to the banquet?" she asked.

"No one invited us," he said.

"Uh, I could probably get you an invite," she offered. "I do know the king."

"Thank you, but we'd rather not. We have our grubs."

"Well, I'll leave you to it," Sarah said. She headed for her room. They seemed quite content sitting there roasting their grubs. If they were happy, there seemed to be no reason to rock the boat. She zipped open her duffle bag. She had to decide whether to wear the dress she had, slightly wrinkled, or go in her military uniform. Neither idea really appealed to her. She didn't really know if the Tau had a dress uniform. Even if they did, she did not possess one. She couldn't remember much about the party at Emperor Sing's. She remembered military guests were there, including Zuto. But the event was so fuzzy in her mind she had no idea what anyone wore. And the dress she took to that party was back on Mars. At least it wasn't that horrible green dress. It would have to do.

Sarah was just about ready to go when there was a knock at the door. She opened it to find Billy Hawkins standing there. "I didn't really think you'd come." Sarah opened up her clipboard and sent a message, then closed it and placed it on top of a small table. She didn't expect to need it anymore that evening.

"Well, it's not like I've got much else to do," he said. "I'm closing up Burger Heaven. There just aren't any customers anymore."

"I'm sorry about your business, but I'm glad you came. Free food awaits," Sarah said. She latched her arm around his elbow. "It's just down a ways." There was a bit of a line forming.

One guy in a white jacket was checking off people. "Name?"

"Meadows," she said.

"Ah, there you are." His attention turned to the guests now joining the line behind them.

They soon reached the door. Another guy in a white jacket announced, "General Sarah Meadows and Mister Billy Hawkins."

"General?" Billy whispered. "You're a general? You didn't tell me you were a general?"

Sarah grinned at him. She whispered, "At least they don't have a receiving line. Those are just awful." Another usher escorted them to their table. Billy ended up sitting with Sarah on one side and Ting on the other. He seemed a little uneasy sitting so close to a Tau, a species he'd never seen until a few days before. Sarah had Billy next to her and Goth on her other side.

Sarah was a bit surprised to see that Goth, Tepo and Ting were all sitting there. "I didn't think you guys were coming?"

"Marshal Zuto made us," Goth explained.

"Who's this Marshal Zuto?" Billy asked.

As if to answer his question, the announcer said, "Marshal Zuto, Supreme Commander of the Tau Army." Zuto was escorted to the King's table by one of the ushers.

"Oh," Billy said.

Sarah noticed Zuto was wearing the very uniform she had passed on.

"Ambassador Tremont of Almeria," came the next introduction. Sarah thought he looked quite a bit like Dragon, but smaller. Almerians grew bigger with age. It seemed odd this one's name was easy to pronounce. He also rated the King's table.

Sarah told Goth, "If you got that embassy job, you could go to these types of things all the time."

"I'm not getting it. I'm not important enough," Goth insisted.

"What embassy job?" Billy asked.

"They need a military attaché for the Tau Embassy on Mars," Sarah said. "Commander Goth would like to have it, but he doesn't think he has the rank or the connections."

Billy seemed surprised. "The Tau have an embassy on Mars? I've been away a while."

A few minutes later everyone stood. The announcer said, "His Royal Majesty, King Karl Phillip Geste III, and Princess Estonia." Karl and a female were escorted by two ushers to their table.

"That must be his daughter," Sarah said. "She's been living on Almeria. I've never met her."

The first course was some sort of soup. It was edible, but the spices seemed strange to her and Sarah didn't really enjoy it. She noticed Billy slurped it up. Goth also managed to consume his without any difficulty.

Then came a dish with meat and various vegetable along with a delicious sauce. Karl had once fixed this for the Gompers gang, though she had forgotten what it was called. That was followed with a baked vegetable dish. Then the desert was fungus bread. Sarah tried to restrain herself and eat it slowly. She wasn't fighting for it like they did at the Gompers bullpen. She looked up and caught Karl watching her. She didn't know if he made the menu just for her, but she strongly suspected the possibility.

As the servers carted off the plates, Karl rose to speak. "Ladies and gentlemen, I thank you all for coming, and especially on such short notice. As we work through the difficult times ahead in rebuilding our world, I just wanted to take the time to thank those who have continued to support me. Living in exile was a challenge, a challenge that would have been unbearable except for the efforts of some of you here. I wanted to especially thank a few of you. Would Commander Goth, Crewman Topo and Crewman Ting come up here?"

Goth looked like he wanted to hide underneath the table. He looked at Sarah.

Sarah shrugged. "Don't ask me."

The three of them approached the King's table with all of the enthusiasm of a child going to the dentist for the first time. "Only a few weeks ago, there was an attempt to kill me. These brave soldiers came to my rescue and thwarted the attack. They weren't even assigned to protect me. I just wanted to express my gratitude. A servant behind Karl handed him three gold medals, each with a neck ribbon. I hereby bestow upon you The King's Medal of Valor. It is to recognize acts of gallantry. I can think of none more deserving than the three of you." He placed a medal over each of their heads. "Congratulations and thank you." The audience all started to applaud.

When he sat back down, Sarah whispered to Goth, "At least they didn't make you dance in the streets."

Karl resumed his speech. "And, I'd like to acknowledge the tireless and unyielding support of Emperor Sing of the Tau. And also to my very good friends, Marshal Zuto and Ambassador Tremont. And there are plenty of others who I am grateful to as well. But, I won't make everyone fall asleep listening to me recite a bunch of names." He took a sip of water. An aide came up behind him. That aide was holding a sword.

"And one last thing I'd like to address this evening. There is one person who has been my friend, ally and confidant. She is the one who vanquished Earthforce from this world just days ago. She is the one who convinced me now was the time to return to Chiron and take back my scepter."

Now Sarah was the one who wanted to hide underneath the table.

"To her I owe a debt beyond anything I can ever repay. As I stand here tonight, reunited with my daughter, and once again ruling this world I so dearly love. And while I truly think she'd be happier with a recipe for fungus bread, which she will find when she returns to her room, the question arose of how can I best show my enormous gratitude to her. And that answer was not easy. We have no real history of women involved in military service on this world. On Mars and Earth, they have served for generations, but not here. Perhaps that will soon change." He took another sip of water.

"My daughter asked me if gender were not the issue, what would I do? I asked my advisers. There is, frankly, no real precedent. I was told I am the king. Do what I want. So, if Sarah Meadows, General Sarah Meadows would kindly come up here?"

Sarah didn't just want to hide; she wanted to flee the room. She approached the King's table.

Karl moved down to the end of it. "Kneel, please," he whispered.

She did as instructed. Karl drew the sword. "Sarah Meadows, I hereby appoint and bestow upon you the title of Knight Commander of the Planet Chiron. May you henceforth be known as Lady Sarah Meadows." He tapped her shoulders with the sword, then sheathed it. "Arise Lady Sarah." He held out the sword. "And you get to keep the sword." Karl went back to the podium at the center of the table. "The term Lord Sarah didn't seem right, in our language or hers."

People started applauding as she went back to her table. She smiled at everyone, then sat back down.

"I would have rather had to dance in the streets," Goth said.

"Me, too."

37
GOING HOME

Billy walked Sarah back to her room. "Want to come in?" Sarah asked.

"Nah, I should be going," Billy replied. "I like you Sarah," Billy said. "But..."

She said, "I intimidate you, don't I?"

"A little. I just want to go back to Earth and open up a Hamburger Heaven Two somewhere. Somehow, I just don't see you, with all those titles and stuff, being happy cooking french fries and slicing onions," Billy said.

She tapped him on his chest. "That's where you're wrong. I love slicing onions. I love onions. But you're probably right about moving to Earth. It was great seeing you, Billy Hawkins." She grabbed him and kissed him.

When she finally released him, he said, "I sure wish I'd been a better chess player." He started toward the exit. "By the way, I made a ton of money while I was here. I'm really rich."

"Damn, I should have tried to sell you some insurance," Sarah said.

Sarah got up early the next morning and decided she needed one more session in the bath tub. The bath tub would've been a better prize than some sword. Unfortunately, it would not fit on the shuttle.

About the time she finished getting dressed, once again in her military uniform, there was a knock at the door. One of these guys in white who were suddenly popping up all over the palace stood there at her doorway. "The King commands and requests your immediate presence in his chambers."

"He does, does he? Lead on my good fellow."

Karl was sitting at a desk. Estonia was sitting in a nearby chair. "Ah, Sarah, I understand your ship awaits to take you back to Mars," Karl said.

"Yes, I was just getting ready to go."

"Sarah, I've heard so much about you," Estonia said. "I wish you could stay longer."

"Well, you both have a lot of work to do. Maybe you'll make a state visit to Mars sometime," she said.

"I'd like that," Estonia said. "I've never been there. Papa thought it best if we lived apart. Those were rough times."

"Sorry to put you on the spot last night," Karl said. "If I'd told you my intentions, you would've gone and hidden somewhere. I really can't thank you enough. And that includes the time you pulled me out of the sewage vat."

"Sewage vat?" Estonia asked.

"I'll tell you about it, later," Karl assured her. "Until whenever, then. Oh, that fellow you were with last night? Any wedding bells in the future?"

"Nope. He just dumped me, actually," Sarah said.

"Dumped you? What a fool," Karl said.

Sarah said, "Billy wants to go to Earth and sell hamburgers. I don't think I'd be all that popular with the Earth government, somehow."

"Billy? Is he the Billy who made you eat dirt as a child?" Karl asked.

Sarah said, "Damn, you've got a good memory. One and the same, but that was long time ago."

"Safe travels, Sarah," Karl said.

"Nice meeting you," Estonia added.

Goth and his crew were lingering around her room when she got back. "Hi guys. I was saying goodbye to the king."

"Are you ready to go?" Goth asked.

"Sure."

They walked along toward where the ship was now parked. It was about a kilometer from the palace. Sarah noticed a sign in the window of a storefront. People were inside painting. The sign read FUTURE HOME OF GOMPERS INSURANCE. And there stood Don Don right by the door.

"It didn't take you very long to show up," Sarah said.

"We'll have this place up and running in a few more days," he declared.

"I'm sure you will," Sarah agreed.

"By the way," Don Don said, "we changed the manual. Military leave is only for Martian Defense Force, not some alien army. You're fired for unauthorized absence." He seemed very pleased with himself. "And don't try using your Gompers card any longer. It's cancelled."

Goth nodded to Topo. Topo took his sidearm, a Tau standard energy particle pistol, out of its holster. "General, would you like for us to kill this horrible man for you?"

Don Don's face changed from smugness to outright fear. He turned and fled toward the back of the store.

"That was joke," Goth said.

Seeing Don Don run away like that, Sarah started laughing. She was laughing so hard she nearly fell over. She was laughing so hard her side started to hurt. As she regained her composure, she said, "Indeed it was, Commander. Take me home."

They walked the rest of the way to the ship. Parked next to it was another ship. Bercy and his crew were cleaning it. That crew all snapped to attention.

"General," Bercy said.

"We're going to Mars. I guess you guys are going to be here for a few weeks," Sarah said.

"Yes," Bercy agreed. He handed Sarah a small envelope, then returned to attention.

"Well, carry on," she said.

They got in Goth's ship and began flight preparations. They soon took off and climbed up into the morning sky. When they were in space, the crew activated the hyperspace generators and they vanished into the nothingness of that dimension.

"Are you dropping me at Fremont Station?" Sarah asked.

"No," Goth said. "We are going directly to Mars City. The ambassador wants to interview me for military liaison."

"Oh, that sounds promising," Sarah said.

"It will be a waste of time," Goth said. "I never get promoted."

"That's the spirit." Sarah opened her duffle and took out her new sword. She swung it around for a few minutes. "Nice sword and all, but, he could've given me an island or a moon or something."

Ting opened a cabinet. He took out a familiar black pouch and handed it to Sarah. "They left some of these behind."

"Earth Force Banana Pudding. How thoughtful. You guys are

the best." She put her sword away and opened the packet. She took the provided spoon and dug in. It seemed to have just enough stickiness that it clung to the spoon and did not float away.

Sarah dozed for a bit. Then, they came out of hyperspace and were approaching Mars.

"Tau shuttle sixteen to approach control," Goth said. His new transponder and navigation links made this stage much easier than his earlier arrivals to Martian space. "Request clearance for Mars City spaceport."

"This is approach control," a friendly voice answered. "We are transmitting course and vector. You are cleared for pad four." The ship easily glided down through Mars' thin atmosphere and was landing at the spaceport in no time. Topo powered down the engines.

Sarah unbuckled herself and stood. She said, "Registry computer on."

"Why do you want that?" Goth asked.

Sarah responded with, "Stand at attention when I am addressing you, commander." She waited for a moment. The registry computer beeped. "Recognize General Sarah Meadows, personnel action." It beeped again. "Personnel action, Goth, Commander, notation of foreign medal. Awarded Medal of Valor by Planet Chiron, by order of the King of Chiron. End"

"I noticed that foreign honors can go in personnel records," Sarah said.

"Well, thank you," Goth said.

"Do not interrupt a superior when she is addressing you, commander," Sarah snapped. "Action number two, subject Goth, Commander." It beeped. "I noticed something very interesting in the regulations a while back. Commander Goth is hereby issued a field promotion to the rank of captain, with all privileges and honors accordingly, by order of Sarah Meadows, General, Army of the Tau. End report." Sarah took the envelope Captain Bercy had given her and tore it open.

"Captain Goth," she removed his rank insignia and replaced them with a more colorful set, "It is my great pleasure to bestow upon you your new rank insignia. It has been a great honor to serve with you."

"I don't know what to say," Goth said. "Maybe my wife will be proud of me."

"Captain, I am quite certain your wife already is quite proud of you." She picked up her duffle bag.

"Topo and Ting, it has been a pleasure to have served with you." Sarah opened her duffle bag. She took out a small hammer and handed it to Ting. "You can't have too many hammers."

"And Topo," she removed her boot knife with its sheath, then twirled it around so the handle faced him. "I'd like you to have this. Don't carry it around any of those invisible people."

She opened the hatch and headed out the gangway into the spaceport. Her eyes were watering. She was determined no one was going to see some silly human girl cry.

38
DRINKING ALE ON A QUIET MORNING

Sarah had not slept so well in, well she couldn't remember when. She got dressed and decided to spend the day venturing around Mars City doing whatever whimsical thing came up. Goth didn't seem particularly whimsical, but there he stood right outside her door. "Goth?"

"I was looking for you," he said.

"Found me, you have," Sarah noted. "I was just heading down to this place to have a drink and relax for a moment. Care to join me?" She took him over to the nearby bar.

The waiter looked over Goth, then asked, "What would you like?"

"By chance do any of your distributors have any of this green drink they sell of Planet Chiron?" Sarah asked.

"Never heard of it," the waiter informed her.

"Of course. Martian Red," Sarah said. "Goth?"

"I don't like anything."

"Water," Sarah suggested. Their drinks quickly arrived. "What's on your mind?"

"I just came from my interview at the embassy," Goth said.

"And how did that go?" Sarah took a sip of the beer. She was going to have to figure out how to get that green stuff from Chiron.

"They had this letter of recommendation from some general," Goth said.

"Did they now." Sarah took another drink. "And?"

"They had this letter from the King of Chiron," Goth said.

"Impressive," Sarah said. "So, what happened?"

"They offered me the position. I'm the new military attaché," Goth said. "I go home for a few days, then I start. My wife can even come to Mars to live, if she wants to."

"You don't know if she wants to?" she asked.

"Have not asked her. Told her I wouldn't get the job," Goth explained. "I'll talk to her when I get home. Surprise her."

"Sounds like a plan," Sarah agreed.

"I need to be going," Goth said.

"Well, I'm really happy for you," Sarah said. She finished her beer, then went back over to her apartment. There was a message waiting for her on the terminal.

She changed into the old baggy clothes she used to wear back in her student days. She'd worn them to discourage men from hitting on her all the time. It had just led to a creepier class of men hitting on her. She hopped on Mag Lev and headed out to Dry Gulch. It was not being hit on that concerned her.

She got off at the depot and ventured down the escalator. Some old guy was sitting on the sidewalk. She thought he was the same guy from her last trip there. He started rubbing his crotch as he looked at her. That seemed familiar as well. What a wonderful town. She headed down L Street until she reached the Old Nag Bar & Casino.

Sarah entered through the batwing doors. There were some men playing cards on green velvet tables. A large bar ran down the side of the establishment. There was a large mirror on the wall behind the bar. A few men sat on stools drinking something from a bottle. A few others loitered in the back, next to the piano. There was a large painting of a naked lady hung above the piano. There were no gaming machines or dealer robots here. This was old time gambling. At night they even played an old Earth game known as faro, which used a dealer—a female dealer who usually had a lot of cleavage.

And, at a table next to the bar, sat the Rt. Honorable Becky Hudson, former Foreign Minister and newly elected Mayor of Dry Gulch. There were two glasses of beer on the table. It looked like Martian Red Ale. One of them was half empty, the other hadn't been touched. Becky pointed at the empty chair across from her. "Sarah, how good of you to come."

"I almost didn't," Sarah replied.

"I wasn't too nice the last time I saw you. When I heard you were back on Mars, I wanted to make amends," Becky explained.

"You sure heard fast," Sarah pointed out. "I just arrived yesterday."

"Well, I still have a few friends at the Ministry," Becky said. "In fact, it's those friends I wanted to talk to you about."

"How so?"

"Well, for years now, actually ever since the Martian Republic was founded, we've been bullied constantly by Earth. It's always been a chore trying to appease them while still not looking too weak," she said. "You've now gone off and gotten them off of Tartarus, then driven them out of Chiron as well. From the Ministry's point of view, this is a disaster." She finished her beer. "Where's that useless bartender?"

Sarah pushed her untouched glass over to Becky. "Have mine."

"Really?"

"And from the view of the Tau and the folks on Chiron, things couldn't be better," Sarah said. "It's all how you look at it."

"I don't give a fuck about those damned aliens," Becky said. "Where's that bartender?"

"Take mine, really," Sarah said again.

Becky said, "Well, there are those who are quite angry with you."

Sarah nodded in agreement. "Including most of Earth's government, I would think. And the stooges like you who work for them. I was happy to vote for the new Chancellor."

"You don't understand," Becky said. "I was going to offer you something, a job with the Insurance Commission. I've got connections. Anything to keep you from running around stirring things up for a bit. The hell with you. Sit in your little apartment and think you're important. See if I care. Where's that bartender?"

"No, seriously, have mine," Sarah again offered. "I don't want it."

"Gave up drinking have we?" Becky asked.

"The Tau do not drink with enemies," Sarah stated.

"And you really think you're one of those damned lizards! The hell with it. I tried." Becky looked around again. The bartender brought her another Martian Red. She chugged half of it down.

"My glass not to your liking?" Sarah asked.

"What are you implying?" Becky demanded.

"Put something in my drink? I pass out. Those two goons

from Earth over by the piano dump me in one of the many abandoned wells underneath this two-bit town. Your pals at Earth can be quite vindictive," Sarah said.

"That's ridiculous." Becky stood. "You've gotten really paranoid, my dear. I've got a town to run." Becky headed out through the batwings.

Sarah sat at the table for a moment. She had been watching the men over by the piano in the mirror behind the bar. They definitely were from Earth. Life would've been so much simpler if she'd stuck to selling insurance. "Pick on the unemployed Martian girl why don't you?" she said aloud to nobody. She got up and exited through the batwing doors. She picked up her pace as she headed for the cover of the corner of the building. Two point four seconds later the two guys from Earth came charging out through the batwings.

About the Author

David B. Riley is the editor of numerous horror and weirdwestern anthologies. He is also the author of four novels and more than 100 short stories. He writes horror, science fiction and steampunk and is an active member of the Horror Writers Association.

David presided over *Science Fiction Trails* magazine for a decade is now publisher of *Story Emporium* magazine. He lives in Colorado and works in the hotel business when he's not working on literary endeavors.

More Books from
WolfSinger Publications

Time Warp: Book One – William Paul Lazarus

Forced to leave his own planet because of a civil war, Prince Anton flees into the unknown universe with only his all-knowing, automatonic horse, Thurgose, for company. En route to Earth, the closest inhabited planet, Anton quickly finds enemies are chasing him and he must veer to another planet where heralded fighters face off against weeds and poaching creates serious dangers.

His spaceship damaged, he and Thurgose return to an Earth where every thought is captured by computers, as ambitious residents battle for the chance to get pills that will make them immortal.

Trapped inside a military complex, Anton must find a way to escape, get back his ship, and somehow evade his enemies in the heavens above and on Earth.

To do that, he has only a woman who has deserted her post to help him and an energy-deprived Thurgose.

Time Warp: Book Two – William Paul Lazarus

Trapped on Earth as his archenemy Wyron hovers dangerously in the sky above, Crown Prince Anton can only rely for assistance on his fantastic automatonic rocking horse Thurgose and a friendly bureaucrat named Bonnie. They try to hide with Outsiders, people who have rejected society's push for ratings to achieve immortality, finding Bonnie's brother among them.

Wyron won't wait and attacks, forcing the Americans to turn to the only ones who can save them, Anton and Thurgose.

With his ship repaired and joined by a human crew, Anton sets off for an epic battle.

Fanny & Dice – Rebecca McFarland Kyle

"I'm leaving Hell for good, Eurydice…"

When she heard those words, Eurydice had a choice: remain in Hades' realm or escape to Earth with her kinswoman, Persephone.

She knew the Earth wasn't what they'd left. Demeter hadn't summoned Persephone to bring Spring for quite some time…and the last dead crossed the River Styx many years before. She hadn't expected to arrive in a world where trains rode across the prairie on metal tracks instead of chariots and men settled disputes with six guns instead of swords.

Eurydice will face perils both immortal and mortal, from gun and axe to her own heart….

Seventh Daughter – Ronnie Seagren

Some people are destined from birth to do great things.

Gil Orlov is born in the shadow of totality of a solar eclipse, the seventh daughter of a seventh daughter. She is the culmination of a carefully planned genealogy begun by her great-grandmother. Gil's purpose, the goal of her family—defeating a Vision of the world in flames, reduced to a lifeless cinder.

But the power she should have is muted or lacking. Gil and her six sisters begin an arduous journey to a place of power high in the Peruvian Andes known as Killichaka—the Bridge to the Moon. They must make it to this ancient temple in time to complete a ritual during the totality of the 1937 solar eclipse. If they are successful, Gil's powers should be restored—giving her the ability to prevent the global disaster her ancestors warned of.

To succeed they must first survive the journey and locate Killichaka. Against them is the environment, the elements, their own doubts and fears as well as the 'Other' and a force that would gleefully see the world fall into chaos—an entity known as Supay.

Lost Trails – Edited by Cynthia Ward

Ah, the "Western frontier"!

We learned all about it as children. We learned it was full of brave white American pioneer men killing the native inhabitants, who didn't realize the land they'd occupied for millennia belonged to the newcomers.

We learned it was full of heroic white American gunmen shooting each other in high noon standoffs. Those few characters who didn't fit the above roles were generally helpless Mexican peasants; treacherous Mexican bandits; or the occasional rancher's wife, school marm, or prostitute.

Omitted from the history lessons and the movies and TV shows were—the whole wide world. Well pull up a seat next to the fire and we'll tell you those stories—follow the Lost Trails of those who were omitted as they tell us their stories of the Weird West.

The Station – A David Smith

The distant future. Humanity has reached the stars...and found no life.

On a remote space station, lone crewman Lt. Robert Bradley awakens to starless space and complete darkness. When he summons the courage to venture outside, Bradley becomes the first human to embark on humanity's greatest journey.

He will develop a new understanding of the universe and witness the destinies of countless sentient life forms.

Blind Eye - F. Lynn Godfriaux

Mattie Lamont Tyler loses both parents in an apparent car accident, then finds herself estranged from her only sibling when her sister Angela elopes with a new boyfriend. But Mattie, a photojournalist with (ironically) a phobia of guns and violence, is blind to dangers around her until Angela ends up on the critical list in an ICU six hundred miles from home and Mattie's husband, a Southern Ute who appears to be a quiet, unassuming weather forecaster, stops answering his cell.

Before she can figure out what's going on, Mattie is kidnapped by Hawk, a ruthless stranger with accusations Mattie does not understand. Her own survival and the lives of her loved ones depend on whether Mattie can see beyond her "blind eye" into unknown inner strength.

From the plains of Oklahoma to the mountains of Southwest Colorado, Blind Eye sweeps the reader into a frantic race against greed, lies, and pre-meditated murder.

Check out these and more great books at:
www.wolfsingerpubs.com

www.ingramcontent.com/pod-product-compliance
Lightning Source LLC
Chambersburg PA
CBHW060635260626
47161CB00008B/2895